End Run

A Drew Gavin Mystery

Steve Brewer

Philadelphia

ISBN 1-890768-25-1

First Printing, October 2000

This book is a work of fiction. Names, characters, places and incidents are either the product of the author's imagination or are used fictitiously. Any resemblance to actual events or locales or persons, living or dead, is entirely coincidental. Although the author and publisher have made every effort to ensure the accuracy and completeness of information contained in this book, we assume no responsibility for errors, inaccuracies, omissions, or any inconsistency herein. Any slights of people, places or organizations are unintentional.

Library of Congress Cataloging-in-Publication Data
Steve Brewer, 1957-
    End Run: a Drew Gavin mystery / by Steve Brewer.
      p. cm.
    ISBN 1-890768-25-1
    1. Sportswriters--Fiction. 2. Albuquerque (N.M.)--Fiction.
    3. Professional sports--Fiction 4. Political corruption--Fiction.
    I. Title.
PS3552.R42135 E54 2000
813'.54--dc21

                     00-040772
                     CIP

10 9 8 7 6 5 4 3 2 1

Dedicated to my friend Frank Zoretich, in thanks for his whipsaw critiques and artful encouragement.

Thanks also to my wife, Kelly, George Phocas, and Connie Shelton, for believing in me.

The fireplace poker lashed at his head. It seemed to move in slow motion, no blur, no whir of sound. Swinging right at him, clear and silent and slow, but still too quick to dodge, to fend it off.

In that instant the anger drained out of him, and his mind flashed on buying the fireplace set, years ago, back when love and money and ambition all sat in a row, waiting for him.

He'd used that bronze-handled poker to tend scores of fires, squatting before the stone hearth, watching the orange flames lick and quaver. But now it was a weapon, swinging at his head. . . .

And the last burst of thought, the final blip of consciousness before the poker connected: My God, how has it come to this?

ONE

Reunions are funny. You go to see how everyone else turned out, and instead come away thinking how the years have changed you.

Drew Gavin had no intention of attending his ten-year reunion at the University of New Mexico. He'd received notices in the mail for months, inviting him to homecoming banquets and tailgate parties, urging him to pledge money to his alma mater. Most went into the trash unopened. He had no spare money to give away, not on the thirty grand a year he made as a sportswriter, and he didn't want to attend parties arranged just so his peers could trumpet their successes and show off their spouses. Lately he felt he was in a rut, and he didn't need his fellow alumni digging it any deeper.

Even the homecoming game, usually a source of pleasant gridiron memories, felt wrong this year. Some idiot had scheduled the game against Brigham Young University, and the Lobos almost never beat the Utah school. This year promised to be no different; UNM had a record of 1-2 and they were lucky to have won the one. They'd have a better chance if the homecoming queen and her court lined up against the Cougars.

The acres of blacktop parking lots around mud-colored University Stadium were packed full of Winnebagos and pickup trucks and people. Grills spewed sweet-smelling barbecue smoke and coolers hid icy beers. Fans with painted faces whooped and laughed. The tailgate parties were always the best part of a Lobo game. Four hours from now, these same fans would be grimly frowning over another loss, shaking their heads and blaming the referees.

Drew showed his press badge to a snooty guard to gain admittance to the news media parking lot and found a slot for his Jeep. From the lot it was a short walk to the elevator that would carry him up to the tall-windowed press box four stories above the playing field. But Drew had an hour until kickoff, so he decided to roam the tailgate parties first. Sometimes he ran into people he knew or fans who recognized him from the photo that ran with his twice-weekly column in the Albuquerque Gazette. They'd often share their beer, and he figured he could use a brew to wash down another dose of watching the Lobos lose.

It was a great day for football—the last Saturday in September, the temperature in the seventies, not a cloud in the turquoise sky. Drew inhaled deeply, smelling the barbecue and exhaust fumes and freshly mown grass. Radios blared pregame shows and thumping rock 'n' roll. Horns honked in the snarl of traffic around the packed lots.

He carried his laptop computer, his stat books, and his pens in a satchel slung over one shoulder as he threaded his way through the clumps of revelers, hunting a familiar face who might spare a cold one.

Then he saw the class reunion tent. He remembered from the mailings that the class of 1989 would have a party tent set up in the parking lot before the game. It was easy enough to spot. The white canvas tent was maybe thirty feet square and decorated with red ribbons and banners proclaiming that ten years had passed since graduation.

He hesitated outside the tent. Inside there'd be free drinks and food. But there'd also be his old classmates—the bankers and lawyers and doctors who'd made something of themselves since college. Drew was stuck in the same job he'd taken right after graduation.

He glanced down at his clothes: frayed jeans and yellowed sneakers and a purple polo shirt that said "Hula Bowl" on the chest—another freebie. Half his clothes were labeled with sporting events, one of his job's few perks. He tucked at his shirttail, and wished he'd taken time to shave.

At least he still had all his hair. He'd let his body slip since the days when he suited up as a six-foot-four defensive end. A diet of beer and Hungry Man TV-dinners had moved more of his 250 pounds to his waist. He still had a broad chest and meaty arms, but he didn't do much to keep in shape anymore. His ankles were too gimpy for running, and weight lifting seemed like vanity now that he had no reason to put his muscles to work.

Mentally, he'd changed even more. At twenty-two, you think nothing can hurt you—the whole world stretches before you like an all-you-can-eat buffet. By thirty-two, you've been hurt a few times, particularly in the romance department. And the buffet has dwindled so all you can see sometimes are the dips and the nuts.

Drew squeezed through the tent door and into the thick herd of chatting alumni. Crowds made him uncomfortable. A big guy like him had a larger "bubble" of space he didn't want invaded. He turned his broad shoulders sideways and edged along, muttering "Excuse me" over and over as he made his way through the crowd. He saw a few people he recognized— a couple of Land's End types who'd been big in student government and were lawyers now; a wide-eyed woman who'd been a cheerleader; a couple of aging jocks like himself, sniggering and ogling the women.

He'd nearly reached the bar when he spotted Helen across the way. She still wore her black hair long, past her shoulders, parted in the center above a high, smooth forehead. Her olive skin was dark from a summer of lazy tanning, making her ready smile seem even brighter. She wore jeans and a light-weight black sweater, and she was as tall and trim as he remembered.

Their eyes met across the tent and he was unable to breathe for several seconds. She waved, smiling, and it was an invitation he couldn't refuse.

"Hi," was all he could manage when he reached her.

"Hello, Drew. It's been a long time. Funny how we can live in the same city and never run into each other. What's it been? Five years, six?"

Drew felt like he'd been gut-punched. The sight of her still weakened him, still hurt him deep inside.

"I was wondering if I'd see you here," she said. "I volunteered for the reunion committee, and I kept checking to see if you'd signed up for any events. But we never heard from you."

"Been pretty busy. I'm on the road with the team a lot. And going to practices and all."

She nodded, her eyes roaming him.

"Covering the game today?"

"Yeah, I probably ought to get up to the press box."

"Don't run off yet. Tell me all about your life."

"Not much to tell. Same old sports stuff. Somebody wins, somebody loses. Writing it up for the Gazette. Drinking after work with the guys from the office."

"I saw your address on the reunion lists. You're living in that high-rise over on Montgomery, the Monte Vista?"

He nodded. The building had a reputation as a place for swinging singles, not that he did much swinging. He spent most of his time at home in front of the tube, watching ESPN.

"Seems like a nice place," she said. "I've just seen it from the street, driving by."

"It's all right. What about you?"

"Freddie and I built a house up in the foothills. It's a long drive into the heart of the city, but it's what he wanted."

Drew frowned. She had to mention Freddie. If this conversation had to happen at all, at least she could've left Freddie out of it.

Then Freddie Graham himself popped clear of a group of people to Drew's left. He staggered over to them and threw a possessive arm around Helen's shoulders.

"Drew Gavin!" he shouted. "The eternal jock. How's it hanging?"

Freddie wore a polo shirt stretched tight over his stomach and khaki slacks and loafers without socks. His dark red hair was parted high on the side and slicked back. He reached out a manicured hand, which Drew swallowed in one of his own. Freddie shook it vigorously, as if he was glad to see him, as if Drew hadn't threatened years ago to break that very arm.

"Fine, Freddie."

"Good, good. I read your stuff in the paper sometimes, but I never see you around town. Why is that?"

Drew didn't want to talk to Freddie. He wanted to stand and stare at Helen, soaking her in as he had when they were in college. Back then, he'd watch her for hours at a time, until she'd get embarrassed and make him turn away. Looking at her then had been a constant reminder of his good fortune. Now it had the opposite effect.

"I think Drew travels in different circles," she said.

"Yeah," Freddie said, his voice still too loud. "Guess you don't spend much time among the country-club set."

"Only when I'm covering a golf tournament."

"Yeah? You cover golf?"

"Not often. I hate it."

The smile slid off Freddie's freckled face.

"Well, it's good to see you," he said nervously. "We've gotta run now. I see the mayor across the way. Need to go say hello."

"You go ahead," Helen said without looking at him. "I'll catch up. I want to visit with Drew for a minute."

Freddie had hold of her arm and he pulled slightly, "I need you with me. Business."

Helen peeled his fingers loose and gave him a pat on the shoulder.

"I'll be along in a minute, Freddie."

Freddie's eyes danced from Drew to Helen and back again, but he didn't argue.

"Good to see you, Drew," he said as he maneuvered away through the crowd.

Helen smiled at Drew. "Freddie's all business, all the time."

"Looks that way. He treating you well?"

She lifted a shoulder. "He tries hard to keep me happy."

"When he's not too busy with business."

"I'm used to it. That's the way I was raised."

Drew nodded, remembering.

"So you ever settle down and get married?"

"No. Never found the right woman, I guess."

"Too bad."

"Well, I found her," he said, and he couldn't believe the words were falling from his mouth. "But I let her get away."

She looked down, embarrassed, and Drew felt like a fool.

"Sorry, guess that was out of line."

Her quiet smile returned.

"It's okay," she said. "I still think about you sometimes. The other day, I heard an old Chuck Berry song on the radio and I remembered how we used to drive around town, singing along to those old songs. It made me smile."

"You thought I was crazy, but I'll always believe rock 'n' roll went downhill after the Beatles came along."

"You still listen to the oldies?"

"More than ever. Pop gave me his record collection."

"How is your father?"

"Not so good. He had a stroke a year ago, left him paralyzed down his right side. He's living in a nursing home."

"I'm sorry to hear that. It must be hard for you."

"His retirement fund pays for it. And his mind's okay. He's still the Coach."

Silence loomed between them. A cheer went up from inside the stadium.

"I'd better go," he said. "It was good to see you."

"You, too. Take care, Drew."

He turned away, the memories eating at him, but he caught movement from the corner of his eye and looked around to see Freddie Graham backed into a corner of the tent by a blond guy in a Hawaiian shirt. Something felt wrong. The guy talking to Freddie was too young to be at the reunion, for one thing, and he looked angry, poking Freddie in the chest with his finger. And Freddie had paled. The freckles on his face stood out like measles.

Drew glanced back at Helen, but she was facing the other way, already engrossed in conversation with a woman in a Lobo sweatshirt. He started to leave the tent—Freddie's problems were none of his concern—but he found himself snaking through the crowd toward Freddie and the man with the shaggy blond hair.

"Is there a problem here?"

Relief showed for an instant on Freddie's face. The blond man turned to face Drew, who saw at once he was a tough customer. He had squinty eyes with no life behind them, convict eyes. He was a few inches shorter than Drew and probably fifty pounds lighter, but he didn't back down.

"None of your business, hoss," he said. "Run along."

Drew suddenly felt warm all over.

"Maybe you're the one who'd better leave," he said. "Looks

like you're bothering people."

"It's okay, Drew," Freddie stammered. "A little misunder-standing—"

"You gonna make me leave, asshole?" the blond man snarled.

"If that's the way you want it."

The blond man glanced around the tent, checking out the crowd. Without warning, he looped an overhand right at Drew's face. Surprised, Drew ducked to his right, taking the punch on one side of his thick neck.

"Hey!"

The guy swung again, but Drew got a forearm up in time to block it. He grabbed the man's wrist in both hands and twisted hard. The guy's eyes widened as Drew twisted his arm behind him in a hammerlock. He bent the arm up between the guy's shoulder blades, hard enough so that the blond went up on his toes.

Drew leaned close to his ear and said, "Time for you to leave, stud. We're going to walk out of this tent. You try anything and I'll take this arm home as a souvenir."

He pushed him along, the man on tiptoe to ease the pressure on his arm and shoulder. The crowd had gone silent and Drew felt eyes on him, but he didn't look away from his captive. He marched him into the parking lot, and gave him a push as he let him go.

The guy spun around, ready to try it again, but football fans were thick outside the tent, and cops roamed the parking lot. He rubbed his shoulder, glaring at Drew.

"You don't know how to mind your own business," he said. "That could get you hurt."

Drew suddenly felt weary.

"Why don't you go home?" he said. "Don't ruin the game for everybody else."

The blond glanced around again, deciding, then he pointed at Drew.

"I ever see you again, you're a dead man," he said. He smiled, a cold smile that revealed bright, perfect teeth.

"Yeah, yeah. Get out of here."

The blond turned on his heel. Drew watched him go until he was out of sight. He wondered whether he should go back inside the tent and try to explain what had happened. He heard murmurs behind him, people who'd come out of the tent to watch. Drew sighed and trudged away toward the press box, rubbing the side of his neck.

TWO

Vicente "Three Eyes" Sanchez sat in the red leather barber chair Sunday morning, a sheet around his neck and his black-and-tan dachshund, Oscar, panting in his lap. Oscar sneezed occasionally from the bits of gray hair floating in the air as Max Reyes clipped away furiously, making sure his most important customer got the full treatment.

Three Eyes didn't make it easy for Max. He refused to remove his eyeglasses or his eye patch for the haircut, so Max had to work around lots of obstacles.

Three Eyes was nearly blind. He'd worn the patch over his left eye since spearing his face on a handlebar in a bicycle accident when he was nine years old. Over the years, the overworked right eye had gradually lost vision until the glasses he wore over the patch were thick as welder's goggles. Without his glasses, Three Eyes couldn't see a thing.

Max knew better than to ask him to remove the glasses so he'd have an easier time snipping away at his thinning hair. Three Eyes had so many enemies, he couldn't afford to sit blindly in the barber chair at a predictable hour every Sunday.

Max sighed in exasperation while he worked his scissors around the arms of the eyeglasses. He didn't complain, though. Max Reyes didn't want to find another shop, one where he'd have to pay rent.

Max's Barber Shop was a front for Three Eyes' bookie operation. From the sidewalk, passersby could see the mirrored walls and the two old-fashioned barber chairs and a counter covered with scissors and brushes and vats of blue antiseptic holding black combs. A weathered sofa buried under ancient magazines sat against the wall across from the chairs, in case Max ever had enough customers that someone had to wait.

You had to brave your way past a steel door marked "Employees Only" to see the real moneymaker. Back there, in a large room Max rarely visited, were long tables where Three Eyes' people sat with old-fashioned black phones to their ears and pencils in their hands, recording wagers on everything from who'd win the Super Bowl to who'd be the next Pope.

Max gave up some things in exchange for free rent. He couldn't hire a partner to man the other chair, because Three Eyes didn't want a stranger sniffing around the place. He lost customers who wouldn't visit his shop because they feared Three Eyes and his thugs. And, he had to keep the shop open every Sunday to explain the comings and goings of the book-ie's people. Damn few men wanted to waste their Sundays getting a haircut, so Three Eyes was often the only customer all day. It was understood that he didn't pay. They'd had this arrangement for twenty years.

"Tell me, Vicente," Max said. "You ever think about retiring?"

Three Eyes snorted. "To do what? Go fishing?"

"I think about it sometimes. We're not getting any younger. Wouldn't you like a rest?"

Three Eyes shook his head, another habit that annoyed Max. One of these days, he would move his head at the wrong moment, and Max would snip off one of his big ears. And that, Max knew, would be his last act on Earth.

"I got no time to rest," Three Eyes said. "I'm too busy making a buck."

Three Eyes was worth a fortune, but it was always the same

with him: Make more money, take more bets, punish those who paid late. Greed was a powerful force, one to which he'd surrendered years ago.

Max, on the other hand, barely scraped by with his limited clientele. No retirement fund for him. Sometimes he thought about chucking it all, getting some relief from a lifetime of seven-day workweeks, maybe even going fishing. He'd never tried fishing, but he kept hearing how relaxing it was. After twenty years of catering to Three Eyes and his revolving gang of toughs, Max could use a little relaxation.

The bell above the door jangled as two men entered. One was a stocky Navajo with a ragged scar down the right side of his face. The other was a tanned blond with squinty eyes and the whitest teeth Max had ever seen. Max caught himself frowning at the sight of them, and forced a smile under his twitching mustache.

"Hi, Zipper, Calvin. Beautiful day, eh?"

The Indian's real name was Luther Yazzie, but everyone called him Zipper because of the scar left by long-ago stitches. The scar looked so much like a zipper, Max had had nightmares about someone pulling it open and Zipper's brains spilling out. But Calvin Cox was the one who really scared him. Calvin was too pretty, with his surfer hair and his tight jeans and the toothbrush he always carried in the pocket of his Hawaiian shirt. Max thought Calvin was like a coral snake, all beautiful colors and deadly poison.

"Hey, Max," Calvin said, flashing his dazzling smile. "You're lookin' good. The rug looks almost natural today."

Calvin never passed through the shop without making a crack about Max's shiny black toupee. Max wasn't proud of the hairpiece. It was hot and it itched and he never forgot it sat on top of his head. But he had no choice. People don't trust a bald barber.

"Don't bother Max," Three Eyes growled. "He's working

on my hair."

Calvin grinned at them. Zipper was impassive. In the decade he'd known Zipper, Max had never seen him smile, frown, scowl, or laugh. The Navajo's face was like a block of stone, one that had been marred by a careless sculptor.

"I been waiting for you boys," Three Eyes said. "Where you been?"

Zipper grunted.

"I would'a been here an hour ago, but Calvin was sleeping in."

Three Eyes cocked the eyebrow over his good eye, which made the eyeglasses and the patch's strap move around his head. Max danced backward, scissors upraised. He'd nearly nicked Three Eyes, and the close call made him catch his breath.

"Sorry, boss," Calvin said, grinning so big that he didn't look the least bit sorry. "I was up late. After I made my rounds yesterday, I brought home a barmaid, and she worked me over good."

Max sighed. Calvin always had some tale of sexual conquest to share, even though nobody wanted to hear it.

"You should'a seen her, boss. Had tits like two pup tents. Tight little ass, make you think you died and went to heaven."

"Probably the closest to heaven you'll ever get," Three Eyes said.

Calvin cackled. "You're right about that, boss. But it's close enough to keep me happy."

Max put the scissors on the counter, and picked up the soft brush he used to sweep bits of hair off of customers' necks. He wasn't quite finished with Three Eyes, but he wasn't taking any more chances nicking him. Not when Three Eyes was yakking it up with his men.

"You know," Three Eyes said to Calvin, "if you paid as

much attention to business as you do to your dick, you'd be a
fuckin' millionaire."

Calvin came closer, reaching out to pat Oscar on the head.
The dog growled at him, but he didn't seem to notice.

"Can't put a price on love, boss."

Max unfastened the sheet from around Three Eyes' neck
and whisked it away with a flourish, nearly pitching Oscar
into the floor. The dog sneezed and glared at him.

"All done, Vicente."

"Yeah?" Three Eyes squinted at his reflection in the mirror.
"Okay. Looks good. You always do a good job, Max."

Max thanked him, thinking: You like it so much, how
about a tip once in a while?

Three Eyes clutched the dachshund to his chest as he wrestled his way out of the chair. He's moving slower these days,
Max thought, getting old. One of these days, Three Eyes
would die and finally be out of Max's life. Maybe then he
could retire.

Three Eyes lifted his old gray fedora from the counter and
clamped it down on his freshly shorn head, making Max
grind his teeth together. Max didn't know why Three Eyes
even bothered with his weekly haircuts. The only time he was
ever without the hat was when he was in the barber chair.

In fact, Three Eyes always looked as if he wore the exact
same clothes: gray felt hat, white guayabera shirt, gray slacks,
shiny black shoes. In cold months, he'd add a gray overcoat.

The Indian didn't change much from day to day either:
jeans and weathered cowboy boots, a plaid, pearl-buttoned
Western-style shirt, a hip-length brown leather coat to hide
his shoulder holster and the big knife on his belt. He wore his
black hair cut short in a flattop, the work of Max Reyes, who
made sure each week that every hair was the perfect length,
the top as flat and smooth as a pool table.

Calvin was the only peacock among them, with his flashy

shirts and the gold chains around his neck and that unnaturally blond mane. Max would like to give Calvin a good trim, make him look respectable. But Calvin seemed as vain about his long hair as he was about his shiny teeth. He'd told Max more than once that he only let women cut his hair. He liked them to rub up against him when they reached for his head. Sick fucker. Max would like to rub against him with his Buick.

"I got business for you," Three Eyes said to his mismatched men.

Max turned away and got his broom to sweep up the miserably few snippets of hair that had fallen from Three Eyes' head. He knew better than to listen too closely when business was being discussed.

He watched in the mirror as Three Eyes pulled a piece of paper from his shirt pocket.

"Time to make more collections." Calvin reached for the paper, but Three Eyes made a point of handing it to Zipper. "Some of these guys are two weeks late. Make them understand that's not acceptable."

Max shuddered at the thought of what Zipper and Calvin might do to the men whose names were on the list. Such thoughts had kept Max from ever placing a bet with the men behind the steel door. Even a sure thing wasn't worth the risk.

"You got it, boss," Calvin said, answering for both of them. Calvin, Max noted, liked to talk as much as Zipper preferred silence. How did they stand each other all day?

Calvin looked over the squat Indian's shoulder.

"Lotta names," he said. "Think we'll be done by tonight?"

Three Eyes hoisted the dog higher so it could lick his cheek. "I don't care how long it takes. Just do it."

"I got a hot date tonight," Calvin said. "Wouldn't want to miss it."

"Thinking with your dick again," Three Eyes grumbled.

"Business first, hah?"

"Sure, boss."

"Any questions?" Three Eyes asked Zipper, who still studied the list as if it were in some foreign language.

The Indian slowly shook his head.

"Okay, come by tomorrow. Tell me how it went."

Zipper nodded and turned toward the door without a word.

Calvin flashed his teeth at the mirror. "See ya later, Max. Let a little air get under that rug, okay? Wouldn't want you to mildew."

The pair breezed out the door. Max welcomed the jingle of the bell that signaled they were gone. He turned back to Three Eyes, his hands clasped before him.

"Anything else, Vicente?"

"No. I'll be in the back. Time to feed Oscar."

Three Eyes lugged the little dog through the back door. Max got a glimpse of the old-timers manning the phone bank before the door swung shut.

He let out his breath in a rush. Christ, what he put up with for free rent. He needed to retire, find a hobby. Maybe fishing. At least, out fishing, he wouldn't need the stupid toupee.

THREE

Helen wished Freddie would put the newspaper away. They'd slept late and were sitting in their robes across from each other in the sunny breakfast nook of their sprawling home. She'd prepared coffee and grapefruit and toast—which was about the extent of her culinary skills—but Freddie didn't stop reading the Sunday Gazette to eat. His hand appeared, fumbled for a slice of toast, then disappeared behind the newspaper.

Helen sighed. When it had no effect, she sighed again, louder.

"What's the matter, dear?" Freddie said from behind the newspaper.

"Are you about finished?"

He collapsed the Gazette into his lap to look at her.

"Just reading what your old boyfriend wrote about the Lobos. I was so busy during the game, shaking hands and shit, I bet I only saw half the plays."

"You didn't miss much."

"That's what Drew seems to be saying here. He really laid it on heavy when it came to those fumbles in the fourth quarter. That kid, what's his name—"

He popped open the paper and scanned the article.

"The halfback. Here it is, Jamal Moore. Listen to this: 'Moore raced down the field with eight minutes to go in the fourth quarter, but he failed to take the ball with him. The pigskin bounced off his knee and tumbled along the ground for five yards before Brigham Young defensive back Stanley Stevens snatched it up. Moore was nearly to the end zone before he realized he'd forgotten something.' That's gotta hurt."

Helen stared out the French doors at the well-tended lawn and the twin sycamore trees, which showed their first traces of autumn gold. The house was set in the rolling foothills of the Sandia Mountains, surrounded by wild chamisa and piñon and cactus, but Freddie had insisted on a weekly gardener and a square of irrigated lawn, no matter the cost.

"Imagine being that kid," he continued. "You fumble a couple of times, cost your team the game. Then you read this the next morning. Just makes you feel worse."

Helen turned back to Freddie, who smiled smugly, waiting for her to say something.

"Sounds accurate to me."

"I think old Drew is living in the past," he said. "He's sore because he's not down on the field with the rest of the jocks. So he takes it out on this kid."

"I don't really want to talk about Drew—"

"I saw the way he looked at you yesterday. Football's not the only thing he misses, I'll bet."

Helen glanced down at her hands in her lap, caught herself picking at her cuticles and forced herself to stop. She'd get another scolding from Noreen, her manicurist, if she showed up at her Wednesday appointment with wrecked nails.

"The problem with guys like Drew is they think muscles count for something. It's brains, Helen—that's what matters in this world. He can't admit the better man won."

"Freddie—"

"You notice the way he looked? Needed a shave. Sloppy clothes. I think the old boy's letting himself go."

"Can we talk about something else?"

He grinned mischievously, then set the newspaper on the table.

"Don't like me to bring up the past, sweetheart? What would you like to talk about?"

"There's that benefit on Friday night. The one at the Hilton? Cheryl and Sandra are coming over later today to finish the preparations."

"Sounds like I need to get out of the house. I can't stand those two."

Helen frowned at him. "They've worked really hard to put this thing together."

"Which one is this again? Crippled children or something?"

"Muscular dystrophy. A black-tie dinner and a silent auction. I told you about it last week."

"So many of these things—I can't keep 'em all straight."

"You're the one who encourages me to get involved with them," she said icily. "You always say, 'It's good for business.'"

"I know, sweetheart. And it is. You want to be a player in the community, you've got to put on your monkey suit and be seen."

"It's a good cause, Freddie—"

"Sure it is. They all are. But they end up costing me money."

Helen looked out into the yard again. The patch of grass was green and lush. She caught herself wishing for a weed, a dandelion. Her life felt like that lawn, pristine and prosaic and predictable.

"Speaking of money," he said, "let's not buy anything at that auction, okay?"

"Why not?"

"What could we possibly need?" He gestured broadly at the well-furnished house. "We always buy stuff we don't need, just for appearances' sake."

"You're the one who cares about appearances."

"Usually, yeah. But it's a silent auction, right? Nobody'll know if we give it a pass."

"What's the problem, Freddie? It's not like we don't have the money."

Now it was his turn to stare out the window.

"You might be surprised," he said.

"What's that supposed to mean?"

"Nothing. Little cash flow problem. I've got a lot of irons in the fire right now."

Helen knew nothing of their financial situation. Freddie insisted on handling the household accounts himself. His study, full of files and bills and stale cigar smoke, might as well be a tomb in Egypt for all she knew of what went on in there. Freddie always wanted to feel he was running things. He didn't want her to work. He didn't want to have children. Helen obediently built her life around charity balls and ladies' lunches and dinners at the Petroleum Club with her table-hopping husband. All good for business, if not very fulfilling. Freddie's business was mostly a mystery to her. She knew that, for a lawyer, he spent damned little time in courtrooms. Too busy wheeling and dealing, cooking up mergers and buyouts with her father.

"Do I need to be worried?" she asked.

He ran a hand through his red hair before his face split into its familiar grin.

"Not at all, sugar. I wouldn't want you to crease that beautiful face with worry lines. Leave it up to old Freddie. He's looking after things."

What things? she wondered. What cash flow problems?

"Does this have something to do with that man who cornered you at the reunion yesterday?" she asked.

"I told you—that was a case of mistaken identity. That guy thought I was somebody else."

"Good thing for you Drew got in the middle of it," she said flatly.

Freddie's face flushed. "I had things under control. Wasn't any reason for him to muscle in."

She opened her mouth to argue, but the phone on the kitchen counter rang, and Freddie leaped up to answer it.

"Hello? Oh, hi, Nick! How are ya?"

Freddie turned so he faced Helen, the curly phone cord wrapped halfway around him.

"Golf this afternoon? Sounds great!"

He smiled and waggled his eyebrows at Helen. He'd found his out for the afternoon visit by Cheryl and Sandra. Nobody—especially not Freddie—turned down an invitation from Nick Casso.

Freddie listened for a full minute, nodding along. Then he said, "I've got those papers in my study. Can I call you right back? I'll trot down there and have everything in front of me. Okay? Bye."

He untangled himself from the phone cord and hung up.

"Sorry, hon. Duty calls."

Freddie trotted down the hall, his bathrobe flapping, eager to do her daddy's bidding.

Helen stacked the newspaper on the table. Drew Gavin's byline lay before her on the sports page. She picked up the paper and scanned the terse account of another Lobo failure.

Her gaze strayed again to her manicured lawn outside her perfect home. And she sighed.

FOUR

Curtis White was smoking one of his smelly French cigarettes just outside the back door to the newsroom, which was a good thing for Drew, since he'd forgotten the card key for the employee entrance. On Sundays, the lobby was battened down tighter than the American embassy in Beirut. He could've stood outdoors a long time waiting for one of his colleagues inside to open the door. As it was, he only needed to wait until Curtis finished his smoke.

"Shit, man, you don't look so good," Curtis said by way of greeting.

"Don't feel so good, either. Thanks to you."

"Hey, man, not my fault. I told you not to eat that worm."

Drew definitely remembered Curtis egging him on about the worm in the mescal bottle—it was one of the few things he did remember from the night before at Champions Sports Bar—but he didn't want to start an argument. Curtis would argue about which direction the sun came up, given the chance, and Drew didn't want to delay his entrance into the newsroom any longer than necessary. He felt too crummy to hang around outside.

It was a warm sunny day, but Drew still had the shakes from his pounding hangover, and the bright sunlight didn't help. He'd searched his battered old Jeep for sunglasses before braving the freeways, but they didn't turn up. They were probably in the bartender's lost-and-found collection at Champions.

He squinted at Curtis, who seemed in no hurry to open the door. Curtis looked none the worse for wear, as always. The man could drink everybody else under the table—hell, under the floor—and feel no ill effects the next day. It wasn't fair.

Curtis wore a lime-green knit shirt over chocolate-brown pants that were nearly the same shade as his skin. His hair was twisted into three-inch-long dreadlocks that pointed in every direction, and his eyes had that sleepy look that drove women wild. Curtis stood six-and-a-half feet tall, giving him a couple of inches over Drew, but he weighed maybe one-hundred-and-eighty pounds soaking wet. His body was all angles and sharp-edged planes. He looked like you could cut yourself on him, but that didn't scare the women away.

"Got a hangover, huh?" Curtis said, a smile spreading across his face.

"I was recovering until I got a look at that shirt."

"What's the matter with this shirt?"

"It's so loud I could hear it in the Jeep."

"Man, you don't know fashion, that's all. This shirt's hot. This color is the style."

Curtis pronounced "style" as if it were the secret password that opened all doors. For him, that was probably true.

"You should talk. Look at you, wearing those same dog-ass clothes. No wonder women give you the breeze."

Drew looked down at his own clothes. Faded Levis, Converse sneakers, a blue rugby shirt with a "Sun Bowl" logo on the chest.

"This is how I always dress."

"That's what I'm saying."

Curtis blew a smoke ring into the still air and watched it drift away.

"Are you about through with that thing? I need inside."

"You waiting on me? I thought you just swung by to insult my threads."

"Come on, Curtis. The sun's burning a hole through my skull."

"Gotta stay away from those worms, man. They'll kill you."

"I'm gonna kill you in a minute, you don't open that door."

"Chill, man. I got it."

Curtis flicked away the butt. He pulled his card-key from his hip pocket and swiped it through a reader on the wall. The door unlocked with a click, and Drew pulled it open.

Drew and Curtis had known each other since college, though they hadn't become friends until both were working at the Gazette. If Drew sometimes felt that all his football dreams had been shattered because his ankles had let him down, Curtis had no complaints. He'd stayed healthy and talented through his basketball career. He just hadn't been focused. He was more interested in a good time than a good future. He didn't seem to let the past bother him, either. He drifted from one party to the next, from one woman to another, seemingly happy all the time. Curtis was his best friend, but sometimes he made Drew's teeth hurt.

"Yo, gentlemen," Curtis said loudly to the assembled sportswriters. "Mr. Gavin has graced us with his presence."

This announcement was greeted with the usual jeers and sneers. The sports desk was a tightly knit team, but they'd drink Jim Jones punch before they'd admit it.

"Gavin, you look like shit," shouted Spiffy O'Neill, the old master of the desk.

"And you don't smell so great, either," said Chris "Sparky" Anderson, who sat at the desk across from Drew's.

All the noise made Drew's head hurt.

"Thank you, one and all," he said, raising his hands as if

accepting applause. "I couldn't let a day go by without seeing you guys. I might go normal."

"No way," said Spiffy.

"Not a chance," added Sparky.

Dave Hogan, who answered to Filthy, grunted his agreement without looking up from his glowing computer terminal. Hogan was the desk's copy editor, fixing grammar and writing headlines, and they rarely got a word out of him. The man had tunnel vision when it came to his work. And he didn't seem to do anything besides work. He sure as heck didn't spend much time at the laundry. He was wearing the same clothes he'd worn yesterday and the day before, and the wrinkles suggested he'd slept in them, too.

"Benedict here?" Drew asked, glancing around the mostly empty newsroom.

"No way," Spiffy said. "You're not gonna get that sucker to come in on a Sunday."

Most of the writers were intimidated by sports editor Greg Benedict, who was a snake on two legs, but Spiffy had been working at the paper when God was a boy and he professed to fear nothing except maybe getting his clothes dirty or scuffing his shiny loafers.

Drew slumped into the armless chair behind his desk and swiveled it so he was speaking to Spiffy, who sat in the back row by the tall windows. Curtis's desk separated theirs, but he'd wandered off somewhere, so their view of each other wasn't impeded by his spiky dreadlocks, as it usually was.

"I didn't think I could face Benedict today," Drew said. "I've got a pounder of a hangover."

"Ah, that would explain the green around your gills," Spiffy said brightly. "Let me guess: You went out last night with Curtis."

Drew nodded somberly.

"I keep telling you, that young man will put you in an

early grave."

"I feel like I dug my way out of one."

Spiffy smiled, which made him look even more like a leprechaun, one who wears a snap-brim hat indoors and whose wide necktie features a painted hula dancer.

"You've got to take care of yourself when you're young, my boy. Otherwise, you'll look like me when you get old."

"You're in better shape than I am right now."

"It's all a facade, my boy. Smoke and mirrors. On the inside, I'm a little old man."

Spiffy liked to play this game, talking himself down. Drew knew there were widows lined up around the block for a chance to go dancing with the Spiffster.

A portable television hung from a bracket on the ceiling, and a cheer rose from the NFL game that played there.

"Packers just scored," Filthy Hogan said without looking up from his computer monitor. Drew didn't know how Filthy could see the computer through his smudged eyeglasses, much less the TV.

Heads swiveled to watch the replay. Brett Favre scrambled to his left, then sent a pass zipping back across the field to a wide receiver who'd gotten open in the end zone.

"Hit him right in the chest," Drew said.

"That catch was self-defense," Sparky said from the other side of the desks. "If he hadn't gotten his hands on it, it would've smoked a hole through him."

"That youngster's got quite an arm all right," Spiffy agreed. "I'm reminded of Staubach in his salad days—"

Drew swung his chair back around to face his cluttered desk. Once Spiffy launched into stories about the good old days, you could be caught up for hours. Drew's sudden departure from the conversation meant Sparky would get both barrels.

He thought of his workmates—with the exception of

Curtis—as the Dwarves. They were mostly small men who'd spent their lives watching sports rather than playing them. And they all answered to nicknames that ended in "y," most bestowed by Greg Benedict. Even the one woman on the sports staff, a shovel-jawed Oklahoman named Henrietta Morehouse who didn't work Sundays because she was busy at church, answered to "Henry."

Drew and Curtis White had no nicknames, partly because their names didn't lend themselves to such playing around and partly because Benedict despised them. Curtis always said that was a good thing—"Else, he might call me 'Whitey' and I'd have to kill him"—but Drew often felt left out. Another reason to hate Benedict.

The sportswriters sat at the back of the newsroom, as far from the public entrance as the editors could put them. Newsrooms were once smoky, noisy places, but the Gazette's had about as much atmosphere as an insurance office, with gray industrial carpeting and rows of beige desks. The noise of constantly ringing telephones was dulled by the carpet; smoking was only allowed outdoors; and newspeople in general seemed a more sedate bunch these days than you'd see in *The Front Page*.

The only part with any personality was sports, where the language was rough and the jokes bitter and the desks were buried under stat books and game programs and other detritus. A fabric-covered wall to Drew's left separated the sports department from the quieter environs of features, where the reporters wrote about gardening and food and the arts. The Wailing Wall, as it was called, was decorated with old photos and mangled tennis rackets and golf clubs bent like paper clips. Here and there were pinned up handwritten quotations from staff members, dated and signed, predictions of victories or particularly pithy sayings. Some of the statements were so old the paper had yellowed and curled, including one Spiffy had scrawled years ago: "This sports department will never have a woman on its staff." That was Henry's favorite, and she wouldn't let anyone remove it.

The desks in sports faced the rest of the newsroom and its glowing computer monitors. The center of the room was dominated by the copy desk, where the desks were set in an oblong meant to duplicate the old horseshoe-shaped "rims" that were around back when everything was done with paper and paste. These days, thanks to computers, a story never touched paper until it hit the big presses at the far end of the building.

The Gazette was a morning newspaper, which meant most of the Sunday workers wouldn't arrive until later in the afternoon. The copy desk sat empty, and only a few industrious reporters wandered about the city desk at the other end of the room. The top editors had glassed-in offices that ran along one wall, and all were dark except for the one occupied by the editor, Bob Goodman. Near as Drew could tell, Goodman lived in that office. He was usually the first to arrive and the last to leave, which Drew figured could explain his three divorces, his baldness and the jitteriness that left chewed-up pencils scattered around his desk. Drew considered Goodman the consummate high-strung newsman, though he was prone to personnel mistakes, like hiring Benedict.

One of Goodman's better hires, a twenty-six-year-old police reporter named Teresa Vargas, bustled around the city desk. She was a Las Cruces native who'd gone to UNM and then worked a few years at the Santa Fe paper before moving up to the Gazette. Drew watched as she picked up a phone and stood hip-cocked, listening. He'd caught himself watching her a lot in the months since she'd arrived at the Gazette. Partly, that was because she was easy on the eyes—slim and dark with an easy smile that made him think of Helen. Partly, it was because of her bohemian fashion tastes, which reflected her time in Santa Fe. Four or five earrings pierced each ear and a like number of bracelets jangled around each wrist. She tended toward black clothes with neon-colored shoes and accessories to match. Today, she wore black jeans and purple shoes and a purple bowling shirt. Her lipstick and nails were the same shade of purple and she wore a little girl's purple bow in her spiky black hair. If other reporters showed up to work looking that way, Goodman would usher them into his office for a little talk. But Teresa Vargas had already proved she could kick ass on the blood-and-guts police beat, and the brass seemed content to sit back and marvel at her.

Maybe that's what I need, Drew thought glumly. Get the attention of the editors. Start wearing purple lipstick like Dennis Rodman.

Later, he was engrossed in stat sheets from Saturday's Lobo loss when Teresa appeared at his desk.

"Hey, tiger," she said. "Got a tip for you."

He smiled when he looked up, and she twinkled back at him. He could feel himself blushing. Someone behind him, probably Spiffy, snickered.

"Yeah?" he said, rocking back in his chair and crossing his arms over his chest. "What kinda sports story would you have?"

"Might be a hot one." She was chewing gum and cracking it between sentences. "I was doing my rounds on the way into work and I was at the cop shop, going through the arrest reports."

"Yeah?"

"One of them's missing. A sheriff's department report. They're numbered and I always check the sequence. I asked the duty sergeant and he said he didn't know anything about it. Blew me off. I waited until his back was turned and then I used a pencil on the next report, kind of scribbled on it, to see what might've been written on the report that was missing.

You know, it leaves an impression—"

"Bet they don't like you scribbling on their reports."

"Not if they caught me, they wouldn't. But I erased it before anybody noticed."

"You get a name?"

"Yeah. Jamal Moore."

He sat up straight. "Jamal Moore? Are you sure?"

"Yeah. I couldn't make out what he was arrested for or anything. I mean, I wasn't going to scribble on the entire report. But I got that name. Then I saw his name in your story just now, and I put two and two together."

Drew scratched at his chin. "I wonder if it's the same guy?"

"How many Jamal Moores could there be in Albuquerque?"

"I don't know, but I'll look into it. Thanks for the tip."

"You bet, tiger."

She breezed off toward the city desk, and Drew watched her go. Jamal Moore? If the Lobos' star halfback had been arrested, that would be big news. Might even get Jamal bounced off the team. Of course, the way he's been fumbling the ball, that might be for the best. Jamal was a local kid, out of Highland High School, and Drew had assumed he'd have a bright future with the Lobos. Except lately he couldn't hang onto the football if it had handles.

Drew returned to his Monday story, doing the postmortem on Saturday's game, but his mind kept slipping back to Jamal Moore and how to check out Teresa's tip. An hour later, the story walked in the door all by itself.

The employees' door was all glass and Curtis, returning from the break room with a Pepsi in his hand, spotted someone out there before he could take his seat. Drew saw Curtis heading toward the door, and he swiveled his chair to see what other doofus had forgotten his card key. But it was no employee tapping his knuckles on the door. It was a beefy black man with a shiny shaved head. He wore a red nylon sweatsuit and sneakers, but that was the only relaxed thing about him. His face bore a scowl, and he held his body straight as a drill sergeant. Curtis threw open the door, and Drew heard the stranger mention his name.

Before Drew could finish thinking, "Uh-oh," a smirking Curtis led the man to his desk.

"This brother's looking for you."

The man leaned over Drew's desk, placing his big fists on the piles of newspapers and notes that covered the desktop.

"My name's Buck Moore," the man rumbled. "I want to talk to you."

Drew skated backward a foot in his rolling chair. The man wasn't quite as large as Drew, but his expression said he was mad. He had beer on his breath, too, so Drew quickly added it up: A big, angry man who's been drinking wants to talk to me in person. Oh, shit.

Lots of pissed-off crazies wander into newsrooms, falsely assuming that barking at a reporter will get them better coverage. That's why the lobby is manned by security guards during the week and kept locked tight on weekends. But this guy had come to the employees' entrance, and Curtis had blithely let him in. Drew cut his eyes to Curtis, who stood off to one side, smiling at his predicament.

"Yes, sir," Drew said. "What can I do for you?"

"I've got a son. His name's Jamal Moore. That ring a bell with you?"

"Yes, sir."

"You roughed him up pretty good in the paper this morning," Moore said. "You blamed the loss on him, and that's not fair."

Drew scooted back another foot in his chair, until it bumped up against the front of Curtis' desk. Still not far enough to be out of slapping range if Moore decided to take a swat at him, but at least it gave him a little room to maneuver.

"He put the ball on the ground twice in the fourth quarter. The Lobos had a chance before that."

Moore glowered.

"You can't blame the whole game on one kid, on two plays. It's not fair. You hurt people when you write shit like that."

"I'd hurt the readers if I did it any other way."

The other sportswriters sat mutely, watching the argument unfold. Drew didn't expect any help from the Dwarves. They could all assault Moore and he might not even notice. And Curtis was too busy grinning to join in. Bastard.

Moore reached out and jabbed Drew in the chest with a stiff forefinger.

"Lay off my kid."

Drew narrowed his eyes at the angry man.

"You'd better keep that finger to yourself. Unless you want to lose it."

Moore glanced down at his extended finger, then back up at Drew. His arm flexed as if he wanted to push Drew again, but then it dropped to his side.

"I've had about enough of your newspaper and its snide reporting."

"Then maybe you'd better cancel your subscription."

Moore shot him a baleful look and turned toward the door.

"Hold on a second," Drew said. "I've got a question for you."

Moore stopped where he was and glared at Drew. "Yeah?"

"I heard a rumor that Jamal got arrested last night," he said offhandedly. "Is that right?"

Moore's eyes widened briefly, then he reset his face into a scowl.

"The hell did you hear something like that?"

"Doesn't matter. Is it true?"

"I'm not talking to you about anything. Go fuck yourself."

"So you can't deny he was arrested? Have you seen him since last night?"

Moore strode back up to the desk, and pointed his finger at Drew's face, an inch from his nose.

"I told you to lay off my kid. He's a good boy. He wasn't arrested for anything. He was home with his mother and me after the game. You print anything else about him, and I'm gonna come looking for you. You got that?"

Drew tried to grin, but it didn't seem to take. Moore glared at him a moment longer, then stalked out the door. The Dwarves turned in their chairs to watch him cross the parking lot. Drew was surprised to see Moore fling open the door of a Bernalillo County Sheriff's Department car and climb behind the wheel.

"Look out, Drew," Curtis said, laughing "You messing with the law."

Drew scowled at him.

"Yeah, and he's messing with a man with a hangover. Who made the worse mistake?"

The Dwarves laughed, but Drew didn't join them as he watched the cop car roll away. If Moore's with the sheriff's department, he thought, maybe that's how that arrest report turned up missing. Certainly something to look into. As soon as this hangover passes.

FIVE

Zipper wheeled his spotless, twenty-year-old Pontiac through Sunday afternoon traffic on San Mateo Boulevard, gripping the wheel tightly at ten and two o'clock. Calvin Cox grinned, watching the Navajo drive. The man was so intent, he never even blinked.

"Hey, Zip, you in a hurry?"

"Gotta lotta stops to make," Zipper said, barely moving his lips.

"Thought maybe you were getting yourself psyched up."

"I'm always psyched up."

"Psych-o's more like it." Calvin laughed at his own lame joke.

"You should talk. Crazy motherfucker."

Calvin fished the toothbrush out of his pocket and stuck it in the side of his mouth. He sometimes went at his teeth for hours at a time with the dry toothbrush. Other times, like now, he just sucked on it.

"Least I don't go around with a toothbrush all the time," Zipper muttered.

"Watch out now, Zip. You're gonna regret that when we're old men and I'm sitting around with pearly whites while you're gumming your oatmeal."

Zipper grunted. They'd had this discussion at least once a week for the two years they'd worked together. Calvin knew Zipper didn't expect to reach old age. Not in this line of work.

Zipper whipped the Pontiac across two lanes of traffic and made an abrupt right turn into the potholed parking lot of Joe's Place, a concrete bunker of a bar with painted-over windows. The place was tucked back from the street between two strip malls, and he nearly drove past it every time business required them to stop in and see Joe Serna.

Serna was a fat slob who barely kept his business afloat, but he still found money to place weekly bets with Three Eyes. The man was one of those compulsive gamblers who'd bet on any sport, even ones he knew shit about. Serna would bet on the fucking weather.

Two pickup trucks were parked in front of Joe's Place. Calvin recognized one of them, a blue Chevy, as belonging to Joe himself. The other might belong to a customer or an employee. Zipper's mouth twitched.

"You want me to handle this one, Zip? I like old Joe. I could give him a little talking-to."

"We'll both go."

"Okay, but keep yourself under control. Joe's a good customer."

"Joe's late on his payment. That makes him a bad customer."

Calvin pocketed his toothbrush, and they got out of the Pontiac and eased up to the bar's dimpled steel door. Inside, it was dark as a vault, lit only by a few Budweiser neons behind the bar, and they paused to let their eyes adjust. Joe recognized them right away. Sweat popped out like jewels on his bald head, and his mouth worked soundlessly under his black mustache. One customer, a gray-bearded guy wearing a railroad engineer's cap, nursed a beer at the bar across from Joe. He turned on his barstool to get a look at them.

Calvin didn't waste any time. He strode across the saloon and clapped a hand on the old-timer's shoulder.

"Time to go," he said.

"The hell you mean? I've got a beer here—"

Calvin squeezed the bony shoulder until the geezer's eyes went wide.

"Joe needs to close down for a while. He's got some personal business."

"But—"

Calvin thought maybe he'd have to slap the old man, get his attention, but the guy looked down and spotted the butt of the pistol jutting from Calvin's belt.

"See you later, Joe," the customer said quickly. "Sorry."

Calvin let go of the old man's shoulder and gave him a slap on the ass as he headed for the exit.

"Good thinking," he called behind the customer.

Zipper stood just inside the door where he'd stopped to let his eyes adjust. The old man edged past him and out the door. Zipper's eyes never left Joe's face, and it was as if the power of the Indian's stare caused the sweat to pour down Joe's forehead.

"Hi, fellas," Joe said anxiously. "Three Eyes send you around?"

"That's right, Joe," Calvin said brightly. "You're late again."

Joe stammered an apology, but his gaze never shifted from Zipper. Calvin might be the attention-getter, with his loud voice and louder clothes, but Zip was the one everyone feared.

Zipper stepped up to the bar and rested his brown hands on top of it. He slid his hands back and forth, as if checking the bar's smoothness.

"You fellas want a beer?"

"No thanks, Joe," Calvin said, still keeping his tone light. "Zipper here don't drink. Ain't that right, Zip?"

Zipper didn't take his eyes off Serna and didn't acknowledge the offer or Calvin's ribbing answer.

"Come here, Joe," he said softly. "Let me see your hands."

"My hands?" Serna's hands went behind his back. He had to force himself to reach across the bar to Zipper, who studied the hands intently.

"You got nice hands for a fat man," Calvin said. "You go to a manicurist?"

Serna's trembled as he watched Zipper.

"Why you want to see my hands?"

"Trying to decide which finger to take back to Three Eyes."

Zipper drew the big hunting knife from his belt so quickly, it was as if it had materialized in his grip. With his other hand he grasped Serna's wrist and held it tight so the bartender couldn't jerk free.

"Jesus Christ, don't cut me, Zipper," Serna said breathlessly. "I'll pay up."

Zipper rested the blade across Serna's knuckles. One downward thrust, and all four fingers would get shorter.

"Hey, Zip, don't cut his hand," Calvin called. "How's he gonna draw beers?"

Zipper didn't reply, didn't even look up when Calvin vaulted over the bar and came up close beside Joe Serna.

"See, Joe?" Calvin said, his voice barely above a whisper. "You gotta be careful. You stiff Three Eyes, next thing you know, you got Zipper hacking on you with that big knife."

Serna gulped and nodded.

"You owe Three Eyes four thousand dollars," Calvin whispered in his ear. "This makes Three Eyes unhappy. And when the boss is unhappy, Zipper gets weird like this."

Calvin looked past Joe's head to Zipper, slipped him a wink.

"Let him go, Zip. You cut off his fingers, Joe won't be able to work. Then how's he gonna get the money?"

Serna nodded vigorously, his jowls bouncing around. He squinted and blinked, either against tears or sweat, Calvin couldn't tell.

"Listen to him, Zipper," Serna croaked. "I'll get the money. I swear it."

Zipper lifted the knife and turned away. By the time he made it to the door, the knife was back in its sheath. His expression had never changed.

"Look here, Joe," Calvin said, stepping back to give the fat man room to turn around behind the bar. Serna was so relieved to keep his fingers, he didn't see the punch coming.

Calvin swung hard, a right uppercut that sank so deeply into Joe's gut that Calvin could swear he felt backbone. Foul air blew out of Serna's mouth and he doubled over, then dropped to his knees. Calvin kept his fist cocked, ready to deliver another, but Joe's eyes were swimming around in his head.

"That's so you don't forget, Joe. You don't deliver that money in two days, I'm gonna turn Zipper loose on you. Your fingers will be the least of your problems."

Serna, still fighting for breath, managed to nod.

Calvin leapt back over the bar, landing between two stools. He leaned over the bar to look down at Serna.

"Two days, Joe," he said, and he followed Zipper out the door.

They got into the Pontiac and Zipper cranked the engine and swung onto San Mateo.

"That was good, Zip. That stuff with the knife. Joe didn't know you were just fuckin' around."

"I wasn't fuckin' around. I was gonna cut him."

Calvin let his eyes go wide at Zipper, but he was laughing on the inside.

"You in a bad mood, Zip?"

"I'm tired of these fat fucks not paying up," Zipper said. "Gonna start taking pieces of 'em home with me."

Calvin leered at him. "Gonna start scalping them?"

"That's not funny, shithead."

"Hey, c'mon, Zip, I'm just kidding around."

Calvin tried to look hurt, but he wasn't much good at it. The grin kept fighting itself back onto his face. He plucked the toothbrush from his pocket and stuck it in his cheek.

"I think this job's getting to you, Zip. You're not the same carefree fella I used to know."

The thought of Zipper ever being carefree caused Calvin to laugh uproariously, but the Navajo just stared through the windshield, pushing the Pontiac through traffic.

"Who's next on the list?" he asked.

Calvin fished the list out of his pocket. Zipper had handed it over to him as soon as they were out of Three Eyes' sight. The boss entrusted the weekly list to Zipper, but only Calvin knew reading it was a struggle for him.

"Our next contestant," Calvin boomed in a fake TV announcer's voice, "is Mr. Freddie Graham from Albuquerque, New Mexico."

Zipper chewed on that, and Calvin could tell he was running Three Eyes' inventory through his head.

"Idn't he that fuckin' lawyer?"

"That's right, Zip. He's a rich motherfucker, too."

"And he's behind on his payment?"

"That's why he's on the list. I went to see him yesterday. Tracked him down at this reunion thing outside the stadium where the Lobos play. I told him he had until midnight to pay up, or he was going to go on the list."

"Why didn't you rough him up then?"

"All kinds of people around. Then this big fucker, must be a friend of his, got into the middle of it, tried to run me off."

"What did you do?"

Calvin shifted in his seat.

"Nothing. Lotta cops nosing around. But I'm gonna keep my eye out for that fucker. I see him again, I'll pop a cap in his ass."

Zipper grumbled.

"I hate fuckin' lawyers," he said finally.

"Me, too, Zip. That's why this one's gonna be so much fun."

SIX

Freddie Graham steered into the shady parking lot of the Albuquerque Country Club in his silver Porsche, gunning the engine before whipping into an open slot. His golf clubs rattled in their leather bag. The Porsche's trunk wasn't big enough to hold the bag, so Freddie had strapped it in next to him with the seat belt.

He got out of the car and let his hand trail along its sleek fender while he went around to the other side to get his clubs. Freddie had known since he was a poor kid on Chicago's South Side that he'd drive a sports car like this one day. Too bad the little fucker cost so much. Six hundred dollars a month, after a big down payment. It cost a lot to keep up appearances. These days, every dime counted. If he didn't eliminate his debts, and damned quick, he'd look out his window some day soon to see a repo truck towing the Porsche away.

He snatched up the clattering bag, slung it over his shoulder and stalked off toward the country club, his cleated black-and-white shoes clacking on the asphalt.

The Albuquerque Country Club featured the same white stucco walls and red tiled roof as Freddie's house. Inside, the building was cool tile and dark wood and open spaces designed for mingling. All good for business. So was the bar, where many a deal had been cut over the years.

Freddie hadn't grown up frolicking in the corridors like

many of his peers. He'd been the youngest of seven red-haired boys born to a hard-drinking firefighter and a weary, rosary-counting housewife. He'd come to New Mexico to attend law school, bucking the family tradition that sent every one of his dumb-ass brothers into the Chicago fire brigades. Meeting Helen had been a way into the country club life. Nick had been a member of the club's board so long, it took only a wave of his hand to get a person admitted. Nick even agreed to pay the membership fee in perpetuity, as a gift to his daughter. Funny how Helen never came down here except for the occasional game of tennis. It was Freddie who hung around the bar and teed off with Nick.

Freddie glanced at his stainless steel Rolex as he breezed through the lobby. Nick expected him to be punctual, even though Freddie had to drive all the way down from the foothills, and Nick lived only three blocks from the golf course.

Freddie saw Mark Bellows and Chip Williams huddled over drinks at the far end of the lobby. Normally he would've joined them, see if maybe he could grab a piece of whatever they were cooking up. But Nick was waiting, and he had to make do with a smile and a wave as he hustled out the back door toward the links.

Nick Casso paced beside his golf cart. He wore lemon-yellow pants, a white polo shirt, and a knitted hat that looked like it belonged on a pimp. He pointedly glanced at his watch, and Freddie practically sprinted over to him.

"You're late," Nick barked in greeting.

"Got caught in traffic. Sorry."

Nick scowled at him, his heavy eyebrows jutting like devil's horns from his creased forehead. Like the eyebrows, Nick's hair was jet black, and Freddie suspected Nick dyed it to keep himself looking young and competitive. Like he needed to worry. In this town when Nick said a word, any word, in his

Greek-tinged baritone, his bidding was done.

Nick Casso had grown up in his family's grocery store, a dusty place long ago given over to the wrecking ball. He'd watched his old man, Demetrius Casso, fleece the locals from the time he was big enough to crawl. Demetrius had come over from the old country at the turn of the century and had ended up settling in a desert town way out in New Mexico. By the time Demetrius passed away in the 1960s, he owned half of downtown Albuquerque. Nick had taken over the family businesses, and mostly through force of will had turned them into multimillion-dollar industries. There wasn't much that happened in the city these days without Nick's blessing.

At the top of that list was whatever occurred within Nick's own family. For some reason, he had decided Freddie would make a good husband to his only child. From there, it was just a matter of Freddie insinuating himself into Helen's arms. Nick took care of the rest.

Freddie had worked hard during his nine-year marriage to keep Nick happy. Most of the time, he managed. The only displeasure Nick brought up with any regularity was the lack of a grandson. Freddie kept putting that off, figuring another in the Casso line would just be competition for the riches, once Nick finally kicked the bucket. Freddie had worked too hard over the years, had eaten too much of Nick's shit, to start sharing this late in the game.

"Let's get started," Nick growled. "You tee off."

Freddie was a fine golfer, a three-handicap in college, but he usually let Nick win their twice-monthly contests. Besides, he stayed so busy making sure Nick was comfortable, his drink replenished, his cigar lit, that he couldn't concentrate on his game.

He hurried to the first tee, still trying to make up for being late, spiked a tee into the turf and set a ball on top of it. Then, without so much as a deep breath, he selected a club and gave the ball a good smacking. It sailed long but veered left, and he heard the unmistakable sound of a ball ripping through cottonwood leaves before it landed in the rough.

"Damn," he said for Nick's benefit.

"Too bad," Nick said smugly. "You rushed it."

Freddie thinking: Shit, yeah, I rushed it. Already had you yelling at me about being late. Wasn't about to take my time and piss you off more.

"Let me show you how it's done," Nick said as he waddled up to the tee.

Freddie stood head-and-shoulders taller than the bandy-legged Greek, but he managed to look small as Nick set up his shot. Nick had a nice swing for a guy who wasn't much taller than your average golf club, and he hit the ball long and straight. They watched it bounce on the fairway and roll to a stop in a good lie to the green.

"See there? You gotta remember to breathe."

"Right you are, Nick. Thanks for the tip."

Freddie didn't dare look at the other golfers who snickered around the first tee. He slumped into the golf cart as Nick took the wheel and zoomed off down the fairway. Nick always insisted on steering the cart, and he drove balls-out, the way he did everything. Freddie always came away from these games glad to be alive.

He waited until they were out of earshot of the other golfers before he spoke up.

"I called that guy in New York," he said over the whir of the cart. "Just like you said."

"Everything all right?"

"Yes, sir, he's coming out Monday to talk it over further. I told him we'd meet him at your office first thing Tuesday morning."

"That's good," Nick said without taking his eyes off the

asphalt trail. They hurtled over a bump and Freddie grabbed onto his seat to keep from sailing out.

They stopped when Nick spotted Freddie's Titleist sitting between the gnarly roots of a cottonwood. Freddie sighed at the sight, and Nick grinned.

"You got those numbers worked up?" he asked. "The ones for the New York guy?"

"Yes, sir. Well, almost. A little more research to do on the constitutionality of using the lodgers' tax, but it's pretty much ready to go."

"Good. I don't want this fucked up. This is a big opportunity."

"Don't worry, Nick," Freddie said as he got out of the cart. "I'm taking care of business."

Nick gave him an oily smile as Freddie shambled over to his trapped ball.

"Good thing you're better at business than you are at golf, eh?"

Freddie forced a grin. "You said it, Nick."

Then he turned away before his father-in-law could see the hatred in his eyes.

SEVEN

Helen Graham had just set the scones and teapot on the table when the doorbell rang.

Cheryl Alstad and Sandra Chavez turned their heads in unison, and Helen thought they resembled a couple of ponies, spooked by a noise in the night. She'd had such uncharitable thoughts about the women before. Cheryl had a long, horsey face, and she wore her blond hair cut into blunt bangs. Sandra was dark and pretty, but flighty and twitchy, and she had a whinny of a laugh.

The women had their hearts in the right place, though. They worked hard on the charity fund-raisers, and they did it because they wanted to, not because their husbands insisted such events were "good for business." For Helen, their commitment meant less work for her. She'd get a full share of the credit for the event, when her biggest contribution was store-bought scones.

Helen told the ladies to serve themselves, then walked briskly to the door, her sundress floating around her bare legs. She wasn't expecting anyone, but she didn't bother with the peephole. Up here in the foothills, you pretty much had to be searching for her house to find it. She flung open the door and took a step back at the sight of the two men standing there. One was a Native American, a stout man with short black hair and a suture scar running down one side of his wide face. The other looked like a surfer, and he flashed a dazzling smile at the sight of her. Helen wasn't certain, but he looked like the man Drew had hustled out of the reunion tent the day before, the one who'd mistaken Freddie for someone else.

"Can I help you?" she asked, then frowned at the surprising quaver in her voice.

"You must be Mrs. Graham," the blond said brightly. "We're looking for your husband. Is he home?"

Looking for Freddie? Then this must be the man from the reunion. But who was he? And why had Freddie lied about not knowing him?

"Freddie's not in at the moment," she said. "Is there something I can help you with?"

The men exchanged a glance, then the blond turned back to her, leering.

"Sure like to take you up on that. Bet you could help me in ways I've never dreamed."

The Indian grunted at his partner, who quickly backpedaled.

"We have some business with your husband. Sure he's not here?"

"Quite sure. But I'll be happy to give Freddie a message for you."

Again, the men looked at each other before the blond answered.

"Maybe we could just come in, take a look around. Make sure Mr. Graham hasn't sneaked in while you weren't looking."

Helen pushed the door closed a couple of inches, ready to slam it if they insisted.

"I'm afraid that's not possible. I've got a house full of company at the moment."

She made a vague gesture toward the expensive cars Sandra and Cheryl had parked in front of the house.

"I really must get back to my guests. Can I tell Freddie what you want?"

The blond started to say something else, but the scarred Indian stopped him with a hand on his arm.

"Tell Mr. Graham that Zipper and Calvin stopped by to see him," he said. "Can you remember that?"

"Calvin and, um, Zipper, was it?"

"That's right. He knows who we are."

"He does."

"Sure," the blond said "Everyone knows us. Maybe you'd like to get to know us, too."

He gave her a wink.

"Maybe some other time," she said hoarsely. "I'll tell Freddie you stopped by."

She quickly shut the door and peered out the peephole as the men walked toward a big black car. Not until they drove away did she take a deep breath.

My God, she thought, why would Freddie be mixed up with men like those? What "business" could they possibly have with him?

She composed herself and returned to the dining room, making a silent vow to ask her husband some stern questions.

EIGHT

Drew went looking for Jamal Moore in the Lobos' swank workout facility on Sunday afternoon. Players in gym shorts horsed around among the weight machines and treadmills, already recovering from the grim loss of the day before. The sight made Drew frown. He'd always been depressed for days after losing a game, which meant he spent much of his college career in a funk.

The one bright spot had been Helen. The mere sight of her always cheered him up, no matter how dire the Lobos' fortunes.

They'd met a dozen years before at a crowded sorority party, populated by some of the same idiots who'd been in the reunion tent at yesterday's game. Drew and some of his jock buddies had lurched drunkenly into the party, one of those tea-and-crumpets affairs that were out of fashion even then. Drew's football season had ended early because of a broken ankle, and he wore a plaster cast on his left foot. Helen had been standing off in a corner by herself, and one look had told him she was different—mature, self-assured, a grown-up among girls. She'd matched his stare with a frank one of her own.

He must've been a sight, flushed with a beer buzz, his clothes awry, limping around like Frankenstein. But she'd smiled at him, and it had been encouragement enough.

What followed had been a true romance, one that

should've had a soundtrack — swelling strings and flowery lyrics. They'd spent every available minute together. Drew would come out of the athletic dorm to find Helen waiting for him, sitting on a bench, smiling as soon as she saw his face. Or, he'd pick her up at the mansion where she lived with her millionaire father. He'd roar up in the beat-up Chevy he drove then, Elvis blasting from the speakers, cold beer on the floorboard, and Helen would run out to meet him while Nick Casso stood in the doorway, glowering.

Drew and Helen finished their junior year in each others' arms, spent the summer at swimming pools and in smoky bars. Helen even came to football practice in August, sunning in the bleachers while Drew sweated and stormed around the field, knowing she was watching.

Their senior year had been the best time of Drew's life. The Lobos for once finished with a winning record. He was named to the All-Western Athletic Conference defensive team, even though he'd missed three games for ankle injuries. After the season, he and Helen had left town for the Christmas holidays, running off to Durango, Colorado, for skiing and scenery and sweet nights together. Then it was back to the school grind in the spring semester, finishing up his bachelor's degree in journalism so he'd have a career in the newspaper business when he graduated. The constant through it all was Helen, always there, always loving, always ready to laugh. They never talked about marriage, but he'd assumed that would be next, right after graduation. They might not have had any money or a place of their own or any of the household goods newlyweds desire, but they'd make it work somehow. Hell, he always figured Helen was smarter than him anyway. She'd find some great career, he'd get a newspaper job, they'd get by. And if it meant thumbing their noses at her old man, so much the better.

Assumptions are dangerous. Drew was so occupied with

his unspoken plans and his homework and his senior parties, he neglected Helen, leaving her ripe for the plucking.

And Freddie Graham had been there to steal her. Freddie was a few years older, already finished with law school and starting his career, and he'd maneuvered Helen away as slickly as an attorney working a technicality. At first, Drew didn't even notice. He was busy with finals and graduation was just around the corner. But while Drew was hitting the books, Freddie was taking Helen to romantic dinners and out dancing. And smooth Freddie had Nick Casso's blessing, even though Freddie bore a striking resemblance to Howdy Doody.

Drew thought Helen had taken the easy way out. Dating him had been two years of rebellion against her father, who hadn't been pleased that his only daughter had taken up with a jock, one with a poor background and a dim future. Drew had grown up in a rundown house near the Rio Grande Zoo, close enough to hear the lions roaring at night and to get the occasional wind-borne whiff of elephant dung. It was just a few blocks from the country club neighborhood where the Cassos lived, but it was a long drop in status.

You work for a daily newspaper, you're going to make your share of goofs, and you learn to shake them off. Get back on that horse and ride. But losing Helen was the biggest mistake Drew ever made. He took a deep breath and rubbed at his eyes, trying to take his mind off her. Only losers live in the past.

Drew was such a familiar figure around the weight room that most of the players didn't pay him any attention as he roamed around, lost in his thoughts. A few nodded or waved, but Drew didn't see Jamal until he went back to the hot tubs near the shower room.

Jamal lounged in a Jacuzzi, letting the water jets soothe muscles no doubt aching from the pounding he'd taken from the Brigham Young team. Drew walked over to him, thinking: Too bad they don't have a therapy to help you hang onto the football.

Jamal was a handsome kid, compactly built and well-muscled. He wore his hair in tight cornrows that made his head look streamlined. Usually, you could count on Jamal to beam a front-page smile, but today his face went sullen when Drew spoke to him.

"How's it going, Jamal?"

Jamal grunted, but said nothing.

"You're sore at me, huh? Your dad came by the newsroom, all mad because of the way I wrote my story."

Jamal cut his eyes at Drew, then looked away, his face a study in resentment.

"Look, Jamal, that's the way it goes. You get the headlines when you have a great game, and you get 'em when it all goes rotten. You've got to learn to roll with it."

"Don't tell me what I've got to learn, man. You don't know me. You don't know nothin' about me."

"No, maybe not. But I've got some pretty good guesses. Like, I'm guessing you went out partying after the game last night. And you got into some kind of trouble."

Jamal's eyes narrowed.

"What you talking about, man?"

"Didn't you get arrested last night? One of our reporters saw your name on a rap sheet down at the sheriff's department."

"Not me, man. Don't know what you're talking about."

Jamal didn't seem surprised Drew was asking such questions. Maybe his dad already had warned him a sportswriter might come sniffing around.

"I looked in the phone book, Jamal. Aren't any 'Jamal Moore's' listed. I'm thinking you're the only one in town."

"Wasn't me."

"Yeah? Then where were you last night?"

"That's none of your fuckin' business."

"Come on, Jamal."

"Fuck off, man. I'm not talkin' to you no more."

Drew opened his mouth to ask it a different way, but Jamal was looking past him.

"Hey, coach! This guy's botherin' me."

Drew turned to find Ted Meyers, the strength coach, swaggering toward them. Meyers was a walking testament to the shaping power of weight lifting, one huge muscle with a head attached, and the weight room was his bailiwick.

"What's going on?" he rumbled.

"This guy won't leave me alone," Jamal complained. "I'm trying to get a soak here. I'm naked. Can't a man get some privacy?"

"Let's go, Drew. Give the kid some space."

"I'm interviewing him."

Meyers frowned. Even his eyebrows looked muscular.

"You got a problem, take it up with the AD. But for now, I need you to go away."

Drew knew the athletic director would be no help, even if he could find him on a Sunday. The AD made no secret of his disdain for the news media. If Drew pushed too hard, Meyers could ban him from the weight room altogether, which would make his job tougher in the future.

"Okay, Ted, whatever you say," he said, moving toward the door. "But I've got some more questions for you, Jamal."

Jamal huffed, but said nothing more.

Drew padded away through the carpeted weight room. Jamal had always been cooperative before, seemed to love getting his name in the paper. Was he hiding something, or was he just pissed because Drew had told the truth about those fumbles?

NINE

Chuck Gavin cocked one side of his mouth into what passed for a smile since his stroke, and carefully formed his words: "Hi, son. You look like hell."

"That's what everybody keeps telling me."

Chuck used his good hand to gesture toward the puke-green upholstered chair the nursing home designated for his guests. Drew pushed Chuck's wheelchair out of the way and perched on the chair. Chuck sat on the edge of the bed, his feet in his slippers and a plaid robe belted around his thick waist.

"You going somewhere?" Drew asked.

Chuck shook his head. It only swiveled one direction.

"Thought you'd be stopping by. Figured I should get out of bed, look like a real man."

Chuck didn't feel like a real man, not anymore. He was half a man, the other half frozen with paralysis. In the year since his stroke, he'd learned to dress himself and feed himself and sign his name with the wrong hand, but he hadn't been able to get his mind around the notion that half of him didn't work anymore.

"Had that dream again last night," he said. "The one where I'm still coaching the Bulldogs. Only this time, you were in the dream, too."

"Was I playing?"

"No, you were up in the stands. You kept hollering at me,

'Sit down, I can't see. Sit down!' Now what do you suppose that means?"

"Got me. I never understand dreams."

"I woke up sore as hell. I was ready to climb up into the stands and rearrange your face. Tell you to move to a different seat where you could see better."

Drew leaned forward. Chuck hungrily eyed the paper bag he clutched in one hand.

"Don't be mad at me," Drew said, "or I'll keep these cookies for myself."

He reached into the bag and pulled out a package of Oreos—the big package, with three rows of perfect black and white cookies.

"Hell, it was just a dream, wasn't it? Hand 'em over."

Chuck had always had a sweet tooth. He used to carry Milky Ways into the stadium, gnaw on them while trying to come up with a defensive strategy. It helped him think. But they didn't want you thinking too much at the Mesa del Oso Retirement Village, and they were stingy with sweets. Unless you counted green Jell-O, which Chuck wouldn't touch.

He knocked down three Oreos before he said another word. Then he swiped at his mouth with the back of his left hand.

"You got one of those all-day hangovers?"

"How could you tell?"

"It's either that or the flu, and you ain't coughing."

"The flu might feel better about now."

"Party?"

"Just drinking with Curtis after the homecoming game. You see the score?"

"That's no reason to drink. You get drunk every time the Lobos lose, you'll never sober up."

"Don't remind me."

"Something bothering you?"

Drew looked away, out the window, which had a pleasant view—if you liked brick walls.

"It's nothing, Pop."

It took Chuck a moment to organize the words in his head, but then he said, "You can't kid me, son. I know you too well. Something's up."

Drew ran a big hand back over his short dark hair. Damn, Chuck thought, he was a fine-looking young man. Made him proud every time he saw him. Even with a hangover, Drew could whip his weight in wildcats. And he was honest and skilled and had decent manners. Chuck smiled, thinking: I'd pat myself on the back if my one good hand wasn't full of cookies.

"I ran into Helen yesterday."

"Casso's girl?"

"She looks just the same, Pop. She was at homecoming with her husband, this lawyer named Freddie."

"I remember him. Little weasel."

"That's the guy. Anyway, they seem to be doing pretty well, and I guess I got to wondering where my life was headed. Next thing you know, I was drinking with Curtis."

Chuck chewed, lost in thought.

"Never got over her, did you?"

Drew shrugged, said nothing.

"You get that from me, you know. I'm the same way. Never got over your mother dying on us like that. Why do you think I never remarried?"

Drew studied his shoes.

"Don't get your head down, boy. Like I've always told you, it wasn't your fault. She wasn't real healthy to begin with."

"She died giving birth. That's something I've always carried around with me."

The cookie went sour in Chuck's mouth, but he forced himself to swallow. He closed the package and leaned over to set it on the bedside table.

"It's a chance every woman takes," he said. "It was worth it to her. She'd be happy with the way you turned out."

His son's eyes had a haunted look to them, one Chuck remembered from when Drew was a boy, troubled by nightmares.

"Think so? Even the way I feel today? Hungover. No idea where my life is headed."

"You're right where you want to be. Got a good job. Everybody reads your stuff in the paper."

"Is that enough? Shouldn't I be settling down and all?"

Chuck gave him a dismissive wave. Then he turned more toward Drew, using his hand to swing his dead leg around.

"You're not going to be happy with a woman until you get Helen out of your system. You ought to be going out, looking for a good woman, instead of hanging around with Curtis."

"I go on dates."

"Not often enough. And you compare them all to that Helen. Nobody can compete against a memory."

"You got it all figured out, huh?"

"You bet. Take my advice, son. Get out there and play the field."

"All right, I get it. Shit, how are you doing? I come in here pouring out my problems, I didn't even ask—"

"I'm fine. They're treating me good here."

"You need anything? Need me to speak to the nurses?"

"Hell, I can speak to the nurses if I have a problem. Nothing wrong with my mouth, though I think sometimes the whole staff would be happier if I couldn't talk."

"You giving them hell again?"

"Naw, everything's fine. I got another therapy session in an hour. Therapist was out sick on Friday, so they moved it to this evening. She'll be pulling and pushing on me, making me work these dead old muscles until I'm worn out."

"Is it helping?"

"I don't know, son. I can't tell much difference to tell you the truth."

"Keep after it," Drew said. "I want to see you up walking around."

"That'd be mighty fine, wouldn't it? You know, in those dreams I'm always walking somewhere, pacing up and down the sidelines or something. I think my brain must miss walking, even if my leg's not interested."

Drew nodded, looking a little glum.

"Remember how I used to make you exercise every day?" Chuck said. "Even when you were little. When you were six years old, you could do more push-ups than me. Always had you out in the backyard, pushing that tackling dummy around."

Drew grinned. "You about worked me to death."

"Kept you out of trouble. Too bad there wasn't some exercise you could've done to make your ankles stronger. You would've made it to the NFL."

Drew cracked his knuckles, looked at Chuck from under his eyebrows.

"Still wish I'd made it?"

"Sometimes. Be nice to see you rich and famous and all. But you turned out all right. I like opening the paper in the morning, hunting for your byline. If you'd gone pro, your career would be over by now anyway and you'd be sitting right there in that chair, telling me you don't know what to do with your life."

Chuck cackled, making Drew grin.

"You run along now. I've got to get ready for my therapy session."

Drew looked at his chrome wristwatch, then got to his feet.

"You just want me to leave so you can pig out on those Oreos."

"Hell, you ain't stopping me. I appreciate you bringing them by. I'll take two of those and call you in the morning."

He finally got a laugh out of Drew, and that made Chuck feel better. He worried about his son. The boy came by every Sunday, regular as clockwork, bringing treats and checking on him. But he wished he could keep an eye on him during the week. Chuck still would like to be helping him, coaching him, if he could.

Drew bent over and threw an arm around Chuck's neck, giving him a hug.

"Thanks, Pop," he said into his ear. "You always know the right thing to say."

And then he was gone. Chuck wiped at his eyes with his good hand. Goddamn kid.

TEN

It had been dark for an hour by the time Freddie Graham got home. Helen heard his car purr up and met him at the front door.

"They install lights down at the golf course?"

"No, we were done hours ago. Nick and I went to the bar to discuss some business."

Freddie's breath stank of bourbon. He gave Helen a peck on the cheek, and it took all her willpower not to flinch away.

"What kind of business?" she asked as she followed him toward the back of the house. His golf bag was slung over his shoulder, and the heads of the clubs swaying above the rim made her think of cobras.

"Just the usual," he said over his shoulder. "Cutting deals, you know."

"What kind of deals?"

Freddie opened the door to his study and slung the golf bag against the wall with a clatter. He looked at her unsteadily as he shut the door.

"What, suddenly you're interested in business?"

"It must be important to keep you away all evening."

He slipped past her, and stumbled toward the kitchen. She followed close behind. She waited until Freddie had flung open the refrigerator door and was peering inside before she sprung it on him.

"I was just wondering if this business had anything to do

with the men who stopped by here today."

Freddie jerked, hitting his head on the inside of the refrigerator. He rubbed the back of his head as he turned to her, looking annoyed.

"What men?"

"Two men came by while Cheryl and Sandra were here. Said they needed to discuss some business with you."

Freddie frowned. "Did they have names?"

"Calvin and Zipper."

Freddie blanched, which made his freckles more apparent. He turned away, shutting the fridge door without taking anything out.

"You know those men, Freddie?"

"Sure. They're friends of mine."

"One of them, that Calvin, was the man who was at the reunion yesterday. You said he'd mistaken you for somebody else."

"Yeah, well, that wasn't quite the truth. I didn't want you to worry. That was just a misunderstanding."

"They seemed like rough men to me."

Freddie looked her over.

"Did they now? They say anything rough to you?"

"Calvin got a little suggestive, but that's not what I meant. They didn't believe me when I said you weren't here. I thought they were going to force their way in and search the house."

Freddie shoved his hands in his pockets to keep them from dancing around. He chewed on his lower lip.

"What kind of business could you have with men like that, Freddie?"

He tried to turn away, but she snagged the arm of his green golf sweater and wheeled him around.

"Hey, careful! That's cashmere."

"I don't care if it's solid gold. I want to know what those

men want with you."

"And I said I don't want to talk about it. What I want is a drink."

He walked to the wet bar in the corner, Helen right on his heels.

"You want one?" he asked, holding up a crystal decanter of bourbon.

Helen shook her head. Her arms were crossed over her chest and she hugged herself tightly. Freddie poured a stiff drink and drained most of it in one gulp. He studied the level of liquor in the bottle, shrugged and topped off his glass.

"Ah, that's better," he said after another sip. "You go drinking with Nick, you can't just stop suddenly. Give you a hangover. The old man can still put 'em away. Bet he could drink me under the table anytime."

Freddie gave her his Howdy Doody grin, but it wouldn't work this time.

"You're in trouble, aren't you, Freddie?"

"I don't know what you mean."

"Calvin and Zipper. What do they want? I'm guessing it's money."

Freddie squirmed, but she had him cornered.

"All right, yeah, I owe those guys some money. I'll pay 'em, and I'll tell 'em to not come around here, bothering you. Okay?"

"How much?"

"What do you care? I said I'll handle it."

"How much, Freddie?"

He tried to walk away, but Helen stepped sideways to cut him off. He either had to talk to her or climb over the bar to make his escape.

"What's the big deal? I'll take care of it like I always do. Don't worry about it."

"I am worried, Freddie. Those men will hurt you if you

don't pay. Right?"

"Nah. Who'd want to hurt me? Besides, it's not a problem. I'll pay them."

"You said this morning we had cash flow problems. Now you owe these men money. What am I supposed to do? Sit here worrying about you, fending off bill collectors?"

"Stop worrying. Nothing's going to happen to me."

"Are you sure?"

She gave him her level stare for a long time. His mouth worked, but nothing came out. Helen felt fear crawl up her back. Freddie was never at a loss for words.

"Maybe you're right," he said finally. "Maybe I should tell you about it. Just so you won't worry. Can we at least sit down? I feel like I'm being interrogated here."

"Tell me first."

He rolled his eyes.

"Look, I do owe them some money. Not those guys, but their boss. I made a few bets that didn't come through, and I sort of forgot about it, and so they came to collect. I'm sorry you had to deal with them."

"What kind of bets?"

"You know, the usual. Football games, baseball play-offs. It's no big deal."

"How much?"

"Boy, you're not going to let this go, are you? I'll handle it. I've just been so busy with this deal I'm working on with Nick, I've neglected the other stuff. I'll get busy, get the money together and make this go away."

"How much, Freddie?"

Freddie looked down at his shoes for a long time. Helen noticed he was wearing his ridiculous two-toned golf shoes in the house and it distracted her for a moment, thinking what the sharp cleats were doing to her carpets.

"I don't know exactly," he said without looking up. "I

haven't kept track. There's interest and all because I'm late paying."

"Give me a guess."

"Probably around sixty thou."

Helen flushed. She tugged at her sweater and flicked back her hair, but she wasn't aware she was moving. Her brain had locked on the number.

"How could you run up that kind of debt?"

"It just happened. You know how it is. You place a bet and it doesn't pay off, so you place two more, thinking you'll make back what you lost before you have to pay. It's just a run of bad luck."

"My God, Freddie, is that what you'd call it? Bad luck? How about stupidity? That's the term that comes to my mind."

"Hey, c'mon. Don't get ugly about it. I got a little carried away. I'll fix it. I mean, I don't have that much cash on hand. I've been tied up with Nick's deal—"

Helen's brain sparked.

"Get the money from him."

"What?"

"Ask Daddy for the money. Tell him we'll pay him back."

Freddie pushed past her, looking as if he needed to run, but he stopped a few steps away and turned to face her.

"Can't do that. Nick wouldn't understand."

"So what? He has the money. At least he won't break your legs for not paying on time."

"C'mon, sweetheart. Nobody breaks legs. That's only in movies."

"Those men looked capable of it."

"Capable, sure. But why would they do that? They need me to pay them, that's all."

"I could get the money from Daddy."

"No, don't do that. Nick already thinks I'm a screw-up. I

don't need to prove it. Besides, he can't know about the gambling. It would scotch the deal we're working on."

"What deal?"

"Can't talk about it. Strictly hush-hush."

"You can't talk to me about it? What is wrong with you, Freddie? You think I'd blab to everyone about your deals, about how you've landed us in debt? About how criminals are coming to the house?"

Helen watched as his face flushed. She saw the fear in his eyes. He peeled off his sweater and tossed it onto a nearby sofa. His golf shirt was wrinkled and wet with sweat, and his red hair stood up crazily.

"I know you can keep a secret," he said. "It's just this deal could be big, very big. It could have us sitting pretty for years to come. If Nick found out about the gambling, he'd toss me out on my ear."

Helen fell into a chair, exhausted.

"So what do we do?" she asked. "Should we call the police?"

"Nick owns the cops in this town. He'd hear about it before sunup. I just need some time. I can get the money together if I have a few days. Call some friends, get a loan, whatever. But I don't know how much time I have. If they came by here on a Sunday—"

"If they find you before you've got the money together, they'll hurt you."

"Nah, they wouldn't—"

"They would, Freddie. I saw it in their eyes."

Freddie fell onto the sofa and sat with his elbows on his knees, staring at his shoes.

"You may be right," he said finally. "But what am I going to do? I can't leave town. There's too much going on right now."

Helen wiped at her eyes with her wrist and sat up

straighter.

"There's the cabin," she said.

The Grahams maintained a small cabin on the far side of the mountains. It made a nice weekend getaway, a staging area for skiing on the eastern slopes of the Sandias.

"What do you mean? Sell the cabin? That would take too long—"

"I didn't mean sell it, though we could if it comes to that. I meant you could go there for a few days and hide out. From the cabin, you can make your phone calls and round up the money. It's not even long-distance from over there."

Freddie straightened up on the sofa, and some color returned to his cheeks.

"That's not bad, sweetheart. I could take care of everything from the cabin. Will you come with me? We could make a little vacation of it."

"I don't want a vacation. I want this problem solved. And we can't leave the house empty. What if those men come back? They might burn it to the ground."

"They wouldn't do that. I'm telling you, it's mostly just a misunderstanding—"

"I don't want to hear any more. Go pack a bag. You need to get out of here."

Freddie ran his hands through his hair and swallowed heavily.

"I'm sorry, Helen. I really am."

"Just go."

ELEVEN

Drew awoke Monday to a ringing noise. He slammed a hand down on his alarm clock, but the ringing continued. He crawled out of bed and stumbled into the living room in his underwear to answer the phone.

"Hullo?"

"Hi, Drew. This is Helen. Helen Graham."

He was surprised, but he tried to hide it.

"Hi, Helen. What time is it?"

"It's after ten."

"I should've been up an hour ago. Guess I went back to sleep after I turned the alarm off."

She said nothing for a moment, and it was as if he could feel her smiling over the phone line.

"What?"

"You haven't changed a bit. Remember how I had to give you a wake-up call every time you had a final exam?"

"Yeah, I was always winging it. Everybody else was up all night, studying. I could barely make it to class on time."

"As I recall, you made passing grades."

"Pure luck."

"You've always been the lucky one, haven't you?" she said, her tone suddenly serious. "I think I need some of your luck. Could you meet me for lunch?"

"I guess so. I need to call the office, but I don't have anything big going on today."

"How about Garduno's on Academy? Say, eleven-thirty? We can beat the rush."

"Okay. But, um—"

"What?"

"Sure this is okay with Freddie?"

"It's about him."

"Oh." He didn't know what that meant, but he'd find out soon enough. "Okay. See you there."

He hung up the phone and stood there, scratching his hairy stomach and speculating. It's about Freddie? Is she thinking of leaving the little red-haired bastard? Finally, after all these years? And what did she mean, she needed Drew's luck?

He didn't feel lucky at the moment. His head hurt from another night of carousing with Curtis. His arthritic ankles ached. And he was cold. He crossed the room to check the thermostat and saw he'd never turned it up after returning from Champions late the night before.

He made coffee, thinking about Helen, trying to ignore the thump in his chest, then began to get ready. He caught himself humming in the shower and felt like an idiot.

He arrived at the restaurant right on time, and found Helen waiting for him on a wooden bench in the tiled lobby. Garduno's is all tricked out like Old Mexico, the decoration laid on with a shovel: ornate tilework and piñatas and bull-fight posters and lots of greenery; mariachi music blaring over hidden speakers; slow-moving ceiling fans made of woven palm fronds.

He reached to shake Helen's hand as she stood, but she gave him a quick embrace. Her hair brushed his chin and her body felt warm and familiar. She smelled like lemons.

Then she turned away to follow a hostess to their table. Drew followed, feeling strange stirrings in his stomach, a tightening of the throat. He took a deep breath, telling himself to calm down, it's just lunch. It's not even about you and Helen and all that past. It's about Freddie, the little shit.

It wasn't until they were seated that he got a good look at Helen's face and saw she'd been crying. Her eyes were red and puffy and she didn't look as if she'd had much sleep. If she's this upset, he thought, maybe she is thinking about dumping Freddie. Maybe I'm being set up as the rebound man. I'd take it. God help me, I'd be anything she wanted me to be.

It took a while to get to it, naturally. First, they had to order, and then they chatted while the waitress brought their soft drinks. Nothing too heavy, just how's work and have you seen any of the old gang and similar nonsense until Drew felt as if he'd burst.

"What's this all about, Helen? What's wrong?"

She looked down at her hands on the table. She was going at her cuticles, just like in the old days. Whenever she was nervous, Helen worked her hands over until her fingers bled.

"Freddie's in trouble," she murmured. "I think some people want to hurt him."

Drew thought, I'd like to hurt him. I'd like to make him disappear forever.

"He's run up some debts. Gambling. And he doesn't have the money to pay."

"What kind of gambling?"

"Betting on sports," she said. "He lost a few, then figured he could gamble his way out of debt. That only made it worse."

He tried to look grim. "Dumb."

She nodded and dabbed at her eyes with her napkin.

"I think he's sick, Drew. Like a compulsion. I mean, I've always known Freddie had a gambling streak in him. It's part of what makes him a good businessman. But I never expected anything like this."

They fell into silence while the food arrived. Helen picked

at her salad, but Drew was famished. He shoveled enchiladas into his mouth.

After a few minutes, when it was clear she wasn't going to take up the conversational thread, he swallowed mightily and said, "I'm sorry you've got problems, Helen. But I don't see what this has to do with me. Did you just need somebody to talk to?"

"Partly." She looked away, not able to face him when she added, "I also thought you might be able to help."

Drew set down his fork.

"I thought of you because of what happened at homecoming. That man that you hustled out of the reunion tent? He's one of the ones who's after Freddie."

Drew said nothing, but he was thinking about the blond man at the reunion, with his narrow eyes and dazzling teeth. No wonder he'd been so mad when Drew interrupted his conversation with Freddie.

"Freddie's in over his head, Drew. He's not a tough guy. He likes to think he's a big shot. But the only clout he's got comes from Daddy."

"And Daddy's not willing to pull his fat out of the fire this time?"

"Freddie won't even talk to him about it. He and Daddy are in the middle of some sort of business deal, and he says Daddy will boot him out if he hears about the gambling."

Drew grunted. He ate a few more bites, waiting for the pitch.

"What I was hoping was that you could talk to these men. After what happened at the reunion, they'd be afraid of you, I think. They'd at least listen to you. Maybe you could get them to give Freddie more time."

"I don't like Freddie. Why should I care if these guys rough him up?"

She looked down at her hands picking at each other, and

forced them into her lap.

"I was afraid you'd say that," she said. "I don't have a good answer. I thought maybe you'd do it for me. I don't want Freddie to get hurt."

Drew felt a storm building inside his chest.

"I'd do anything for you, Helen. But look out for Freddie? That's asking a lot. He stole you away from me."

"That was a long time ago. I need help, Drew. I don't know where else to turn."

He stared down at his food, his appetite gone. The idea of messing with Freddie's bookie put a cold lump in the pit of his stomach. He should tell her no. He should get up and walk out. But he looked at her face and felt himself buckle.

"You're counting on me being a sucker for you, right?"

"It's not like that, Drew—"

"Sure it is. You need a big guy to help Freddie. You saw me at homecoming, and you thought, hey, here's a big, dumb jock. I used to have him wrapped around my little finger. Why not use him?"

Her lower lip trembled. "That's not true and you know it. I'm sorry if I've insulted you. I just didn't know what to do—"

"Hold on, Helen. You don't have to apologize. You know why?"

"Because you're not going to help me?"

"No, because I will. See, I am a big, dumb jock. Nothing good can come of this, and there's a good chance somebody will get hurt. But I'll do it. Not for Freddie. I wouldn't cross the street to spit on Freddie. I'll do it for you. Because I can't stand to see you hurting. I never could."

Her eyes overflowed, but her mouth gave Drew a quivering smile. He wanted to kiss that mouth, kiss away those tears, and he figured it was good thing there was a wooden table between them. He put his hands flat on the table on either side of his plate.

Helen leaned forward and rested her hand on his.

"Thank you, Drew."

He wanted to yank his hand away, to show he still had some control over himself, but he couldn't do it.

"Tell me what I have to do. Do you even know how to find these guys?"

She put her hand back in her lap.

"No, but I know their names. Two of them came to the house looking for Freddie. They were named Calvin and Zipper, and they work for a bookie named Three Eyes."

"Named what?"

"Three Eyes. You know how they call people who wear glasses 'four eyes'? Well, this man wears glasses and a patch over one eye. So they call him that. That's all Freddie would tell me about him."

"So I'm supposed to go find these guys, somewhere in Albuquerque, based on their goofy names?"

"You can do it, Drew. I know you can."

"Then I'm supposed to rough 'em up?"

"Just talk to them. See if Freddie can have more time to pay."

Drew snatched his napkin from his lap and tossed it onto the table.

"I must be crazy," he said as he got to his feet.

"But you'll do it?"

"I'll do it. For you."

TWELVE

Three Eyes sat at his desk in the back room of Max Reyes's barbershop with Oscar in his lap. The dachshund occasionally tried to move around, even tried to climb up on the desk where the papers were spread out. Three Eyes would say, "Hah, Oscar, don't do that," and the dog would settle back onto his lap, happy so long as he kept stroking its back.

Three Eyes' desk was in the back corner of the room, turned at an angle so he faced the door. Wrong person comes through that door, he has time to drop behind the steel desk for some protection, maybe even pull the .357-Magnum from its bracket in the leghole of the desk and put a round through the intruder's sternum. Or, if there's too many of them, he could slip through the trapdoor under his desk and hide in the musty crawl space under the barbershop. You don't last twenty years as a bookie without being prepared.

Aside from the desk, the windowless room was furnished with long tables along each wall. Metal folding chairs were pushed in neatly under the tables. A dozen telephones were spaced along the tables, making it look like Three Eyes was ready to start a telethon, take pledges.

In a couple of hours, each phone would have one of Three Eyes' trusted men working it, taking last-minute bets on the Monday night NFL game. But now it was quiet, time for him to catch up on his accounting and make sure his associates weren't skimming his profits.

"Sit still, Oscar," he said to the squirming dog. "You'll make me spill my coffee on these papers. Then where would I be? Fucked, that's where."

The panting dog stared up adoringly with red-rimmed eyes.

"You little shit." He patted Oscar on the head, making the dog's head bob, making him suck in his tongue quickly to keep from biting it off.

Three Eyes had owned the dachshund for a year, taking the purebred puppy in payment from some stiff who'd never place another bet with his organization. He'd grown attached to the animal, which surprised him. Three Eyes had no family, no friends other than his employees and maybe Max the barber. He'd let the little dog come into his life, and now he found himself cooing over it and buying expensive dog food and generally acting like an idiot when no one was watching.

"You're making me soft, Oscar, you know that? Old man like me getting a dog. At my age, I shouldn't be buying green bananas. Now I got you to look after. What was I thinking, hah? You little shit."

He stroked the dog lovingly, but snapped his head up when he heard the latch click in the steel door to the barbershop. He squinted as the door swung open, his feet flat on the floor. The cops come through that door, Three Eyes would move so fast, little Oscar better be able to fly.

Calvin Cox's blond head poked around the door, peering in with that stupid grin on his face.

"Hey, boss," he said. "How's it hanging?"

Calvin strolled through the door, with Zipper close behind. Calvin looked as goofy and loose-limbed as ever in his aloha shirt and black bomber jacket, the stupid toothbrush jutting from his pocket. It was always hard to read the Indian's face, but Three Eyes thought he looked pissed off. I probably would, too, if I hung around Calvin all the time.

Better to spend your time with a dog.

"You take care of our business?" he asked them.

"Most of it," Calvin said as he leaned a hip on Three Eyes' desk, talking back over his shoulder like he didn't need to give the old man his full attention.

"Whaddaya mean, 'most'?"

Zipper stood squarely in front of Three Eyes, practically at attention.

"Couldn't find that lawyer, Graham," he said. "We went by his house yesterday, but he wasn't home. His wife wouldn't let us in—"

"But she was a sweet piece of ass," Calvin said. "I would've gone on in, seen what she had to offer, but Zip decided it was time to go."

Three Eyes glared at him, but said nothing.

"We watched the house awhile," Zipper continued. "Guy never showed up. We took care of the others. Put the fear in 'em. They'll all pay up."

"But you couldn't find Graham? What, you just stopped looking?"

"This morning, we went over to his office, in that big building across from City Hall? We talked to his secretary. She said he's out of town."

"Out of town where?"

"She wouldn't say. Started getting kinda huffy with us. I thought she was gonna call security, so we left."

"I wished she had've called somebody," Calvin said. "I'd like to pop one of those rent-a-cops."

"Shut up, Calvin," Three Eyes said matter-of-factly. "I'm listening to Zipper."

"The secretary said she didn't know when Graham would be back," Zipper concluded.

Three Eyes bent over creakily to set Oscar on the floor. The little dog sat, looking up at his master expectantly. Three

Eyes flattened his hands on top of his desk.

"That fuckin' lawyer owes me a lot of money. I been carrying him, figuring he was good for it. I don't like this."

"How much does he owe?" Calvin asked.

"I said 'a lot,' okay? More than everybody else on that list put together. I want him found, and I want you to make an example of him."

Calvin and Zipper nodded mutely.

"Fuckin' big shots think they can skate on a legitimate debt. I want him taught a lesson, and I want that money in my hands."

Zipper nodded and turned toward the door, ready to go track down Freddie Graham. But Calvin had another question.

"How bad you want him hurt?"

"Do whatever you gotta do. Just get that money."

"He's a fuckin' lawyer. Could bring heat down on us."

Three Eyes stared at Calvin coldly.

"I ask you for an opinion?"

"No, I'm just sayin'—"

"Don't talk, Calvin. You give me a headache when you talk. Go do what I told you."

"Okay, boss. All right if we mess up his wife a little, too?"

Calvin had slid off the desk to follow Zipper out the door, but Three Eyes gestured him back. Calvin leaned over the desk, grinning, clearly expecting some lascivious comment from the old man, but Three Eyes snatched a handful of his slick shirt and pulled him close.

"You know who the wife is, idiot? Nick Casso's daughter. You know who Casso is?"

Calvin's eyes widened at being yanked around by the boss.

"Some rich guy, right?"

"That's right. You talk about heat, you mess around with the wife, then we'll have heat for sure. Stay away from her, you fuckin' moron. Take care of the lawyer, do it quick, and get back here with my money. Are we clear?"

"Sure, boss. I was just kiddin' around."

"Do I look like I'm in the mood for kidding?"

"Guess not."

He pushed Calvin away, and Calvin straightened and brushed at his wrinkled shirt.

"You two take care of business," Three Eyes said. "I don't want to see your faces until this problem is solved. Got that?"

"Got it."

"Go."

After the door closed behind them, Three Eyes reached down to pick up Oscar and put him back in his lap.

"See what I have to put up with?" he asked the dog. The confrontation had frightened Oscar, who whined in breathless little squeaks.

"What's the matter, Oscar? You need to go piddle? Come on, Papa'll take you outside."

THIRTEEN

The most important part of being a sportswriter—or any kind of reporter—is knowing who to call. Drew didn't have to ponder Helen's request long before he recognized that the most knowledgeable expert on local sports gambling sat only a couple of desks away from him at the office. He called Spiffy O'Neill.

"Drew, my boy, where are you?" Spiffy said. "Benedict's been looking for you."

"I got tied up. What does he want?"

"I have no idea, but I doubt it's important."

"Listen, Spiff, you ever heard of a bookie they call Three Eyes?"

"Ah, Three Eyes. That would be Mr. Vicente Sanchez, who runs book out of a barbershop in the South Valley."

"You know the guy?"

"Not well. Three Eyes and his bunch play a little rough for my tastes. I prefer to place my wagers through Las Vegas."

"But you know where I could locate him?"

"Look for Max's Barbershop down on Isleta, south of Bridge. You know that area?"

"I can find it."

"Three Eyes operates out of the back of the shop. It's common knowledge."

"Not to me. I'd never heard of the guy."

Spiffy paused, and Drew could picture the old man's glowing cheeks, his wry smile, as he built up to the question.

"Whatever would you want with Three Eyes? I've never known you to place a bet."

"I just need to talk to him. It's a personal thing."

"All right then. Tell me about it when you can. But watch yourself, my boy. Three Eyes plays for keeps."

Before Drew could answer, Spiffy whispered quickly, "Benedict's coming back this way."

"Okay, Spiffster. You never heard from me, right?"

Spiffy said in a loud voice, "Sorry, you must have the wrong number."

Drew hung up the pay phone and walked to his Jeep. He cranked up the engine and headed for the southern end of the city.

Isleta Boulevard is the central artery of the South Valley, an area of irrigated farms and wind-twisted cottonwoods and rundown shops with signs in Spanish. Drew rarely went to the valley unless he was covering a high school game. The rest of the time, the South Valley could be on a different planet from the Northeast Heights where he lived, or at least in a different country, perhaps Old Mexico.

He was past Max's Barbershop before he spotted the sign and the peppermint pole out front. The shop was squeezed into a block of storefronts between a dingy botanica and a boarded-up hardware store.

Drew parked on a side street and walked up the sidewalk, feeling big and obvious, the only Anglo around and the only pedestrian. Low-riders and battered pickups zipped past on Isleta, stirring up road grit.

A bell jangled as he entered the barbershop. He took a deep breath and looked around, but it resembled any other barbershop—nothing to indicate what went on behind the scenes. A barber in a white smock and a ridiculous shiny black toupee was combing his mustache in front of the mirror, and he turned and asked Drew if he could help him.

"Just looking for Mr. Sanchez," Drew said breezily, not slowing as he passed the barber chairs. "Back through here, right?"

"Hey, wait a minute," the barber said, but Drew turned the knob and swung open the steel door before he could try to stop him.

The room was eerily empty, except for an old man in a fedora who sat at a desk at the far end. The walls were lined with tables and chalkboards, and the hardwood floor was dusty and scarred.

"You Sanchez?" he asked as the door swung shut behind him.

"Who the fuck are you?"

"Name's Drew Gavin. I need to talk to you."

The old man eyed him warily as Drew pulled a chair from one of the tables, swung it around toward Sanchez's desk and straddled it like a horse, resting his arms on its back. The desk was covered in papers—yellowed ledgers, slips with scrawly handwriting. A heavy black phone sat on one corner of the desk, next to an incongruously modern plastic box. Drew looked closer and saw it was a caller identification device like the one Benedict kept on his desk. Call comes in and Benedict doesn't recognize the number, he just lets it ring until one of his staffers picks it up. The sports editor used the gizmo to protect him from irate readers. Drew wondered why the bookie needed one.

Beneath the brim of his hat, the old man wore thick eyeglasses and a black patch over one eye. He squinted at Drew, sizing him up. His thin lips worked against each other, like he was pulling up a wad of spit. A dachshund was curled in the old man's lap, and it raised its head to look Drew over.

"Nice dog," he said. Another thing reporters know: Always try to make the interviewee comfortable. Compliment their office decor or the photo of their ugly children, anything to make them think of you as a human rather than as an arm of the news media.

"His name's Oscar," Three Eyes said automatically.

"I get it. Like Oscar Meyer. He's a wiener dog."

"I named him after Oscar de la Hoya, the boxer. Why the hell would I name my dog after a wiener?"

"Right. De la Hoya, he's the best."

"Then why do I keep losing money on him?"

The old man stroked the dog, patted its head.

"Got him about a year ago. Idiot doctor told me I had to give up cigars. Oscar gives me something to do with my hands."

"How do you keep him lit?"

Three Eyes scowled.

"Or I guess, sometimes, a wiener dog is just a wiener dog."

Drew knew he should stop clowning around and get down to business. He didn't fear the old man, but he didn't like having the steel door behind him, where anybody could walk in and jump him before he could get turned around. He remembered the cold eyes of the smiling blond man he'd manhandled at the reunion.

"I know you," the old man said, his hands still busy with the dog. "You played for the Lobos. Now you work for the newspaper."

"That's right."

"I remember back in, what, '88, something like that, the Lobos were playing Air Force up in Colorado Springs," Three Eyes said. "Kept it close, but they were losing."

"As usual," Drew interjected.

"Air Force had the ball on the ten-yard line, pushing to score, and you came blasting through the line, sacked the quarterback, knocked the ball loose. You remember this?"

Remember it? It had been the shining moment of Drew's

junior year. He nodded.

"Lobos recovered the fumble, kept the ball till time ran out."

"We still lost."

"Yeah, but you kept 'em from scoring. Cost me a fuckin' bundle."

It took Drew a second to swallow that. His big moment, his personal victory in that loss to the Falcons, reduced to a point spread by this geezer. Christ.

At least Three Eyes made no bones about what he did here in this back room, didn't try to act innocent, which should make it easier for Drew to get to the point.

The door cracked open behind him, and Drew wheeled around. The barber's shellacked toupee peeked through, followed by wide eyes and his twitchy mustache.

"Everything all right in there, Vicente?"

"Sure, Max, sure. Go count your combs or something. I'll handle this guy."

When Drew turned back, Three Eyes had a giant pistol pointed at his chest.

"Jesus, what's that for?"

"Just so we got no misunderstandings," Three Eyes said. "I don't know why you're here, what you want. I don't want you to write about me in the newspaper."

Drew raised his empty hands to shoulder height.

"No way. I don't even want my boss to know I'm here."

"Good. Put your fuckin' hands down. I'm not gonna shoot you. Not unless you do the wrong thing."

Drew wasn't sure what the "wrong thing" might be, but he was certain he didn't want to cross that line.

"I just came here to talk. I need a favor. For a friend of mine."

Referring to Freddie Graham as a "friend" made his teeth grind, but he reminded himself he was doing this for Helen, not for Freddie.

"Why should I do you a favor?" Three Eyes said. "What you ever done for me?"

Drew shrugged, had no ready answer. He couldn't take his eyes off the big gun.

Three Eyes turned the pistol on its side and set it on the desk. The gun was probably too heavy for the old guy to hold steady, but it remained pointed in Drew's direction and Three Eyes kept his gnarled hand on top of it.

"Who's your friend?" he said wearily.

"Freddie Graham. He's a lawyer?"

The bookie's one eye sparked.

"I know who the fuck he is. He owes me money."

"That's right. He needs more time."

"He sent you here?"

"No. I'm here as a favor to his wife. I, um, we used to be close. She asked me to come here, as a friend."

"Does the husband know about this?"

"I don't think so. He's afraid of you and your men. He probably would've objected to my coming here."

"Probably would object to you messing around with his wife, too, hah?"

"We're not 'messing around.'" Drew's face felt hot. "I'm just doing her a favor."

"This is Nick Casso's daughter we're talkin' about, right?"

Drew nodded.

"I could get my money from Casso, put Freddie's ass in a sling."

"Tell you the truth, I wouldn't care if you did. That's right where Freddie's ass belongs. But it would hurt the daughter, hurt the family. And you don't want to do that."

Three Eyes weighed that for a minute.

"Graham's hiding out," he said finally. "You know where?"

"No. I don't want to know. That's what I told Helen, his

wife. I told her, I'll go see Mr. Sanchez, see what he has to say, but that's my only involvement."

Three Eyes pushed the dog out of his lap, and it landed with a soft thump behind the desk. He leaned forward, his hand on the pistol, and gave Drew his hard look.

"Here's what you tell her: Freddie Graham doesn't get my money, and I mean today, I'm gonna start shipping him home in pieces. First a finger. Then maybe an ear, his nose."

"Come on, Mr. Sanchez, you don't want to do that."

"You think I'm gonna let the little shit push me around? It's not good for business. What if other people find out I let Mr. Big Shot skate? Hah? Then, everybody starts thinking, 'Old Sanchez, he's gettin' soft. Maybe I won't pay him either.' Pretty soon, I'm out of business."

Drew tried to give him back the same unflinching stare, but it was tough with the gun aimed at him. He clutched his hands together in his lap. Maybe Sanchez wouldn't notice they were shaking.

"You carve up Freddie Graham, it's going to be bad for business anyway. How do you think Nick Casso's going to take that? He'll have every cop in the city on your ass."

Three Eyes smiled, which gave Drew a chill.

"You think so? You think Casso owns more cops than I do? Shit. He messes with me, I'll have him arrested."

Drew tried to return the smile, but he could feel it wasn't working.

"Besides," the old man said, "the last thing Graham wants is to get his father-in-law involved. I hear they got some kinda deal going. Casso finds out Graham's in trouble with me, and it's all over."

"What kind of deal?"

"The fuck should I know? Go ask Freddie, if you can find him. But you better find him before I do. He might not be talkin' if I find him first. I might feed his tongue to Oscar."

Drew nodded once, stood up and walked to the door, a crawly feeling between his shoulder blades.

"Would you like that, Oscar?" he heard the old man say. "You want some tongue? Even if it comes from a lawyer? Might be too tough, hah?"

FOURTEEN

Helen Graham paced her kitchen, her bare feet cold on the tiles. Four paces one way, pause by the telephone on the counter, then turn and four steps back. No matter how hard she looked at it, the phone wouldn't ring.

Drew had promised he'd phone as soon as he was done with the bookie, but it had been hours since lunchtime and still no call. Helen had spent most of that time in Freddie's study, sorting through the files in two oak cabinets. Freddie's filing system was haphazard at best, but she'd managed to find pending bills and records of their investments and his business papers. An hour with a calculator confirmed what she'd feared: She and Freddie were in trouble, even without the debt to Three Eyes hanging over them.

Bills were past due. Helen found a form letter from Southwestern Bank, threatening foreclosure on the cabin because Freddie had missed two mortgage payments. The credit cards were maxed out, and the itemized statement included some unexpected expenses: bills from hotels right here in town, florists bills for arrangements she'd never seen. Freddie had some explaining to do.

She paused in her pacing to ask herself the same set of questions all over again: How could this have happened? How had she let Freddie talk her into leaving all financial matters to him? Why hadn't she noticed something was wrong? How could she have been so stupid?

The answers, she knew, lay in her upbringing as the overly protected daughter of Nick Casso. Helen's mother had died of breast cancer as Helen started high school, and her motherlessness had been one of the links she later had in common with Drew. Not that her mother was any prize. Barbara Casso spent most of her days floating around the mansion in a peignoir, a cigarette in one hand and a martini in the other. Putting up with Nick, she seemed to think, was duty enough in the world, one that merited its own anesthetic. Still, she had been Helen's confidante, and when she was suddenly gone, Helen lost her moorings.

The cancer that killed Helen's mother was a force of nature, swift and sure, one Nick couldn't control with his money and his power. He'd reacted with cold rage. By the time he shook himself out of it, his daughter was nearing graduation and he vowed he would protect her, no matter how much it stifled her. He sent her to UNM so he could keep her living at home. He provided for her every want and need—sports cars and party dresses and sorority dues. Nick wanted Helen to major in business, so she could take over the family fortune one day. But Helen had opted for psychology in hopes of understanding Nick and maybe herself. The switch was a step toward building a life of her own. Drew Gavin had been the second step.

But she'd eventually collapsed under her father's pressure. Nick was determined his daughter would have a safe, happy future and insisted Drew wasn't the one to provide it. He'd done everything he could to thwart the romance, more than Drew had ever known, and breaking off the relationship was more a form of surrender than an act of will.

Now, she thought, I've done it again. I let Freddie run everything, let him set me up as the princess, insulated from the world. And this was the cost. Everything I've built with Freddie is on the brink of collapse. I have nothing; everything's in Freddie's name. She thought she'd finally broken free of Nick Casso's orbit, but she'd simply been circling Freddie, who still followed her father as faithfully as the moon follows Earth.

She thought about leaving him, especially if the hotel and florist bills meant he was having an illicit romance. But she didn't know where she'd go if she left. She'd never held a job in her life, and a decade-old degree in psychology was worthless. Where would she go but back to her father? She couldn't stand that. Nick would never let her live her own life.

The phone trilled. She raced to answer it, more breathlessly than she had intended.

"Hi, Helen, it's Drew."

"Thank God. I was beginning to think something had happened to you."

"No, I'm fine. But I had to hurry back to the office after I met with Sanchez, and then I got caught in a meeting with my boss."

"You're at the office now?"

"Yeah."

"So you can't speak freely."

"Good guess."

"Can you tell me what he said? Is Freddie in danger?"

"I think so."

"A lot?"

"I'd keep out of sight, if I were him."

"That's what he's doing. But for how long?"

"Sanchez said he wants the money today, or things will happen to Freddie."

"Like what?"

Drew paused.

"I really can't say. Too many people around."

"But it's bad?"

"Real bad."

"Oh, my God."

Helen's knees felt weak. She leaned her hips against the counter, one hand to her forehead.

"Sorry," Drew said after a moment. "I did what I could. But this guy, he's past the talking stage. Know what I mean?"

"Yes."

"Are you going to be all right?"

"I need to talk to Freddie."

"You guys better come up with some way to pay this guy."

"We'll figure something out."

"Okay."

Helen wanted to hang up the phone. She wanted to scream and cry and break dishes. But she just stood there, the phone to her ear, waiting.

"Guess I'd better get busy," Drew said finally. "Sorry it didn't work out better. I tried. I really did."

"I know you did. It was foolish of me to ask you. I should've known it was too late."

"Didn't hurt to ask. But I couldn't persuade him."

"It's all right, Drew. Thank you."

"Sure."

Another awkward silence. Helen's throat felt tight, her eyes hot.

"Well," he said, "call me if I can help. I don't know what I could do at this point, but I'm willing."

"I know."

"I want you to be happy, Helen."

"You always did."

She hung up the phone and let the tears fall.

FIFTEEN

It was chilly in the cabin, but Freddie Graham was afraid to build a fire in the stone fireplace, afraid someone might see the smoke. He'd stashed his Porsche around back, out of sight from the gravel road so nobody could tell he was there. But he kept peeking out the front curtains, just in case.

Calling it a cabin was like calling a yacht a canoe. The A-frame building had a certain rustic quality, in keeping with its wilderness surroundings, but it was more comfortable than most people's regular homes. Large windows opened onto the deck that ran the width of the house. From the east-facing deck, the view was of rolling hills covered with piñons and junipers, a green tumble that hid the cabin from its neighbors. But Freddie had stayed behind closed curtains all day.

He sat on the leather couch, leaning forward over the coffee-table, which was buried under a laptop computer, a phone, his black briefcase and the documents he'd brought with him from home. He knew Nick Casso needed the paperwork completed right away, but he could think only of the danger he faced.

He needed to pick up the phone, call Stan Faulkner, the president of Southwestern Bank, see about getting a loan. Stan would hand over sixty grand, no questions asked, to Nick Casso's son-in-law. But Stan also had a big mouth, and Freddie couldn't afford for the debt to get back to Nick.

Freddie's head felt as if it would implode. He rose from the sofa, paced to the little kitchen notched into one corner of the room and poured himself another drink from a bottle that sat open on the counter. He shouldn't be drinking, not when he had so much work to do, so many calls to make, but bourbon seemed the only thing that would soothe his nerves.

He glanced at the papers on the coffee-table. This was Nick's project—his baby. Mostly orchestrated by Freddie, who'd get no credit, of course. He didn't care, as long as it meant a bundle of money headed his way.

It could all come crashing down if Nick found out about Freddie's gambling. Freddie knew this, had known it all along, but he couldn't seem to stop himself. He'd scan the Gazette sports page, get a look at what that idiot Drew Gavin or the others said about a coming game, and he'd know who was going to win. He could feel it, deep inside. How could he skip the chance to capitalize on that knowledge?

It had worked for years. He'd easily made more from Three Eyes than the old bookie had lifted off him in the past, if somebody wanted to sit down and tote it up. But lately, Freddie had lost his intuition. He'd bet against the line, and his team wouldn't cover the point spread. He'd bet a favorite, and some star would pull a hamstring or some rookie would fumble the ball. Freddie figured it was a temporary run of bad luck—he'd pull out of it any day. So he kept betting, and he kept losing.

Now he was sixty grand in the hole, and he had to come up with the money damned quick. He had investments—the house, the cabin, his Porsche—and he might be able to liquidate something. But none of that could happen fast enough, and wouldn't Nick get wise if suddenly Freddie took out a second mortgage or put the cabin on the market? Nick had eyes and ears everywhere. Too many people trying to curry favor with him to mind their own damned business.

Time was at a premium. His New York contact, Martin

Woodward, had flown into Albuquerque today. Freddie had talked to Woodward on the phone, made it sound like he was just using the cabin as a quiet place to wrap up his work. He sure as hell didn't need the man to know he was hiding out.

Freddie felt lonely, and he picked up the phone, thinking maybe he'd call his secretary, Trish, tell her to get over to the cabin. They could have a little party, take his mind off his troubles. Trish was a trouper. She understood his needs and his apprehensions, unlike Helen. Marrying Helen had given him power and connections, but not much in the way of passion. In bed, it always felt like Helen's mind was elsewhere. Trish approached lovemaking with the same quiet intensity that she poured into her work. A few hours in the sack with her might be just the thing.

He wondered whether Three Eyes' men had quizzed Trish about his whereabouts. He could trust her to keep it quiet that he was at the cabin, but they might be keeping an eye on her, could follow her here. A quick tumble wasn't worth the risk. Besides, he had all this work to do, if he'd just focus.

Damn it. He couldn't think of anything but Three Eyes and his debt and the goons he'd seen once or twice, the ones who'd come to the house. He could close his eyes and clearly see Calvin's wild hair, his beaming teeth, his cold blue stare. Every time he pictured the guy, Freddie wanted another drink. And the thought of Zipper made him want two.

He had to do something. He had to get Three Eyes off his back, so he could focus on Nick's deal. He snatched up the telephone and dialed the familiar number for Three Eyes' bookmaking operation. When a man answered, he asked to speak to Mr. Sanchez.

"This is Sanchez. Who is this?"

"Hello, Mr. Sanchez. It's Freddie Graham."

"I been looking for you."

"Yes, sir, I know. You sent some people by the house. They

frightened my wife."

"Too bad. We hate to drag family into these things. But you owe me a lot of money."

"That's what I wanted to talk to you about. I was wondering, could I get an extension? Pay you something now, you know, and the rest later?"

Nothing on the other end of the line. He thought he could hear Three Eyes talking to someone else, thought maybe he said the name Oscar, but the old man clearly had cupped his hand over the receiver, and it made Freddie nervous. Was Three Eyes somehow tracing the call? Should he hang up and risk pissing off the old man further?

"Where you at, Graham?"

"I'm out of town. Business, you know. But I'll be back soon, and I'll get your money. I just need a little time—"

"You're time's up, stupid. I told you twice already, pay up or take the consequences. Just a little while ago, I sent my boys looking for you again."

"They won't find me. Not until we work something out."

"You better hope they don't. Be too bad for you."

Freddie felt sweat tickling down his ribs. Calling Three Eyes had been a bad idea.

"I'll get you the money, Mr. Sanchez. I promise."

"Hah! A fuckin' lawyer! What's your promise worth?"

"You know I'm good for it."

"No, I don't. I know your father-in-law, Nick Casso, he's good for it. Maybe I should ask him to give me my money."

"No, don't do that. It won't work. You talk to Nick, he'll cut me of out the business, and you'll never get your money."

"I'll get it, or they'll find you floating in the Rio Grande."

"Just a little time—"

"Your time's up, big shot."

The phone clicked dead, and Freddie stared at the receiver in his hand. Then he softly thumped himself in the forehead with it, over and over, muttering, "Stupid. Stupid. Stupid."

He snapped his head up when he heard a noise outside. He listened, the phone dangling in his hand. His breath caught in his throat as he recognized the sound: the rumble and pop of gravel under the tires of an approaching car.

SIXTEEN

Where the hell was Freddie?

The New York guy would be walking in the door of Nick Casso's office any minute, and Nick had nothing to show him. No documentation, no marketing strategy, nada. Freddie, the fucking freeloader, was the man with the papers. Nick normally did business with a handshake and a scowl, but he had to admit, without Freddie and his numbers and pie charts, he felt a little naked.

First thing Tuesday morning, he'd called Freddie's house, but nobody answered. He'd taken that to mean Freddie was on his way to Nick's sixth-floor office in the old First National Bank building downtown. But he hadn't shown.

Nick paced around his office, waiting for nine o'clock to roll around so he could check Freddie's office. He knew better than to call any earlier. Freddie's fellow lawyers might be in already, running up those billable hours, but they couldn't be bothered to answer a goddamn telephone. And the secretaries, he knew from experience, didn't arrive until the last second.

"That's what's wrong with this country," he grumbled. "Nobody remembers how to work."

Nick had worked hard all his life, from the time he was big enough to stock shelves in his father's grocery. He'd made a fortune off his own sweat and brains. But this deal was the biggest yet, and he'd be damned if he'd let Freddie screw it up.

What Nick had in mind, the reason he was meeting with

this guy Woodward, was to buy his way into the exalted ranks of the men who owned National Basketball Association franchises. It would be his greatest achievement, his legacy, and it meant he'd make a shitpile of money.

What was an NBA franchise, after all, but a license to print your own money? Even the crummiest NBA team, a bunch of guys who could barely find their way from one end of the court to the other, was worth a fortune. Sure, it cost tens of millions up front to get into the high-stakes game of team ownership. But it took no time at all for the revenue stream to start flowing the other direction. Ticket sales alone were worth a bundle, but they were the least of it. There were the concessions, where you charged five bucks a pop for a cup of warm beer or two bucks for a box of popcorn. There were multimillion-dollar TV contracts, advertising deals, merchandising agreements for clothing and shoes and pennants and programs. Get the Albuquerque Mustangs up and running, and pretty soon every pimply-faced teen in America wants a cap with the team logo to wear backward on his head. At $29.95 apiece.

Freddie had gotten a tip that the league was looking at another round of expansion to new cities around the country. Nick practically slavered over the opportunity, particularly after he and Freddie figured out a way to build a state-of-the-art arena, one that would look attractive to the other NBA owners and to the sharpies who managed the TV contracts. Get the taxpayers to build the damned thing on city-owned land, and it wouldn't cost Nick a penny. All he had to do was make sure the City Council was lined up to make it happen, then put up the money for the team.

They had a good shot. At half a million people, Albuquerque wasn't as large as most NBA cities, but its basketball fans were known nationally for their rabid support of the Lobos. UNM's eighteen-thousand-seat arena, The Pit, was packed for every home game. Albuquerque had become an annual stop for NBA teams during the exhibition season, and the town had turned out in force for those games, too, for a chance to get a look at veterans dogging it through the pre-season or the latest crop of rookies fumbling around, trying to find their rhythm in the big league.

With a bigger arena, the NBA could be persuaded that Albuquerque was ready for a team, as good a market as any of the newer locales: Charlotte, Orlando, Vancouver, Toronto. And once the team was up and running, Nick would be rolling in dough, all because some guys in short pants were hurling a ball at a hoop.

They were so close. Freddie had figured out the loophole that would get the city to pay for the arena without the risk of taking the bond issue to the voters. The city had a lodgers' tax, paid on every hotel room rented by a visiting conventioneer or local adulterer, and that money just sat in the city coffers, designated for use in ways that would improve tourism. All Nick needed was a quick vote of the councilors and the city would issue eighty million dollars in municipal bonds to pay for the arena, the bonds to be paid off by the lodgers' tax. And the council should be no problem. Bunch of hicks, trying to prove they were as important as their counterparts back east or out in California. They'd be drooling down their shirtfronts for the chance to attract an NBA team.

The tax scam had worked in other cities. Get the city fathers to pony up millions to build an arena, then get an agreement that said all income—from parking to popcorn—went to the team owner. Tell the citizenry: It'll mean new jobs and new business opportunities, it'll give the city another attraction to lure conventions to our wonderful climate, blah, blah, blah. People wouldn't care how much it cost if it meant they'd get to see the big boys play ball.

But none of this would work without Freddie's documents. Where the hell was he?

Nick glanced out the window. The old bank building stood on Central Avenue, Albuquerque's unofficial Main Street, and he had a view to the east past a few other aging office towers, past the railroads that glinted in the morning sunshine, to the green hills of the Heights and, beyond, to the craggy face of the Sandia Mountains.

He circled his desk and flopped into his leather armchair. The corner office had tall old-fashioned windows on two sides, so he could swivel one way and see the mountains in the distance or he could turn the other way and look down on Central's traffic and storefronts and pedestrians—men with their suits and briefcases and the women in their running shoes and skirts, all taking their good sweet time getting to work.

Nick had been at his office since seven o'clock, going over the stock market page in the newspaper, making a few calls to the East Coast. His secretary had, by God, arrived by eight, and was already busy in the outer office. Nick could hear the computer keys clicking through the open door. The secretary, Anna, was ugly as a mule, but she'd been with Nick for thirteen years and knew his business nearly as well as he did. She also knew his moods, which was why she hadn't said jackshit since she arrived. She knew when even the kindest word would draw a tongue-lashing.

"Anna!" he shouted. "Call Freddie's office. See if anybody answers over there. He's supposed to be here already."

Fucking Freddie. Why did I trust that moron to manage this deal? It was fine when Freddie was just collecting information and putting together some papers, but here it was— nut-cutting time—and Freddie was AWOL.

"He doesn't show up," Nick said to himself through gritted teeth, "he ruins this deal, and I'll fucking kill him."

Anna appeared in the doorway, holding a slip of pink "While You Were Out" paper in her hand.

"I called over there, got Freddie's secretary, Trish?"

"Yeah?"

Anna looked down at the paper, as if she needed help remembering what Trish had said.

"She said Freddie's out of town."

"What?"

"That's what she said. I asked where he'd gone, and she said she didn't know, that Freddie called her Sunday night and told her to tell everybody he was out of town on business."

"Jesus H. Christ! His business is right here, right now. How could he leave town?"

Anna gave him a shrug to indicate it was beyond all human understanding, then ducked around the corner toward her desk.

Nick felt a stab of heartburn in his chest. He snatched up the phone, dialed Freddie's house again and listened to it ring four times before the answering machine picked up.

"Freddie, goddamnit," he shouted into the phone, "this is Nick. Where the hell are you? Your secretary says you're out of town! You damned well better make it to this meeting!"

Nick slammed the phone down. He stood up. He sat down. He stood up again and circled his desk, muttering and cursing. His chest felt like it was being squeezed by a big rubber band.

"Mr. Casso?" Anna's voice came through the intercom. "There's a Mr. Martin Woodward here to see you."

The NBA guy. Nick had never even met him. Freddie had talked to the guy, got him interested, with Nick's blessing. And now Freddie wasn't here to make the introductions.

Nick stalked toward the door to the outer office but stopped before crossing the threshold. He plastered a big smile on his dark face and walked on through, extending a hand, saying, "Mister Woodward! A pleasure to finally meet you."

SEVENTEEN

Zipper parked his shiny Pontiac in the littered asphalt lot in front of the apartment building. The curtains were closed in Calvin's upstairs apartment. Zipper shook his head. Nearly ten o'clock in the morning, and he would have to drag Calvin out of bed. Again.

He got out of the car and clanged up the iron steps, not caring whether he awakened anyone else. Anyone who lived in such a goddamned ugly building deserved to be disturbed. The fourplex was a gray concrete cube with a metal balcony set across the front like a rusty brow. Windows were cut into the walls like deep-set eyes. The whole building looked like it was scowling.

Zipper couldn't abide such squalor. He lived alone in a brick house downtown, a little two-bedroom number that dated from the turn of the century. His house had a wooden porch where he could sit and watch the sunrise while sipping his morning coffee. It had a neat yard he kept trimmed and weeded. Inside it had gleaming hardwood floors and white plaster walls. The furniture was simple, but in good shape, and Zipper took pride in the quiet and cleanliness and order.

Of course, he thought, hardly anybody ever sees it, hardly anybody ever stops by to admire the work I've done on the old house and the yard. Calvin, on the other hand, lived like a pig and he had company nearly every night: one woman after another, falling for the blond hair and the dazzling smile.

Women. You'd think they'd be more forward-looking. You'd think they'd rather meet a man who knew how to take care of himself and his property. Instead, they wasted their sex on losers like Calvin, who was nothing but a swinging dick. No brains, no goals, no plans.

But Calvin didn't have a ragged scar running down the side of his face. He didn't know what it was like to scare people he passed on the street, to feel their eyes on him when people dared to stare. Zipper had learned to live with the scar. It had been there ten years, since he was sixteen, and it had become as much a part of him as his stocky build and his dark eyes. He wondered sometimes whether the scar had shaped him, had led him to become the person he was. A scar like that, a knife wound down the side of the face, marked a man, showed the world he came from a violent past. And it caused people to expect violence from him. That wasn't necessarily a handicap in his line of work, but it definitely hurt his love life.

Zipper told no one, not even Calvin, how he'd gotten the scar. When somebody got brave and asked him, he always replied, "Knife." Then he'd stare at them in his expressionless way until they changed the subject.

He was ashamed the scar had been put there by his own father, Victor Yazzie, who'd cut young Luther one night because he'd dared to stand up for his mother.

Victor would drink for hours at a time, sitting before the fire in their rundown hogan near Shiprock. And when Zipper's mother, Flora, said the wrong thing or burned the mutton stew, Victor would rumble toward her, pin her against the wall and beat her. There was no slapping her around, no shouting or complaining, just a silent methodical beating with his fists.

If Flora had time to see it coming, she'd send Zipper and his brother outdoors, where they stood in the falling snow, waiting for it to be over, hearing their mother's weeping through the walls.

One night when he was sixteen, Zipper could stand it no longer. He left his younger brother waiting beside their battered pickup truck, dogs cowering at his feet. He pushed his way back into the hogan and commanded the old man to stop. Victor ignored him at first, too caught up in his drunken fury, picking his shots to Flora's body. When Zipper stepped between them, his father shrugged as if it were a minor inconvenience and began to beat Zipper instead.

But Zipper had grown during the long summers on the reservation. He was tall enough to look his father in the eye, big enough to punch back, and Victor wasn't accustomed to such a challenge. Zipper hit him again and again, the anger of years of abuse propelling his fists. He hadn't stopped until his drunken father was bloodied and lying on the floor. Then he'd turned to his mother, put his arm around her shoulders and whispered to her that the old man would never harm her again.

When he saw her eyes go wide, he wheeled, but not quickly enough. Victor had picked up a butcher knife from the kitchen table and he slashed once, downward, catching Zipper on the side of his forehead. The sharp knife traveled down his face, cleaving the skin to his chin.

The sudden blood and Zipper's howl of pain stunned his father. He backed up a couple of steps, dropped the knife and plunged out the door into the night. As Flora pressed her apron against the wound, trying to staunch the blood, they heard the pickup truck rumble to life and jounce away down the long dirt road. The old man had fled, and he'd taken with him their only transportation. The family had no phone, no way to get help, and it was a long night of suffering before Zipper's aunt happened by and drove him to the clinic in Shiprock.

The doctor did the best he could with the wound, stitching it tightly and covering it with bandages, but the stitches left a scar of their own, a long white line with dots on either side where the sutures had stabbed through the skin.

The wound had nearly healed by the time Victor Yazzie showed up at his home, sober and begging forgiveness. Flora urged young Luther to accept the apology, so their home could be whole again. He pretended to go along, even offering to drive his father into Gallup to buy celebratory whiskey. No one ever saw Victor Yazzie again.

Once Zipper had buried his father in an arroyo a mile off of Route 666, he drove the truck to Albuquerque, where even a Navajo with a fresh scar down the side of his face could hide. He hadn't been in the city long before he met Three Eyes and soon became a dutiful employee. Perhaps because of his own infirmity, Three Eyes had never made fun of the scar, hadn't pushed when Zipper wouldn't talk about how he'd acquired it. Three Eyes had coined the nickname Zipper, but the Indian didn't mind that. Better to have a nickname, an alias. Someday, someone might come looking for Luther Yazzie. But no one had a warrant out for Zipper.

He banged on Calvin's door. Calvin slept like the dead, and sometimes Zipper had to knock six or seven times before his partner would answer.

This time, Calvin opened the door at once. He was bare-chested, dressed only in a pair of black silk boxer shorts, and his blond hair was flat on one side and sticking straight out on the other. He slipped Zipper a bright smile.

"Morning, Zip. I was just gonna call you. Come on in."

The apartment was dark inside, in contrast to the bright sunshine outdoors, and Zipper stopped just inside the door, his eyes adjusting, his nostrils twitching. Beer and Brut and dirty socks and sex. Walking into Calvin's apartment was like stepping into a porn theater.

Beer cans cluttered the coffee-table and clothes were

strewn over the couch and chair. Some of the clothes clearly belonged to a woman, and Zipper cocked an eyebrow at Calvin.

"Uh, yeah," Calvin said. "I've got company. But I can be ready in a jiffy."

Calvin grinned and scratched at his rippling abdomen.

"Had kind of a long night," he said.

"You better get your ass into gear," Zipper said. "I've already heard from the boss this morning."

"I'll just get some clothes. Brush my teeth. Be right with you."

Calvin hurried through the bedroom door. Zipper looked around for somewhere to sit, but the furniture was too littered and he didn't even want to think what it must look like in the kitchen. He stood near the door, waiting.

A black-haired girl who couldn't have been more than twenty came out of the bedroom, naked except for a pair of skimpy red panties. She smiled at him and lifted one shoulder as if to say, "Yeah, I'm naked. So what?" She had wide, bruised lips and large breasts with brown nipples, and she was a little soft in the belly, but Zipper liked the way she looked and he didn't bother to turn away.

"All my clothes are in here," she said softly as she grabbed jeans and a pink blouse off the sofa.

She turned toward him and held the clothes up to her chest, but they hung between her breasts rather than covering them.

"You're Calvin's partner, huh?"

Zipper nodded.

"Must be fun, hanging out with him all the time. He's a funny guy."

"He's a riot," Zipper said flatly.

"Guess I'd better get dressed. Nice to meet you."

She flounced back into the bedroom, passing Calvin in the

doorway. Calvin had found some nearly clean jeans and he was buttoning one of his Hawaiian shirts. This one was red and yellow and featured erupting volcanoes. Zipper had seen it before.

Calvin had a toothbrush in his cheek, but he talked around it, saying, "Hey, Zip, you want a piece of that? She's probably willing."

Zipper's mouth twitched, but he said, "Just get your shoes on, Calvin."

"Suit yourself. But she's probably just what you need, Zip. A little recreation, you know? You can't work all the time."

"Tell that to the boss."

Calvin rolled his eyes and went back into the bedroom.

Zipper heard Calvin's hand smack the girl's bottom, and she squealed and laughed. They talked in low tones, and Zipper couldn't make out what they were saying. He didn't much care. He just wanted Calvin to get it in gear.

Calvin reappeared a few minutes later, pushing the woman ahead of him toward the door.

"Sorry, gotta go," he said. Then, in his fake announcer's voice: "You don't hafta to go home, but you can't stay here!"

She smiled at him over her shoulder, almost running into Zipper, who still stood by the front door. She made her dark eyes round at getting the bum's rush, but she was smiling, and Zipper could see she thought the whole thing was another of Calvin's jokes.

Calvin gave her a good-bye peck at the door, promised to call her soon and closed the door behind her. He listened at the door, making sure he could hear her clomping down the stairs, before he turned to Zipper.

"The boss called, huh? What's up?"

"He's got a line on that guy Graham."

"Where'd he find him?"

"He hasn't found him yet. The idiot called the boss yesterday, and the boss used caller ID to get his number."

"Used what?"

"That box on his desk? Tells him who's calling?"

"Is that what that thing's for?"

Zipper said nothing, waiting.

"So now the boss knows where Graham is?" Calvin said, finally putting it together.

"Not yet. Somewhere east of the mountains. The phone's unlisted, but he's tracking it down. He wants us to be ready as soon as he finds out where it is."

"We're waiting on him, huh?"

"Yeah."

"How about we get some breakfast? I've got a whopper of a hangover. Hey, we could go to Burger King! Get it, a Whopper for my whopper?"

"Let's just go."

EIGHTEEN

Every Tuesday afternoon, the sports staff trooped the length of the newsroom to a conference room, where Greg Benedict would hold forth for an hour on the state of the staff, next Sunday's paper, sports in general, his jock itch, whatever came to mind. Usually, Drew and Curtis and the Dwarves sat quietly through these forced meetings, waiting on Benedict to run out of steam so they could get back to work.

The staff sat around a long table in chairs designed for the broad butts of editors, much more comfortable than the ones reporters had at their desks. The narrow conference room had tall windows down two sides, one set facing an outdoor courtyard, the others looking into the bustle of the newsroom. At either end were walls covered with tacked-up maps and calendars and page layouts.

The sportswriters tended to sit in the same chairs each week. Drew, because of his size and his animosity toward Benedict, got the seat at the far end of the table from the sports editor. Curtis usually sat to Drew's right and Spiffy to his left. They were the three with the most seniority on the staff, and they didn't want to be too handy when Benedict started passing out more work.

The other Dwarves—Sparky, Filthy and Henry —filled the next chairs, with the interns and the clerks and the other ass-kissers closest to Benedict. The arrangement meant

Benedict had to talk loudly to make an impression on the stalwarts at the far end, but he didn't seem to mind. Benedict talked loud anyway, his eyes always alert to whether people were listening.

He was a short, balding guy with a narrow mustache and a round belly and pale, skinny arms that were always exposed because he wore his sleeves rolled up over his elbows, trying to look like a newsman. The Gazette had a dress code that required male employees to wear neckties—a rule most of the sportswriters diligently ignored—and Benedict kept his cinched up tight. Drew figured the tie cut off oxygen to his brain.

"Okay," Benedict said, "the brass has been on my butt to do more enterprise stories. In-depth stuff, Sunday section fronts, you know the drill. So what I need from you are your best ideas. What have you got?"

The writers exchanged looks. Ideas? How were they supposed to have ideas ready when they'd been given no warning? Writers always are struggling for feature ideas. If I had any, Drew thought, I would've already written them.

When no one answered, Benedict said, "Gavin! Why don't you go first?"

All heads turned Drew's way. Christ, he didn't need this. He was still in the doldrums over his meeting with Three Eyes the day before and his inability to help Helen. She'd sounded so miserable on the phone. Why couldn't Benedict leave him the hell alone?

"I don't want to hog the limelight," he said. "Somebody else can lead off."

"No, go ahead," Benedict demanded. "You're always brimming with things, right? Give us your best shot."

Drew thought: I'd like to give you a shot. To the jaw.

He'd been slumped in the chair, his long legs extended straight out beneath the table. He struggled to a more upright position, buying time, before addressing the rest of the staff.

"You know already that I'm working on a tip that Jamal Moore got arrested," he said. "I've called everyone I can think of, but so far I've got nothing. If it's a cover-up, they're doing a helluva job."

Benedict nodded, waiting for Drew to finish.

"That's fine, Gavin. But I'm asking about features. You got something or not?"

Drew cleared his throat.

"I've been thinking about gambling," he ventured. Since his lunch with Helen, he'd thought of little else. His mind was full of questions, the central one being: How did someone like Freddie Graham, who seemed to have it all, get into such a fix?

"Gambling?" Benedict frowned, pretending to think it over. No matter what Drew said, the sports editor would find a problem with it. "What kind of gambling?"

"Sports book. All these guys betting the rent money on NFL games and baseball and basketball. I hear it's a big business."

Benedict was already shaking his head.

"It's an illegal business. We don't want to give it any attention."

Drew didn't really want to do a gambling story, but he didn't like the way Benedict blew him off.

"What, we just ignore it, and it doesn't exist?"

"We all know it exists," Benedict said, his voice taking on an appeasing tone that made Drew mad as hell. "But the brass wouldn't want stories about it. Might look like we're encouraging gambling."

Drew glowered down the length of the table. Benedict was spineless, always predicting the reaction of the "brass" to back up his decisions.

"We don't have to 'encourage' it," Drew said. "Gambling's

all around us. Indian casinos opening up everywhere. A state lottery. Powerball. We've written about all of them, why not sports book?"

Benedict held up an ink-stained index finger, ready to jump in with a point.

"The difference," he intoned, "is that sports betting is illegal, except in Vegas. Those other kinds of gambling, they're allowed under the law."

"Which is why sports gambling would be a story!" Drew surprised himself by getting loud. Christ, what was the matter with him? Why fight with this idiot over a story he didn't even want to write?

"Why're you suddenly so interested in this, Gavin? Been losing a few bets yourself? You know newspaper policy forbids gambling by sportswriters."

Drew grasped the end of the long table and squeezed it hard. It wasn't quite as satisfying as squeezing Benedict's neck would've been, but it kept him under control.

"No," he said, a deadly calm in his voice. "Nothing like that. You asked for ideas. This is one I've been thinking about."

Benedict shook his head. "I don't think so. Who's next?"

Drew rose to his full height and marched toward the door, his chest thrown out, his fists clenched.

"Where are you going?" Benedict's eyes were wide. Drew had to pass him to reach the door, and he clearly thought he was coming after him.

"I've got a story to write," Drew said, reaching for the doorknob.

"This meeting is not finished!" Benedict sounded shrill now. "We need story ideas!"

"Why bother?" Drew said as he swung open the door. "You wouldn't know a good story if it bit you on the ass."

With the door open, his parting shot was heard not just by

the sports staff, but by half the city desk as well. Heads turned, typing stopped, and an unnatural silence followed him as he trudged to his desk.

He didn't look back to the conference room until he was seated. Somebody had shut the door behind him. Benedict's face was bright red, but he continued with the meeting. The other sportswriters were giving him their attention, though Spiffy's face was crimson from trying not to laugh. Only Curtis White had swiveled around in his chair to watch Drew. He had a big shit-eating grin on his face.

Drew ducked his head, thinking, oh Christ, Benedict will try to have me fired for sure. He'll be in Goodman's office, waving his arms around, shouting about "insubordination." Drew trusted the editor would take his side, particularly if Benedict was wrong about what management thought of the story. Of course, then Drew would have to do the story, and the thought of Three Eyes' big pistol made him wince.

Damn.

NINETEEN

Two hours later, Teresa Vargas climbed out of her black Toyota Tercel in the newspaper's parking lot, covering her mouth with a hand while she yawned broadly. She was exhausted, but the crisp sunset air helped. She breathed deeply, trying to perk up.

The night before had been another sleepless one, with Teresa sitting up in bed, painting her fingernails Midnight Ebony and listening to the minutes slowly click by on her alarm clock. Teresa kept all her fingernail polish and emery boards and cotton swabs in a child's beach bucket beside the bed. It helped pass the time during long nights alone.

Painting her fingernails relaxed her, sometimes even helped her defeat the insomnia that had plagued her since childhood. It was an automatic activity, one that let her whirring mind slow down so sleep could come.

Teresa blamed her sleeplessness on her high energy level, that get-up-and-go feeling that pushed her through her days. She supposed it was a form of mania, but it made her a hard worker and a successful reporter, and that was the most important thing. Sleep was a luxury she could do without most of the time. Once in a while, her body would give out, exhausted from a lack of recharging, and she would conk out for fourteen hours straight. Once caught up, she could go again for weeks. Tonight, she thought, might be a catch-up night.

She'd made her last check of the day at the cop shop, going over arrest reports and jail release forms, searching for news. She'd found a couple of small items, but it had been a pretty quiet day, and she was looking forward to finishing up and going home to bed.

The best action of the day, in fact, had occurred right in the newsroom, when Drew Gavin told off his editor right in front of everybody. The newsroom had been buzzing about it earlier, and Teresa had hated to leave for her rounds and miss out on the gossip.

She was almost to the employee entrance when Gavin came striding out the door, his head down, his brow creased. He looked as if he was still angry. Big guy, too. Benedict better watch himself, Teresa mused. You wouldn't want Drew Gavin going postal on your ass.

He was looking at his feet, and Teresa had to step sideways to keep from being trampled.

"Hey, watch where you're going," she said, faking a snarl.

His head snapped up, and he saw what a close call it had been and his face flushed. Teresa thought it was cute. She wouldn't mind making him blush some more. It softened his face, made it warmer.

"Sorry," he mumbled.

He stepped to the side to give her room, but she danced in front of him, cutting him off, making him look at her.

"Hey, tiger, I was in the newsroom when you popped off to Benedict today. Way to go."

Drew ducked his head. "He's an asshole."

"Yes, he is," she said, "and somebody should regularly remind him of it."

Drew looked a little sheepish, but he returned her smile.

"Guess that would be me."

"It's an honorable calling."

"Probably gonna get me fired."

She gave him a get-out-of-here shove in the chest.

"No way. You're too good. Goodman would can Benedict before he'd let you go."

There it is. She'd made him blush again.

"Think so?"

"Sure." She strolled on past, headed toward the newsroom door, but she said over her shoulder, "Give 'em hell, Gavin."

"Thanks."

Teresa was smiling as she let herself into the newsroom. She glanced back over her shoulder, saw Drew walking toward his old Jeep. She thought he stood a little straighter.

Another yawn pulled at her jaw. I've definitely got to get some sleep tonight, she thought. Maybe I'll dream about Drew. That might be pleasant. Beat the hell out of staying up all night doing my nails.

TWENTY

Drew was grinning as he climbed into his Jeep. That Teresa Vargas was a pistol. He'd been watching her since she arrived at the Gazette, but they'd scarcely said more than "hi" to each other before she'd given him the Jamal Moore tip on Sunday. Drew had what he thought of as "old-timer's disease." New staffers often were around the newsroom for months before he engaged them in conversation. He figured, why bother? Most wouldn't be around long anyway. Seen 'em come, seen 'em go. The good ones, the hot reporters like Teresa Vargas, used the Gazette as a farm club, grooming their talents until they were called up by the big leagues. He figured Teresa Vargas wasn't long for the place. She was too good. Front-page stories all the time, milking the cop beat for all it was worth. Before long, the offers from bigger newspapers would pour in, and she'd be gone. He used to get such offers himself occasionally, but he'd always turned them down in favor of staying in his hometown, looking after his dad, watching the goddamn Lobos lose. Lately, the offers had stopped coming.

He cranked up the Jeep's engine, and spun the radio dial, looking for oldies. He hit upon Buddy Holly singing, "That'll Be the Day." The song perked him up, and he fed gas to the Jeep, roaring toward home.

The DJ played two more Buddy Holly favorites before switching to commercials. By then, Drew was in thick traffic near his apartment building. He rubbed his forehead, trying to push away the headache that had settled in after the argument with his boss. As expected, Benedict had gone straight to Goodman's office after the staff meeting, but he apparently hadn't gotten any satisfaction. His face was even redder when he returned to his desk. Things were awfully quiet in the sports department while Drew furiously hammered out his story on the football team's falling fortunes. He'd sent the story to Benedict without a word, and had left before the weasel could nit-pick it. God only knew what the story would look like in print tomorrow. Benedict would probably find some way to twist the words, give the Lobos a dose of cotton candy when they needed castor oil.

Drew parked outside the Monte Vista and entered through the small lobby. He rode the elevator up to his eighth-floor apartment, walked down the hall to his door and let himself inside.

The place looked the same as always. In the center of the room was his prized possession, a leather La-Z-Boy where he spent more nights than he did in his own bed. In one corner, the fireplace was a dark empty maw. Doors led off the other end of the living room into the kitchen and the bedroom. His chair faced a broad cabinet which held his expensive stereo, his collection of old records, his thirty-two-inch television and the mementos from his football career. The trophies were tarnished. A football sat on a dusty shelf, half its air gone. He'd been awarded the game ball during the last contest of his senior year at UNM. Now it looked like a big brown raisin.

He'd left the curtains open in front of the sliding glass doors to his balcony and he could see the orange lights of the city, strung along streets marching toward the dark, humpbacked mountains. His east-facing balcony was the nicest feature of his apartment, one for which he paid dearly. He liked being up high, looking down at the city. It reminded him of being in the press box at a football game, peering down at the action played out in miniature below.

Home sweet home. Drew wanted nothing more than a beer and his La-Z-Boy and some quiet time to sulk. But the phone started ringing before he could reach the refrigerator. He cursed and hurried across the room to snatch up the phone, expecting it be Benedict with complaints about his story.

It was Helen.

"Oh, Drew, I'm so worried. I can't reach Freddie."

"I thought he was hiding out."

"He is. He's staying at our cabin east of the mountains until he can solve this debt. But I've been calling over there all day, and he doesn't answer. He was supposed to meet my father this morning, but he never arrived. Daddy called here, really furious. I'm afraid something's happened to Freddie."

"Like what? Nobody knows he's there, right?"

"I didn't think so, but why doesn't he answer the phone?"

"Maybe he's afraid it's Three Eyes calling."

"The number's unlisted. He must know it's me, but he doesn't answer."

"What are you going to do?"

"I thought I'd drive over there and make sure he's all right. I should've done that earlier, but I kept thinking he'd answer the phone. To tell the truth, I'm scared. It's so dark over there at night. And what if those men did find him? They might still be there."

Drew thought about Three Eyes and the big pistol. She could be right. The old man had vowed to find Freddie and cut him up into pieces. They might be working Freddie over right now, the ringing telephone a minor distraction from their dirty business.

"I'll go," he said.

"You'll never find it without me. It's all dirt roads over there."

"I'll find it. Give me directions. I'll go make sure Freddie's okay, then I'll call you from over there."

She finally agreed. He scribbled the directions in a notebook he kept beside the phone.

"Okay," he said when she finished. "I'll leave right away."

"Thank you. I know this is a lot to ask. You've already done me one favor."

"Let's hope this one works out better than yesterday's."

"Call me soon."

Drew set down the receiver. Another errand for Helen. Another interruption in his life caused by Freddie Graham.

The temperature's always five to ten degrees colder on the east side of the mountains, so Drew went to his closet and located a lined windbreaker like the ones coaches wear. It was black, which would help if he needed to sneak up on the cabin. He hoped Freddie was there alone so sneaking wouldn't be necessary.

Drew didn't own a gun, but he didn't want to show up empty-handed. He rummaged around in the closet until he found a weathered Louisville Slugger, one he'd used in company softball games before he'd decided free beer and camaraderie didn't make up for the tedium of the games. He hefted the bat, deciding it would do, and headed out the door.

TWENTY ONE

Forty minutes later, Drew located the cabin. The driveway forked off an unnamed dirt road, and he would've driven right past if it hadn't been marked with a reflector that looked like a glowing orange lollipop.

From a distance, the east side of the Sandias appeared to be a long, steady slope up to the fractured lip of the mountain. Up close, it's all rolling foothills and ridgelines, covered in a dwarf forest of juniper and piñon. Dirt roads wind between hills and around hogbacks, leading to ragged cabins and luxury mansions, all hidden from each other and the world. Half the year, snow sits among the trees and ice slickens the road leading up to the ski basin. It was too early yet for snow, but the night air had a sting that warned of cold weather to come.

Drew wanted to approach the cabin with his headlights off in case Three Eyes' boys had beaten him to the place. But the driveway was narrow and rough, and he decided he couldn't do Freddie much good if he got the Jeep stuck in a ditch. He drove slowly, watching for any sign of life, but he was upon the cabin before he was ready.

No lights shone from the A-frame building, and Drew switched off the headlights as soon as he spotted it. He sat in the Jeep, holding his breath and waiting for Freddie to appear on the front deck. No Freddie. He guessed that if Freddie had seen someone approaching, he would've switched off all the lights and hidden under the nearest bed.

Drew got out of the Jeep, baseball bat in hand, and eased the car door shut. The moon was nearly full and it illuminated the squat trees and the cabin's redwood walls. He walked up to the deck, but didn't climb the steps, afraid they might creak. He skirted the cabin, trying to see through curtained windows until he reached the back of the building and found Freddie's Porsche, glinting in the silver moonlight.

So Freddie was still here. Drew couldn't imagine him leaving the expensive car out here in the woods unattended. The car was empty and its doors were locked.

Nothing left to do but try the cabin. Maybe Freddie would come out of hiding as soon as he saw it was Drew, and not Three Eyes, who'd tracked him down.

A door was cut into the rear wall of the cabin, and he was surprised to find it unlocked. He cocked the bat over his shoulder and pushed the door open, ready in case someone came bursting out. The door's hinges needed oil, and they squealed as it swung open.

"Freddie?" he called. "You in there? It's Drew Gavin."

He listened for a long minute, but there was no answer.

"Helen sent me," he shouted, thinking that would make everything clear.

Still no answer. He stepped through the door, the bat raised in one hand, the other hand feeling for a light switch. He found one to the left of the door and flipped it on, bracing for an attack. No one.

Drew ventured inside. A kitchenette filled the corner to his right. A bottle of bourbon stood open on the counter. Another switch was on the opposite wall and he crossed to it, flipped it on, lighting up the living room. He went farther inside, casting cautious glances up the stairs. Before he could decide whether that's where he'd go next, he saw a pair of loafers at the end of the leather sofa.

They were cordovan kilties, with fringe and little tassles,

just the kind Freddie Graham would prefer. The shoes were toes down.

Drew's heart sank as he moved closer. He wanted Freddie to be asleep on the floor. He wanted Freddie to have passed out drunk. He wanted some innocent excuse, but there was none. As he reached the end of the sofa, he saw the blood that formed a dark halo around Freddie's head, soaking the gray and white Navajo rug.

"Aw, shit, Freddie."

Freddie's blue eyes were open wide. His red hair was matted with blood that had turned black and gummy. His white shirt was spattered with the stuff. Something had hit him in the left temple, leaving a ragged hole surrounded by a purplish bruise. He'd fallen beside the coffee-table, stretched out on his stomach with his head twisted to the side, as if he'd been favoring the wound as he fell.

Drew dropped the bat, knelt and pressed a finger to Freddie's neck, the way he'd seen people do in the movies, but he didn't expect to find a pulse. Freddie's skin was cold and stiff to the touch. He was dead, and it looked like he'd been that way for some time.

"No wonder you're not answering the phone," Drew said as he stood.

He took a couple of steps backward, putting some distance between himself and the corpse. He looked around the living room, but there was no sign of anyone else, no weapon. Just a dead lawyer on the floor with a hole in his head.

Drew had promised to call Helen as soon as he arrived at the cabin, but he didn't want to be the one who gave her this news.

"Call the cops," he said under his breath.

He wanted to slip out the door, run back to the Jeep and get the hell out of there. Let somebody else deal with the police. But he'd left fingerprints all over the cabin on his way inside and Helen would tell the cops she'd sent him there.

A phone sat on the coffee-table. A laptop computer sat next to the phone, but the coffee-table was otherwise empty. Drew noted that the phone and computer were pushed together at one end, as if Freddie had cleared the table to put something else there. Probably his feet.

He dialed 911. He got a dispatcher in the sheriff's department, explained the situation and gave her directions to the cabin.

"Are you in any danger there?" she asked.

"No. I'm the only one here. The only one who's alive anyway."

"Okay, hon, just sit tight. We'll have a car there in a minute."

He hung up, looked over Freddie's corpse again. He snatched up the baseball bat he'd dropped near Freddie and carried it outside. He hid it behind the rear seat in the Jeep.

Then he went back inside, out of the chill air, and stood near the glass doors, looking out into the night. He still stood there, his breath fogging the glass, when the first patrol car arrived.

TWENTY TWO

The first two deputies on the scene were friendly enough. They were young and seemed excited to be involved in a murder investigation. They kept Drew out on the deck, where he'd gone to meet their car. "Preserving the integrity of the crime scene," one of them said. They turned on all the exterior lights, asked him a few questions, got him to identify Freddie and radioed headquarters. Then they just waited for the detective to arrive.

A brown and white Ford finally jounced up the driveway. The investigator who emerged from the Ford was a large African-American man with a shaved head. He wore a dark suit and a white shirt with the collar open around his thick neck. Drew recognized him, even though the man had been wearing a sweatsuit when he'd seen him in the Gazette newsroom. It was Jamal Moore's father. Drew's heart sank.

"Lieutenant Moore," called one of the deputies, a Hispanic kid whose name badge said "Aragon." "Good to see you, sir. We've got the scene secured."

Moore scowled at the deputies and Drew. "What's the media doing here?"

The deputies looked around quizzically.

"Not here in any official capacity, Lieutenant," Drew said. "I found the body."

The deputies looked at Drew with raised eyebrows.

"Yeah, he found the body," Aragon said. "He's media?"

"Why, sure," Moore said as he approached the deck. "That's Drew Gavin, the famous sportswriter for the Albuquerque Gazette. Isn't that right, Mr. Gavin?"

"Not famous. But that's me."

Lieutenant Moore came heavily up the steps onto the deck.

"Got us a stiff, hmm?"

Drew winced, but nodded and moved to follow Moore inside.

"You wait here," Moore said.

Drew watched through the open door while Moore circled the body.

"Somebody already call the medical examiner?" he asked.

"Yes, sir!" Aragon yipped.

"Good. Anybody touch anything?"

"No, sir!"

"What about you, Mr. Gavin?" Moore stopped his pacing to stare hard at Drew.

"Not much. The phone. Light switches. I came in through the back door."

"What were you doing here?"

"Looking for Freddie."

"That would be Frederick Graham, the deceased?"

"Yeah."

"You found him like this?"

"Just like that."

"Back door was unlocked?"

"Yeah."

"You didn't see anybody else?"

Drew shook his head. He'd already answered these questions for the deputies, but he didn't say so. No need to get Moore riled. He figured the lieutenant was looking for any excuse to make things hard for him.

"What did you hit him with?"

Drew was so busy fretting over whether Moore would try to spring something on him, he wasn't ready when it came.

"What?"

"You hit this man in the head with something, didn't you?"

"Me? Shit, no. I told you, he was like that when I found him."

Moore sucked on a tooth, but kept his eyes on Drew.

"So, if I was to guess that this man was hit with that fireplace poker over there, and I checked it for your fingerprints, I wouldn't find yours, is that right?"

Drew looked to the tools arranged by the fireplace and back again. The poker stood where it belonged, didn't have any blood on it. What the hell was Moore talking about?

"I didn't touch it. I didn't hit Freddie. He was already dead when I got here."

Moore nodded thoughtfully.

"Matter of fact," he said, "I'll bet that poker's got no fingerprints on it at all. Bet it's been wiped down. But I bet we find traces of blood on it."

"What makes you think that's what killed Freddie?"

"Shape of the hole in his head. And the poker's handy. People get killed by blunt trauma like this, the weapon's usually something the killer grabbed up on the spur of the moment."

"What makes you think I did it?"

Moore shrugged his broad shoulders. "Why not?"

"But I'm the one who called the cops!"

"So? That happens a lot."

Moore skirted the body, then walked over to Drew and stood too close. Drew could feel the lieutenant's breath on his face.

"Don't get me wrong," Moore said. "I'm not saying this happened just now. This man's been dead awhile. Maybe twenty-four hours. The medical examiner can tell us for sure."

"I got here less than an hour ago."

"Sure you did. And you called it in right away. You're a good citizen, right? But say you whacked this man last night. You're worried, afraid somebody's gonna catch you. So you come back over tonight after dark, clean the place up, figure you got all your tracks covered. Then you call us."

"That's crazy."

"That's what I'd do if I whacked somebody. Call it in, make it look like I'm just doing my duty. Explain away fingerprints, anything else we find here."

"I'd never been to this cabin before an hour ago."

Moore pursed his lips and nodded.

"That's what I'd say, too, I was you."

Drew wanted to scream.

"Look," he said, trying to keep under control, "you're saying this because you're mad at me. Just because your kid can't hold onto a football doesn't mean I'm a killer."

The deputies, who'd scooted closer to watch Moore work, suddenly found other things to attract their interest.

Moore scowled. "You think I'd let my personal feelings influence this investigation? That what you're saying?"

"I guess I am. I mean, you come by the paper and yell at me. I've been asking a lot of questions about your son, whether he was arrested Saturday night. Next thing I know, you're trying to pin Freddie's death on me."

He flinched as Moore reached out toward him, but the cop just rested a big hand on his shoulder. His smile made Drew shiver.

"It's not like that at all, Gavin. I'm not happy about the way you've been harassing Jamal, but I wouldn't use my badge that way."

"Then what's this all about?"

Moore squeezed Drew's shoulder and gave him a pat before letting his hand drop back to his side.

"I got a corpse here, that's what. And it's my job to find who killed him. I'm just starting with you, that's all."

"Because I found the body?"

"Sure."

Drew took a deep breath. He needed to rein in his anger. Shooting off his mouth at Moore would only make things worse.

"So tell me," Moore said, his tone genial. "What were you doing here anyway?"

"Freddie's wife asked me to check on him."

"His wife?"

"Her name's Helen. She called me tonight, said she could-n't raise Freddie on the phone all day. She wanted me to come with her to check on him, but I thought it might be danger-ous, so I came alone."

"Why did you think that?"

Drew started explaining about Three Eyes and the gam-bling debts, but Moore shook his shiny head.

"Whoa, whoa, this is too much. We're gonna need to go downtown, talk this over some more."

Drew sighed, glanced at his wristwatch.

"Let me ask you one thing first," Moore said. "What's your relationship with the wife of the deceased?"

"She's a friend, that's all. We went to school together."

"Must be a close friend, she asks you to come check on her husband."

"Not that close. In fact, we hadn't seen each other in years until just the other day."

Moore got a sly look on his face. "She a pretty lady?"

"What? Yeah, I guess so. What's that got to do with any-thing?"

"You two ever been more than just friends?"

"Years ago. In college."

"And she just pops back into your life?"

"Sort of. I mean—"

"And now her husband's dead."

"Yeah, but—"

Moore looked past Drew's shoulder, ignoring whatever he was about to say.

"Aragon!" he shouted to the young deputy. "Take Mr. Gavin to headquarters."

"Am I under arrest?"

"Just routine," Moore said. "We need to get a statement."

"My Jeep—"

"Give me the keys. I'll have somebody drive it into the city for you."

He dug the keys out of his pocket and handed them over. Moore smiled wickedly as he jangled the keys in front of Drew's face.

"Though you're not gonna need it for a while. We've got a long night ahead of us."

TWENTY THREE

Three Eyes Sanchez wadded up the morning Gazette and threw it on the floor.

"How the hell did this happen?"

Zipper and Calvin stood on the other side of the old man's desk. Calvin had his hands clasped in front of him, clearly worried. Zipper stood ramrod straight, as usual. Neither seemed to have the foggiest idea what Three Eyes was talking about.

"I told you idiots to find the lawyer, rough him up a little. I didn't say anything about killing him."

Calvin's narrow eyes widened, showing the blue irises that made women flock to him.

"He's dead?"

"Yes, he's dead. Don't you fuckers ever read a newspaper? Watch the news on TV?"

"We didn't kill the lawyer," Zipper said. "We never found him."

Three Eyes leaned forward, his hands on his desk, the fedora low over his forehead.

"I called you last night and told you where to find him."

"We tried, boss," Calvin said quickly. "I mean, that address you gave us, the one you got from his phone number? It was no good."

"No good?"

"We couldn't find it."

Zipper reached out an arm and thunked Calvin across the chest, stopping him.

"We went over there," Zipper said. "We looked for his road, but it was dark and none of the roads seemed to be marked. We drove around for a long time, hunting for it. Decided to go home and try it again in daylight."

Three Eyes shook his head. How was he supposed to run a business, working with idiots? Couldn't find a rich man's cabin in the woods. Just decided to wait until morning. Jesus, Mary and Joseph.

"We were about to head over there when you called," Calvin added.

Oscar sniffed at the newspaper Three Eyes had tossed to the floor. Three Eyes bent over and pulled the dog up into his lap, where it licked his hand gratefully.

"Sometimes I think this wiener dog's got more sense than both of you," he said.

Calvin flushed, but Zipper stared at a point on the wall somewhere over Three Eyes' head. The Indian sometimes unnerved Three Eyes. You could toss all the insults in the world at him and he'd stand there and take it, like a fucking robot. Tell him to hurt somebody, and he'd do it quickly and well, but he didn't seem to have any initiative of his own, any emotion that would spark him to action.

"So you didn't kill the lawyer?"

Zipper shook his head.

"Then who the hell did?"

"Shit, boss," Calvin whined, "how should we know?"

Three Eyes patted the dog's head some more. It helped him think.

"You know what I'm out here?" he said after a minute. "Sixty large. That's how much that fucker Graham owed me. Somebody's gonna pay."

Zipper and Calvin exchanged a look, but Three Eyes

couldn't tell what they were thinking. Probably hoping he didn't mean to take it out of their pay.

"Hit the streets," he said finally. "Get that money. Get it from his wife, get it from that fuckin' sportswriter who came by here, get it from Nick Casso. I don't give a shit. Find whoever killed Graham and get it from him. But you get that money."

TWENTY FOUR

Wednesday morning, when Drew answered his home phone, the first words he heard were: "Saw you doing the perp walk on TV last night."

"Who is this? Goodman?"

"You looked good," the editor said. "Didn't look guilty at all."

"Funny."

"At least you didn't drape your coat over your head like some of those assholes do."

"What time is it?" The slant of sunlight through the sliding glass doors told Drew it couldn't be much past seven.

"Time for you to get your ass in gear," Goodman said. "The publisher watches TV, too. He wants an explanation."

The publisher, Parker Warrington III, was a corporate gnome whose idea of high fashion was his ever-present bowtie and whose idea of journalism was something akin to marketing breakfast cereal. Worst thing a reporter could do, in Warrington's opinion, was make the paper look bad.

"I didn't do anything, Bob. I just found the body."

"I believe you. But we still need a meeting to make the publisher happy. How soon can you be here?"

"I'll see you in an hour."

The Gazette parking lot would normally be empty at eight o'clock in the morning, but a few cars were clustered close to the employees' entrance when Drew rolled up in the Jeep.

The wind blustered across the parking lot as he trudged to the door. Low, gray clouds had rolled in from the southwest. He shoved his hands into the pockets of his windbreaker and pulled it tighter around him.

As soon as he let himself in the door with his card key, Drew saw editors moving from their window offices to the conference room at the far end of the newsroom. Benedict was headed that way, too, and he shot Drew a dirty look over his shoulder.

They settled around the table as the sportswriters had the day before. Drew sat at his usual place at the end of the table, but Goodman, not Benedict, took the throne at the other end. Benedict sat to Goodman's left, his hands crossed on the table. His pursed-lip expression was probably supposed to show concern, but instead he looked constipated. The table was lined with assistant editors and department heads. To Goodman's right was the only person in a suit. Drew recognized him as the newspaper's attorney, a hawk-faced man named Manuel Quintana. The only other reporter at the meeting was Teresa Vargas, who sported dark red lipstick today. She had a notebook at the ready and her pen was poised, but she slipped Drew a wink.

"So," he said, jerking his head toward her, "am I being interviewed or reprimanded?"

Goodman smiled and looked at Drew over his half-glasses.

"No reprimand yet. Innocent until proven guilty."

"Tell it to the cops who marched me past the TV cameras last night."

"What was that about anyway?" Teresa asked, drawing looks from the assembled brass. "Why the perp walk?"

"The homicide detective's got a hard-on for me," Drew said. "His son was the kid who kept coughing up the ball on Saturday: Jamal Moore."

"The kid's a Lobo?" Goodman asked.

"The dad came by here Sunday and chewed me out about my story. Hurt the kid's feelings, I guess." Drew glanced over at Teresa. "I've been working a tip that Jamal got arrested Saturday night and it got covered up."

"And the same cop is investigating the murder?"

"Lucky break, huh?"

Goodman glanced at Quintana.

"Maybe we ought to talk with somebody at the sheriff's department," he said. "Sounds like a conflict of interest."

The lawyer nodded and made a note to himself.

Teresa scrawled something, too, leading Drew to ask again why she was there.

"Don't worry about Vargas," Goodman said. "She's writing the murder, but she'll consult with Manuel on anything she includes from you. We don't want to get you into further trouble, but we don't want to get beat on the story, either."

Goodman didn't say "again," but Drew heard it implied. TV had played Freddie's murder big on the ten o'clock news. The Gazette's night cop reporter, a tortoise named Dan Packard, had managed only a brief story with no details and probably had been lucky to squeeze that into the final edition before deadline.

Benedict had been quiet so far, but he saw a chance to give Drew the shaft and, naturally, took it.

"You should've called the city desk last night," he scolded. "We could've had a better story this morning if we'd known we had someone inside the investigation."

"Drew had other things on his mind last night," Goodman said. "It's not every day you stumble across a corpse. And it sounds like the cops were giving him a hard time."

"Still—"

"Leave it alone, Greg," Goodman said. "Let's start from right now. Clean slate."

Benedict clamped his mouth shut, but he glared at Drew.

"Take it from the top, Drew," Goodman said. "Start with what you were doing at that cabin in the middle of the night."

Drew cracked his knuckles and stared down the long table of editors. If anyone but Goodman had been sitting at the other end, he might've told them all to get stuffed. But he and Goodman had a lot of history, and he owed it to him to play straight.

"Actually, it began a few days ago," he began, and he told them about seeing Helen and Freddie at homecoming, the fracas with the blond tough, lunch with Helen, his encounter with Three Eyes, the nighttime trip to Freddie's cabin.

The whole time, he was thinking: This is what it's like to be on the other side of the tape recorder, weighing each word, wondering how it'll look in print. Except that, usually, the source isn't worried about being fired by the people who are interviewing him.

"Have you talked to the widow?" Goodman asked.

"Last night. I called after Moore had asked all his questions a dozen times. She already knew Freddie was dead by then, of course, and she was real upset."

"What did she say?"

"Just that she was sorry she'd gotten me involved. I told her I was sorry Freddie got killed. Then this deputy interrupted me and told me he, too, was sorry, but my time was up and Moore needed to talk to me again."

"Could you tell where Moore was headed with the investigation?"

"I told him everything I've told you, and he wrote it all down, but he didn't seem real interested in the bookie. He said a bookie wouldn't kill somebody who owed him money."

"You got any better suspects?" Goodman asked.

"No. If the bookie didn't do it, then I don't have the slightest idea."

Heads swiveled and looks were exchanged. Goodman

stopped chewing on a pencil and leaned over to whisper to the lawyer.

Benedict sneered at Drew, and said, "So that's why you proposed doing a big story on sports gambling."

Goodman looked at Drew sharply.

"You caught me off-guard, asking for proposals," Drew said to Benedict. "It was fresh on my mind. I thought maybe there was a story there."

"No wonder you were so pissed off when I rejected it," Benedict said smugly.

"That's not why I got mad. I was pissed because of the reasons you gave. I still say you don't know what the hell you're talking about."

Goodman touched Benedict on the arm.

"Let's not get started with that again, boys," he said. "Drew's been through enough already."

Drew took a deep breath, his eyes on Goodman.

"Here's what we think, Drew," Goodman said. "You ought to take a few days off while things cool down. I don't think you're in any trouble with the cops, not really. But it might look better if you had a few days to get things sorted out."

Drew felt his guts knot.

"I'm supposed to leave Friday morning for Laramie, cover the Wyoming game on Saturday. And I'm still chasing that Jamal Moore story."

Goodman nodded.

"We can send somebody else to Laramie. And you've definitely got a conflict of interest when it comes to this Moore kid. The murder is a front-page story. Freddie Graham was big in the community. We might need you handy if Vargas has more questions."

Teresa didn't seem to need anything else at the moment. She finished scribbling in her notebook and set her pen down.

Goodman turned to the lawyer and said, "Manuel?"

"Yes, I have a couple of things. First of all, everything you told us, it's exactly what you told the police?"

"It's the truth. Why would I change it?"

"Right. The other thing is this: The police probably will want to question you further, do some follow-up. When they contact you, the first thing you do is call me. I don't want you talking to them unless I'm there. Clear?"

Drew nodded glumly.

"Okay, then," Goodman said brightly as he got to his feet. "I think we've covered everything. Now I get to go talk to the publisher."

Drew practically choked on the words, but he said, "You want me to go with you?"

"No, let me handle it. You go on home, get some rest."

Drew stood. All eyes were on him.

"When do I get to come back?" he asked.

"A few days," Goodman said. "Consider it vacation time. You'll still get paid."

Drew headed for the door. Goodman slapped him on the shoulder as he passed.

"Don't worry. This'll blow over in a few days."

Drew didn't even stop by his desk on the way out. He stalked out the back door and across the windswept parking lot to the Jeep. Once inside, he squeezed the steering wheel and gulped air, trying to shake off the anger and anxiety that roiled within him. He'd been suspended with pay, just like pro athletes who screw up some way. But he hadn't done anything. He'd just tried to help a friend.

TWENTY FIVE

Helen pulled the maroon comforter up to her chin and straightened the pillows behind her shoulders. The Kleenex in her hand was in tatters. She tossed it into a wastebasket near the bed and snatched another from a box on the bedside table.

She couldn't stop crying. Everything she could see, smell and touch reminded her of Freddie and what had happened.

Helen's father had ordered her to bed Wednesday afternoon, saying it would be best if she rested after her long interview with the sheriff's homicide investigators. Helen suspected Daddy just wanted to get rid of her, so he could work the phone without her sniffling in the background. He'd been on the phone all day, deflecting reporters and whispering with his business partners. Damage control, she supposed. In his own way, Nick was as concerned about image as Freddie had been.

She wondered what Daddy was up to now. She hadn't heard him growling into the phone for a while, and he hadn't peered into the bedroom for nearly an hour. She slid out from beneath the covers and padded over to the bathroom in search of her robe. Once she had it cinched up tight, she wandered out into the dark hall.

She assumed he still was in the other end of the house where she'd left him. But she heard papers rustling in Freddie's study and she stopped at the door and peeked inside.

Nick was up to his elbows in Freddie's file cabinet, his hairy hands thumbing through folders in search of something. He reached the back of the drawer without finding what he was hunting, muttered a curse and slammed the drawer shut. He was reaching for the next drawer when Helen said frostily, "What are you doing, Daddy?"

He wheeled toward her, then a smile spread across his face at the sight of his baby girl, up and around.

"Feeling better?"

"I can't stand being in bed any longer. What are you looking for?"

"Freddie had some papers I need, and I thought I'd see if I could find them. I didn't want to bother you."

Helen crossed her arms and hugged herself.

"You should be resting," he said. "Sorry if I disturbed you."

Helen walked away toward the kitchen, and Nick trailed along behind her. She kept her back to him while she filled a teapot with water.

"When you were talking to those cops," he said, "they didn't say anything about finding a bunch of papers at the cabin, did they?"

She turned to look him squarely in the eye. "Just his laptop, which they kept as evidence."

Nick scratched his chin, which was already thick with five o'clock shadow.

"Maybe the information's on that computer," he said. "Maybe he hadn't printed it out yet."

Helen shrugged elaborately and set the teapot on the stove. "You want some tea?"

"What I want is a drink, but I don't want to start knocking down martinis until I find those papers. You mind if I go look in Freddie's office again? I was nearly done in there."

"You were going through everything anyway. What makes

you think you need my permission?"

Her voice had an edge to it, but Nick ignored her tone and headed off toward Freddie's study.

The phone on the kitchen counter rang, and Helen scooped up the receiver. She took a deep breath before answering, getting prepared, putting on her game face for whatever Junior Leaguer was calling with condolences.

"Hi, Helen, it's Drew."

Her breath rushed out of her. "Drew, are you okay?"

"I just woke up from a nap. You're the one who must be miserable. How are you holding up?"

Helen took a ragged breath and swallowed a sob.

"The police were here," she said after a moment. "They asked me a lot of questions about you. About me and you, I mean."

"They asked me the same questions," he said. "I told them that was over long ago. I think they were just fishing."

"My God. I'm so sorry I got you involved in this, Drew."

"It's okay. Better that I found Freddie. I keep thinking what it would've been like if you'd been the one who went to that cabin."

She let the phone line fill with silence before she finally asked, "Did he suffer, Drew? Could you tell?"

"I think it was quick and painless."

"Thank you for saying so. I hope you're right."

"I told the cops all about Three Eyes and the gambling debt," he said. "I know you were trying to keep it a secret—"

"Don't worry about that. I told them, too. It's too late now to hurt Freddie's reputation."

"That cop, Moore, didn't seem to think Three Eyes killed Freddie. He said a bookie wouldn't kill somebody because then he'd never get paid."

Helen felt a chill, but said nothing.

"I was wondering, do you think it might've had something

to do with that business deal you mentioned? The one with your father?"

Helen turned away from the counter and was surprised to find Nick standing in the doorway.

"I can't talk about that, Drew. Not now, anyway."

Nick's face was dark. "What's he saying?"

"Daddy, please, I'm on the phone."

"What's that cocksucker saying to you?"

"Daddy!"

"Give me that phone."

She tried to turn away from him, but he snatched the receiver from her hand.

"Gavin? What do you want?"

Nick listened for a moment.

"She doesn't need your sympathy," he barked. "Don't call here anymore."

Nick listened, shaking his head. Helen stood with her hands over her mouth, felt tears coming again.

"Bullshit," he said. "Just stay away from her. We got enough problems right now."

He slammed down the phone.

"Daddy, why did you do that?"

"I don't like that bastard. I never did. Freddie's not even in the ground yet, and here he comes, sniffing around."

"That's not what—"

"Stay away from him, Helen. He's trouble."

Nick reached out to pat her shoulder, but she cringed away.

"You'd better go now, Daddy."

"Why? Because I told off that jerk?"

"Just go."

Nick scowled at her, but then his expression softened.

"Don't you want somebody here with you?"

"I want to be alone. Lock the door on your way out."

Trembling, Helen brushed past him and went to her bedroom. As she got into bed, she heard Nick's Mercedes start up outside and the wheels spit gravel as he roared away.

"Damn you, Daddy," she said as the tears flowed.

TWENTY SIX

Drew set the receiver down gently, as if it might detonate. He ran his hands over his face and massaged his forehead. That bastard Casso, he thought, still coming between Helen and me.

Someone hammered on his door. The building had buzzers down in the lobby, but most people ignored them to come up and bang on the door. Drew took a deep breath before opening it, expecting Moore or Benedict or Three Eyes.

It was Curtis White, grinning and holding out a twelve-pack of Heineken.

"Thought you could use a beer."

"Hell, yes. Get in here."

Curtis pushed the beer into Drew's hands, and ambled past him into the room, looking around like he was considering buying the place.

Drew pulled two bottles from the carton before stowing the rest in the refrigerator. By the time he'd returned to the living room, Curtis was squatting in front of the big TV, fiddling with the color controls. The baseball diamond on the screen went blue, then returned to a proper shade of green.

"There," Curtis said. "How come you're not watching the game?"

"It's baseball," Drew said, handing him a beer.

"That's right," Curtis said. "And baseball's not a sport. It's a pastime."

They exchanged a lazy high-five before Drew fell into his recliner and Curtis perched on the nearby sofa. Both held a not-so-secret contempt for baseball, which left them out in the rain with the Dwarves. Most sportswriters live for the summer game, collecting statistics as if they're jewels and waxing poetic over knuckleballs and double plays and Mark McGwire's greatest hits. Drew preferred contact. Curtis preferred speed.

"Still," Curtis said, his eyes on the TV, "you gotta watch the pennant race. It's required. Else you can't be a real American."

"I see you left the sound off."

"I said watch it. I didn't say you had to listen to those idiot sportscasters."

"Right."

They each took a slug of beer, then Curtis turned to Drew, the baseball game already losing his interest.

"So, what's up?"

Drew frowned at him. "Nothing much. Dead bodies. Interviews with the cops. The usual."

Curtis grinned wide enough that a gold molar flashed at Drew.

"And the brass told you to take a few days off? Recover from your ordeal?"

"Don't think my 'ordeal' had much to do with it. They're only thinking about how it makes the newspaper look."

Curtis made his eyes go round. "The editors aren't putting your feelings first?"

"That'd be a surprise, huh?"

Curtis smiled and sat back. He pulled a pack of Gitanes from his pocket and lit one.

"Why don't you tell Uncle Curtis all about it? I'll be your sympathetic ear."

"Gee, thanks."

But Drew did tell him. The longer he talked, the easier it came. Curtis said nothing, just nodded along, interrupting once to point at the TV screen as a slow-motion replay showed a stocky batter putting one over the fence.

"You listening to me or watching the game?" Drew growled.

"I'm listening. But shit, man, you see that hit? I could hear it all the way here, and they're playing in Cleveland."

Drew had been recounting events more or less in chronological order, and he finished with the phone call and Nick Casso hanging up on him.

"The old man don't like you?"

"Never has."

"What'd you ever do to him?"

"Nothing. Fell for his daughter. He didn't like that."

"You two were hot? Back at UNM?"

Drew nodded glumly. "Wasn't much of a secret at the time. You'd probably remember it if you hadn't been so busy trying to pork the entire cheerleading squad."

Curtis laughed and shook his little dreadlocks.

"Almost made it, too. That one blonde, Mary something, she wouldn't have nothing to do with me."

"Smart girl."

Curtis laughed again, but the mirth slid off his face as he studied Drew.

"Whole thing's got you down, ain't it?"

"Shit, yes. How would you feel, seeing some guy with a big hole in his head?"

Curtis snorted. "Man, where I come from, you grow up seeing that stuff."

Curtis had grown up in East St. Louis, Illinois, before he moved west to play ball at UNM, and he never let anybody forget it.

"Don't bullshit me, man," Drew said. "Your old man is a doctor."

"Still. I saw some shit, growing up. Believe it."

"Okay, tough guy, what would you do now, if you were me?"

"I'd go find who killed Freddie Graham. Jack him up."

"Now that's bullshit, too. You wouldn't mess around in police business."

"Hey, Drew, they messin' in your business. Sounds like that brother who came by the newsroom is after your ass."

"I think he is. But I didn't do anything. He'll lay off eventually."

"What if you handed him the killer? That'd be sweet."

"I tried that. I think that bookie had Freddie killed. But Moore wouldn't believe me."

Curtis shook his head.

"I don't believe it either, bro. Bookie's not gonna kill the man. Might mess him up, make him pay off. But he ain't gonna kill him."

"Now you sound like Moore."

Curtis held up a hand, as if taking a vow. "The truth, the whole truth and nothing but the truth."

Drew drained his Heineken and stifled a burp.

"I'm not going to look for a killer. Who am I, Columbo?"

"No, man, but you've got some skills, you know? Reporting skills. You could make a few calls, do some snooping around."

Curtis set his beer bottle on the floor by his feet and leaned toward Drew. "I know you, man. You can't just sit still. You don't know how to relax."

"Sure I do."

"No, you don't. That's why I'm always trying to get you to party. You're wrapped too tight, baby. Besides, you got some time on your hands. You think Benedict's gonna let you back in the building before this thing's worked out?"

"He'll figure out a way to make me look bad in this deal. Man's a fucking zero."

"He's worse than a zero," Curtis said. "He's the air inside a zero."

"How do you think he got like that?"

"Aw, man, it's 'cause he's new. He came here, what, two years ago? And we were already here, and we didn't like him from the start. He's always gonna be an outsider. He's just passing through, man. The rest of us, we're lifers."

"You got this all figured out."

"Sure. It's all those things. Plus, he's got a little bitty penis."

"Now how would you know that?"

"Just a hunch."

They watched the game in silence for a while until Curtis finally said, "You want another beer?"

"Yeah."

Curtis lanked off to the kitchen, but he called from in there while he opened the beers.

"You know, that Helen's gonna be available again, now that her old man's dead."

Drew shifted in his chair. It was as if Curtis had read his mind.

"Sure make a big impression on her, you find his killer."

Drew grumbled under his breath, then said, "Just bring the beers, will you?"

Curtis returned with a green bottle in either hand.

"Yes, boss," he said, smiling. "Whatever you say, boss."

TWENTY SEVEN

Chuck Gavin slowly dialed the bedside telephone, taking careful aim at each button. It was the third time he'd laboriously dialed Drew's number. It had been busy the other times, and the old coach wasn't happy when the answering machine picked up.

"Damn it, Drew, I know you're there," he shouted. "Pick up the phone."

He waited a second, formulating a message to leave, but Drew answered.

"Hi, Pop. Sorry you had to talk to the machine."

"I hate that damn machine."

"I know, but I've been getting calls from TV stations, so I didn't want to answer."

"I want to know what the hell's going on."

"Well, since you put it so nicely . . ."

"Don't mess with me, son. I've been worried. I saw the newspaper this morning, and there's your name and a picture of Helen's husband and a headline says he's dead, what am I supposed to think?"

"If you're like the cops, you'd think I killed him."

"That's not funny."

"Sorry, Pop. The whole thing's made me a little punchy. I should've called and warned you that I was all over the news with this thing."

"Just tell me what happened."

Chuck sat on the edge of the bed, his right arm and leg dead weight, pulling him over to the side, while he listened to Drew recount finding Freddie Graham's body.

When he was done, Chuck said, "How's Helen taking it?"

"Not good. I called over there a little while ago. She was all choked up. Then her father yanked the phone away from her and chewed me out for calling and hung up."

That fucking Nick Casso, Chuck thought. I should've broken his neck when we were in high school together. "Don't pay any attention to him. He's an ass. Always was."

"That's right. You two knew each other. Long time ago."

"People don't change," he said. "At least, some people don't."

Chuck pinned the receiver against his shoulder and used his good hand to pull his limp arm back across his lap. Don't need to tip over while I've got the boy on the phone. That would make him worry, and I'm enough of a burden already.

"The police gave you a hard time?"

"Yeah, but it's over now. I told them everything I know."

"But they're not letting you work at the paper?"

"That's just temporary. Until this blows over. Don't worry about it, Pop."

"You're getting paid?"

"Yeah."

"Don't let that bastard Casso mess you up at work."

"How would he do that?"

"Just watch yourself."

"Don't worry, Pop. Everything'll be okay."

"You're not going to go poking your nose into it anymore?"

"What makes you say that?"

"I know you. You can't leave something alone. You've got to pick at it."

"That's just what Curtis was saying."

"Curtis is there? How's he doing?"

"Just the same."

"Too bad."

Drew chuckled. It was a welcome sound.

"Call me if you need me. I can't do much to help, but I'm always here by the phone."

"Thanks, Pop. Try not to worry. I'll see you on Sunday."

"Bring me some more of those cookies?"

"You bet."

Chuck let the receiver drop off his shoulder, then picked it up and leaned over to hang it up. He swiveled on the bed and fell back against his pillow.

He didn't like it, not any of it. Too bad that Graham boy got killed, but he was more worried about his son getting starry-eyed over Helen. Chuck always liked Helen, back when she and Drew were dating, but the girl and her father had proved to be nothing but trouble. And Drew's involved with them again. And there wasn't a damned thing Chuck could do about it.

TWENTY EIGHT

Lieutenant Buck Moore spent Thursday morning typing up his investigative notes on the Freddie Graham slaying. Goddamn paperwork. The bane of his existence. In a perfect world, Moore would walk into a crime scene, decide who committed the murder and be allowed to shoot the perpetrator on the spot. Instead, there's endless paperwork, careless prosecutors, idiot judges. A wonder anybody ever gets sent to prison.

In the case of the late Freddie Graham, the perpetrator to be shot would be one Drew Gavin. Gavin had method. He had opportunity. And, he sure as hell had motive. One look at the widow had told the lieutenant everything he needed to know about why Gavin might off Graham. The woman was a knockout, no argument there, and Moore detected a manipulative streak, that poor little rich girl number. He could imagine her giving Gavin the prod: Help me out, Drew. I don't want to be married to Freddie anymore. I want a big lug like you instead. Shit, Gavin would whack the guy at high noon in Civic Plaza for a taste of Helen Graham.

Moore had already told his boss, Sheriff Richard Porter, that Gavin was his No. 1 suspect. But he hadn't told Porter about his run-in with Gavin at the newspaper office, and didn't plan to. Not yet, anyway. If he ended up filing charges against Gavin, he'd have to tell the prosecutors. Just the sort of thing a defense attorney would use to try to get Gavin off.

The Sunday trip to the newspaper office to complain about Gavin's story had been ill-advised, one of those things Moore caught himself doing occasionally. He tried to be a careful man, but sometimes his emotions overtook all reason. And when it came to Jamal, his emotions ran close to the surface.

Plus, he'd been exhausted. Jamal's arrest on Saturday night had required him to stay up all night, covering it up. Getting rid of the arrest report had been the least of it—the duty sergeant owed him many favors going back years. But the young deputies who made the arrest didn't know Buck, and now he'd owe them because they'd agreed to hush it up. Still, it was worth it if he could keep Jamal out of trouble. Jamal had a chance to make it to the NFL. He had the skills and he had the size. But he wasn't talented enough to overcome the taint criminal charges would bring. Buck had to keep the arrest quiet, and if it meant pinning the lawyer's murder on that snoopy sportswriter, so be it. Hell, he was pretty sure Gavin had done it anyway.

He wished the lab boys could've turned up Gavin's fingerprints on that fireplace poker. Sure would make things easier, make the fucking case airtight. But the poker had been wiped down. Only a trace of blood where the hook on the end bent back. Enough to confirm it had been the murder weapon, but not a clear print anywhere on it.

They didn't find much else in the way of fingerprints, either. Nothing that couldn't be explained away in court. Mostly the lawyer's own prints. The wife's. Some from Gavin on the light switches and the doorknobs. A few unidentified smears, could've been left there anytime by ski friends or business acquaintances.

No, the science wasn't strong enough to make it open-and-shut. This would be an old-fashioned murder case: Motive, method and opportunity. And Gavin had all three.

His thoughts were interrupted by his desk phone ringing.

"Lieutenant Moore?" It was Hanrahan from the front desk downstairs.

"What?"

"Man here to see you. A Mister Nick Casso."

So, the father-in-law decides to weigh in.

"Send him up."

Nick Casso. You didn't live long in Albuquerque without hearing about Casso, without feeling his influence. Man owned half the town. Liquor franchises. Tobacco distributorships. Real estate. Companies that manufactured food products for supermarkets and restaurants. Couple of department stores, sold cut-rate clothing. Casso hit all the bases: Food, clothing, shelter, vices. Everything people needed, he was there to supply it.

Casso appeared in his doorway. He was short and beefy, with jet-black hair and eyebrows like two caterpillars. His strong jaw jutted out like it wanted to be hit. He was dressed head to toe in blue polyester, looking as if he bought a cheap suit from one of his own department stores.

Casso extended his hand, giving Moore's big paw a firm grip. No smile, though. The handshake was a formality, not a friendly gesture.

"Sorry about what happened to your son-in-law."

Casso waved off the remark.

"Freddie was a careless man," he said. "It's no big surprise somebody killed him."

"Careless how?" Moore casually picked up a ballpoint pen.

Casso gave him the once-over, his eyes finally settling on the pen poised over the blank pad on Moore's desk.

"We on the record here?"

"Always." Moore tried a grin to set Casso at ease, but it didn't seem to take.

"I didn't come here to be interviewed."

"It's a homicide investigation, Mr. Casso. Anything you or anybody else can tell me about Mr. Graham might be a clue."

Casso squirmed in the hard chair, which wasn't designed for comfort. Moore didn't want people loitering there. He had too damn much work to do.

"Freddie was the kinda guy couldn't find his ass in a roomful of mirrors," Casso said. "I've been carrying him, one way or the other, ever since he married my daughter. He thought he had a good head for business, but it wasn't there. He could handle the numbers, schmooze clients, shit like that, but he'd drop the ball and I'd have to be there to pick it up. Know what I mean?"

Moore thought of Jamal losing his grip on the football, the pigskin tumbling along the turf to be scooped up by his opponents.

"I think so. But why would that get him killed?"

"Don't get me wrong. I don't think Freddie's business dealings led to his murder. He was just a screw-up, okay?"

Moore wrote "screw-up" in block letters on his pad.

"What about the gambling?" he asked. "That an example of Freddie screwing up?"

"It sure as hell was," Casso said, and the color rose in his square face. "I didn't know anything about that until after he was dead. If I had, I might've killed him myself."

Moore felt his eyebrows rise.

"I didn't mean that," Casso said. "Not like it sounded anyway. But I was pretty pissed off when Helen told me Freddie had been gambling away their money."

"Why?"

Casso glanced around the room, and Moore sensed a lie coming.

"We've got a business deal cooking. A big deal. If word got out Freddie was gambling, it could ruin the whole thing."

"Why's that?"

Casso gave him a direct stare. "It's complicated."

"Tell me about it. I'm a pretty bright guy. I like complicated things."

Casso was shaking his head before Moore finished speaking.

"It's all top secret for now. Proprietary information. Just take my word for it. Freddie's gambling wouldn't mix with this deal."

Moore didn't like being put off, but he didn't worry about it. If he needed the information, he could always get a subpoena. Let Casso try to dodge questions when he's under oath. Moore tried another tactic.

"The guy who found the body, Gavin, he thinks Freddie's bookie had him killed."

Casso's face darkened at the mention of Gavin, which Moore found interesting.

"Don't listen to anything that asshole says. He barely knew Freddie."

"Guess he knew your daughter pretty well, though."

"What the hell is that supposed to mean?"

Moore leaned back in his chair.

"Your daughter and Gavin both told me they had a thing in college, back before she married Graham."

"So?"

"Any chance they got something going again?"

Casso glared across the desk.

"That's horseshit. Don't you dare go around saying that. I'll have your ass for slander."

"Take it easy." Moore's voice was low, soothing. "You're saying there's no way something like that's possible?"

"Absolutely no way. Helen's been the most loyal wife you've ever seen, even if Freddie didn't always deserve it."

"Freddie run around on her?"

Casso gave him a dismissive shrug.

"I don't know. Probably. Hell, who hasn't stepped out on his wife occasionally?"

I never have, Moore thought. Rondelle would cut my balls off. Nothing like fear to keep a fellow in line.

"Leave my daughter out of this," Casso said. "She's suffering enough already."

"Is that why you came here today? To tell me to stop bothering the grieving widow?"

Casso eyed him, searching for some hint of sarcasm, but Moore stared back, impassive.

"Partly," Casso said finally. "The other thing is, I wanted to ask you what was recovered from that cabin."

"You mean what evidence we gathered?"

"Something in particular. A bunch of papers Freddie was working on for me. I looked all over his house, and I can't turn them up. You guys take some documents from the cabin?"

Moore ran the inventory through his mind.

"I don't remember any papers. Mostly we just dusted for prints and left things where they were."

"You didn't see a briefcase, something like that?"

Moore shook his head. "This part of that business deal you mentioned?"

Casso frowned. "I need those papers. But like I said, it's all hush-hush, okay? Don't mention it to anybody."

"How can I mention it? I still don't know what the hell it is."

"Doesn't matter. I guarantee you, it had nothing to do with Freddie getting killed. All right?"

"For now."

The men watched each across the desk for a time.

"You a hardass, Moore? You one of those guys that likes to give people a hard time?"

"I'm a homicide detective, Mr. Casso. Only people who

get a hard time from me are the ones who kill their fellow man."

Casso jerked his chin once in what Moore took to be a nod.

"Good enough. So, tell me then, who do you think killed Freddie?"

Moore rocked back in his chair, fiddled with his pen.

"Not sure I could say yet. We have more investigating to do."

"Let me give you a tip. Take a hard look at that guy Gavin. I don't trust him. Never have. I got him out of Helen's life once, and I don't like seeing him mixed up in it again."

Moore felt a smile tugging at his lips. "What would he stand to gain from Freddie's death?"

"I don't know. Son of a bitch is a little crazy, you ask me. Probably thinks he could take up with Helen again if Freddie was out of the way."

"Any chance of that happening?"

Moore watched Casso's reaction carefully, hoping he could read something there, but the rich man's eyes had gone flat and his mouth was a straight line.

"Not if I can help it."

Casso rose to leave. He dropped a business card on Moore's desk, on top of the pad, which was still blank except for the words "screw-up."

"Keep me posted, okay? You got all my numbers there. Call me with any news."

"Or if I have more questions?"

Casso hitched at his waistband. "Whatever. I don't want to be kept in the dark here. You get my meaning?"

He stalked out the door.

The lieutenant thought for a long time about the conversation with Casso, and made a few notes to go into his investigative file. He'd nearly finished typing all his reports, getting caught up for the week, when his phone rang.

"Porter here."

Moore sat up straighter at the sound of his boss's voice. It was odd for Sheriff Porter to phone him. His office was just down the hall.

"I just got a call from the head of the County Commission. Guess what he wanted?"

Moore didn't have to think long. "A quick resolution to the Graham murder."

"That's part of it. Guess what else he said?"

"I give up."

"He said we should leave Nick Casso and his daughter alone."

"No shit?"

"None at all. Now why would he say that?"

"Beats me. Casso was here a couple of hours ago, but I didn't send for him. He came in on his own, looking for some papers the deceased supposedly had."

"What kind of papers?"

"Some business thing. He wouldn't say much about it. Apparently, Graham had them, but they haven't turned up since he was killed."

Porter mulled that.

"That might explain what the commissioner said."

"Which was?"

"He said Casso was involved in something that would mean millions to Albuquerque."

Moore grunted.

"Wonder what it could be," Porter said. "Think it could have anything to do with the homicide?"

"Casso says no. He thinks we should focus on the sportswriter."

"You still thinking that way, too?"

"He looks good for it."

"Okay, Buck. Let me know. But try not to ruffle the rich folks' feathers, okay?"

"You know I wouldn't do that. I'm sure Nick Casso is a fine citizen."

"He's probably a bastard. But he's a rich bastard, so watch yourself."

TWENTY NINE

Most people would enjoy a few days off with pay, but Drew found himself at loose ends Thursday afternoon. He cleaned his apartment, which didn't take as long as expected, considering it only got a thorough cleaning once every six months. When he found himself lining up his sneakers on the floor of the closet, he knew it was time to stop. He played video football on a Nintendo system hooked up to his TV, but the "super-realistic" sounds of crashing pads and thudding bodies reminded him he was going to miss Saturday's Lobo game. He tried to read a mystery novel that had been lying around the apartment for months, but the private eye was a goof and every mention of the raven-haired love interest made him think of Helen.

Wednesday's clouds had blown through the state without dropping any rain, and Thursday was a sunny, cool day. Drew spent an hour on his balcony, looking off toward the Sandias, wondering how Helen was managing her grief, way over there in the foothills. He'd decided to call her—Nick Casso be damned—when the phone rang.

It was Curtis.

"You still in bed, man?"

"It's the middle of the afternoon. I've been up all day."

"Uh-huh, and what you been doing?"

"Nothing."

"Haven't gone out to track down the killer, huh?"

"Would you stop that? I told you, I'm staying out of it."

"You haven't been thinking all day about Helen?"

"Of course not."

"Just checking. Don't want you sitting around, stewing in your own juices."

"I'm not."

"Nice day out. Why don't you put on your sweats? I feel like teaching some white boy how to shoot hoops."

"I can't jump."

"Hell, I know that. Some things even I can't teach you."

"I don't know, Curtis—"

"I'll pick you up in half an hour."

The line clicked dead. Drew knew he ought to skip it. No need to let Curtis make a fool of him on a public basketball court. Besides, he still felt loggy from the beers they'd drunk the night before. But getting outdoors and throwing a ball around sounded better than staying cooped up in his apartment.

When Curtis pulled up in his sporty Z-car, Drew was waiting out front wearing a gray sweatsuit with UNM emblazoned across the chest in faded red. He'd even taped his gimpy ankles in preparation. He'd show Curtis a thing or two this time. He folded into the low-roofed car, breathing through his mouth against the reek of Curtis' Gitanes.

They played at a nearby schoolyard, on an asphalt court with ringing steel backboards and nets made of chain. Sometimes there'd be other guys there after work, enough to get up a game, but it was only four o'clock and they had the place to themselves.

"All right, Drew. Hop out, and I'll show you how it's done. Again."

They warmed up a while, Drew firing clanking jump shots from the top of the key, Curtis sprinting around the court like a gazelle, leaping and spinning and dunking. Nothing made Drew feel heavier or clumsier than watching Curtis move around a basketball court.

"Little one-on-one?" Curtis called after a while. "Make it, take it?"

"Sure. But I hope you aren't expecting much competition."

"Never do. Not from you. Take it out."

Drew dribbled around the free-throw line, waiting for Curtis to come at him, but Curtis loitered near the basket, not even paying attention. Defense had never been his forte.

Drew pulled up and fired a jump shot that banked off the backboard and dropped through the net.

"Ooh, you must be practicing when I'm not around."

"Luck."

"You got that right."

Drew dribbled the ball outside, took two steps toward the goal and threw up a brick that bounced wide. Curtis snagged the rebound without leaving his feet.

"Now that's more like it."

He moved quickly with the ball, taking it beyond the boundary and back in again, driving past Drew, who stood planted with his big arms in the air. Curtis went by him in a blur, driving home a reverse lay-up.

"You call that defense? You're just taking up space under there."

Drew moved his feet, trying to put up some pretense of a battle. It was like trying to guard lightning. Curtis was past him again, throwing up a prayer that dropped in, even though he was looking at Drew rather than at the basket.

"What's this about, Curtis? We haven't played basketball in weeks. Suddenly, you call and want me out here."

"I need to polish my game. Too much time in the office."

"Aren't you supposed to be in the office right now?"

"Benedict thinks I'm out working on a story."

"What story?"

"Lobo football. They're sending me to Laramie 'cause

you're out of action."

Curtis punctuated this news with a thirty-foot jumper that swished through the net.

"You?"

"Somebody's gotta do it. You're on vacation."

"Doesn't feel much like a vacation."

"That's the way the brass is playing it. You need some time off. Sounds better than saying you're a suspect."

"I don't need shit. I'd rather be at my desk than moping around my apartment."

Curtis drilled a twenty-footer. Drew didn't even bother to contest it. The ball hit the edge of the asphalt and skittered away across the playground.

"So what should I know about the game? Lobos'll get beat again, right?"

"Sure."

"Hard to write about losing efforts all the time, ain't it?"

"Tell me."

Curtis trotted after the wayward ball, leaving Drew standing underneath the basket, frowning. Damn, he hated to miss that game. Flying into Laramie was no thrill—it was the worst city to visit in the entire conference—but he felt proprietary about covering the team. If he misses the game, the readers will notice. It'll just make him look more guilty.

He cracked his knuckles, watching Curtis lope back toward him. This was crazy. His whole life, such as it was, would be out of kilter until the cops nailed Freddie's killer. And what's he doing to help? Standing around, playing basketball with Curtis White.

"So nothing else you can tell me to get me prepared for the big game?" Curtis asked.

"A football's the one with the point on each end."

"That's what that is? How do you dribble it?"

THIRTY

Friday morning, Drew drove up into the foothills, asking himself the whole time, "What the hell am I doing?"

It took a while to locate Helen's house among the rolling hills. The narrow streets zigzagged among sagebrush and junipers, sometimes only the roofs of the mansions visible. The search gave him plenty of time to change his mind, turn around and head home to his all-too-familiar apartment, but he kept going.

It wouldn't do for him to be seen at Helen's house so soon after finding Freddie dead. But Drew worried about her, up here in these hills alone. She'd sounded deeply wounded on the phone, and he couldn't get that sound out of his head, the throb in her voice.

He left the Jeep a couple of hundred yards south of the house, off the road behind a clump of junipers, and hiked to Helen's door. If the cops were watching the house, maybe they wouldn't spot him visiting. If they did, hiding the Jeep would probably seem that much more suspicious, but he felt he had to take the chance.

He rang the bell, and the door cracked open after a minute. Helen threw the door wide when she saw it was Drew. It was after ten already, but she still wore her dressing gown, a silky green floor-length number that made him light-headed. Her hair was brushed and she had put on her face, but the makeup couldn't hide the puffiness around her eyes.

She looked past his shoulder before she said, "Drew. What are you doing here?"

"I thought you might need some company. How are you feeling?"

She frowned, then stepped out of the way to let him enter.

"You probably shouldn't be seen here," she said. "People will talk."

"I parked down the road. I don't think anybody saw me."

He looked around the large living room and let a low whistle escape at the leather furniture, the Navajo rugs, the brass lamps.

"Nice place."

"It seems big and empty at the moment. Kind of hollow."

Helen gestured him toward a chair. She perched on the sofa across from him, a heavy oak coffee table between them.

"You want something to drink?"

He shook his head. "I shouldn't stay long. I just wanted to check on you, maybe ask some questions."

She sat back, putting a little more distance between them.

"Are you here for the newspaper?"

"Nothing like that. They put me on leave."

"Because of what happened with Freddie?"

"They're waiting to see how the investigation goes."

"Must be hard on you."

"You'd think it would be nice to get a break, but I spend all my time worrying."

"Worrying about your job?"

"Worrying about you, about what's happened. I know it must be rough."

She nodded, watching him closely.

"It could be worse," she said after a moment. "Freddie and I, we hadn't been getting along that well."

He felt a thump in his chest.

"We seemed to be living separate lives," she said. "Under

the same roof, but that's about all. I think a lot of couples get that way. It was probably just a phase in the relationship. But now we'll never know."

Her eyes filled with tears. Drew couldn't stand to see her hurting. He wanted to spring across the room, envelop her in his arms, kiss away those tears. But he forced himself to sit still.

Helen brushed at her eyes with the back of her hand.

"Sorry. That happens a lot. I'll think I'm fine and then suddenly I'm crying again."

"It's only natural."

"I hope you're right. I keep expecting to feel better, but I guess enough time hasn't passed yet."

"You've still got a lot to go through. I saw in the paper that the funeral's tomorrow."

"God, I'm not looking forward to that. It feels like half the city has already marched through here, telling me how bad they feel for me."

"I kind of expected someone to be here with you today," he said. "I wasn't even sure I should stop by. You know, if Nick was here or something."

"I made him leave. And the rest of them, too. I just needed to be alone."

"And then I come butting in—"

"It's okay, Drew. I'm glad to see you. I keep thinking about how I got you involved in this mess. I'm really sorry."

"No way you could know what I'd find over there."

At the mention of the murder scene, Helen got to her feet and walked around the room, straightening pillows and rearranging knickknacks.

"I try not to think too much about it," she said when she turned back to him. "I mean, about what happened to Freddie at the cabin."

"I can't seem to get it out of my head. I want to know who

killed him."

"I just want it to be over."

Drew felt as if he should be standing, too, but he didn't want to chase her around while she busied herself across the room. He stayed in his chair, raised his voice a little.

"That's why I wanted to talk to you. I thought I might poke around a little."

"Shouldn't you leave that to the police?" she said.

"Maybe I can help."

"What would you do?"

"I don't know yet. Sniff around, see if I can find out whether Freddie had any enemies. Anybody who'd want to do that to him."

"You mean besides the bookie?"

"No matter what Moore thinks, Three Eyes has to be at the top of the list."

"I don't think you should mess with him. Those men of his seem dangerous."

"I'll be all right. What about Freddie's law practice? He ever deal with criminals there, somebody who might hold a grudge?"

"Freddie did corporate work, mostly for Daddy. Daddy was banging around in Freddie's study Wednesday, looking for some papers about their latest deal, but I told him Freddie must've taken them to the cabin. If he's that concerned, it must be something big."

"Maybe there's something in those papers."

"I doubt it. Businessmen stab each other in the back all the time, but they don't literally kill each other."

"Still, you never know. Nobody was supposed to meet him at the cabin, right?"

"No one was even supposed to know he was there."

Drew had run out of questions. He slapped his knees and got to his feet.

"Guess I ought to be going. I just wanted to make sure you were okay."

"You're really going to look into this?"

"A little. What can it hurt?"

She trailed him to the door and stood very close when he turned to say good-bye.

"You might get hurt," she said. "I don't want that on my conscience."

"I'll be fine."

She put her hands on his chest, looking up at him, and for an instant he thought she might kiss him.

"You be careful."

He promised he would, then he was out the door and trudging back toward the Jeep. He felt a little breathless, and it wasn't because of the altitude or the exercise. By the time he got to the Jeep, he was smiling.

THIRTY ONE

Zipper methodically ate sunflower seeds, cracking the shells with his teeth and spitting the hulls out the window of the Pontiac as they drove to Helen Graham's house.

"You're gonna ruin your teeth with those things," Calvin said.

"Hungry."

"I'm hungry, too. But you won't catch me eating bird food."

Calvin stuck his toothbrush in his cheek and gnawed on the bristles a while. It didn't do much to ease his stomach rumbling, but it kept his mouth busy.

Zipper cracked another sunflower seed, making a loud snap. Calvin could practically hear the dentine being chipped away. Indian ought to take better care of his teeth. Not that it mattered much. It wasn't like he ever smiled.

Zipper slowed the Pontiac to a crawl as they neared the Graham house. The big white house sat back from the road at the end of a paved driveway. Junipers and chamisa and sagebrush crowded close to the road, obscuring the house from view. Calvin figured that was a good thing, especially if they had to kick in the door to have their talk with the widow.

Across the road, an old lady in hair curlers and a blue bathrobe bent over in her driveway to pick up her newspaper. She glared at the slow-moving car suspiciously. Calvin gave her his winningest smile, but she frowned sourly and turned back toward her home.

"That old lady spotted us," he said. "Probably gonna write down your license plate number."

Zipper hit the brakes to turn into Helen Graham's driveway, then suddenly pushed the gas again and the Pontiac scooted forward.

"That's your turn," Calvin said.

"Saw something."

Zipper stopped the car and turned to look back over his shoulder. Calvin scooted around in the seat until he was up on his knees, looking out the left rear window. He saw a big guy leaving the Graham house, the widow closing the door behind him.

"Who's that?" Calvin asked.

"Dunno. Maybe we'll wait here and find out."

But the large man didn't get into a car or walk up the driveway toward the road. He headed south through the scrubby trees.

"Where's he going?" Calvin said.

Zipper eased off the brake, let the Pontiac crawl forward. They kept parallel to the man, who lurched along among the trees, looking like freaking Bigfoot.

"There's his car," Zipper said, and Calvin turned to see a Jeep parked off the road behind another clump of trees fifty yards away.

"Think he spent the night with Graham's wife?" Calvin asked. "Maybe he's doing her."

Zipper paused, leaning forward to look around the trees, waiting for the man to reappear.

"Maybe."

"Hey, Zip. Maybe he's the one who killed Graham. You know, he's doing the wife, they want to get rid of the husband."

Zipper cocked an eyebrow, which Calvin considered a personal victory. Zipper moves an eyebrow, it's like somebody else jumping up and down and yelling, "Wow!"

"Maybe," Calvin said, "we make this guy pay the debt."

Zipper watched the gap between the trees until he could see the big man tramping along, then said, "Go to that Jeep."

"You got it, Zip."

Calvin leaped from the car and hauled ass up the road, thinking: Oh, boy, this is gonna be good.

THIRTY TWO

The smile slipped off Drew's face when he recognized the golden boy in the Hawaiian shirt leaning against his Jeep. The guy just stood there, his feet crossed, one elbow back on the Jeep's fender, his long hair moving with the breeze, a big white grin on his face.

"Remember me?" the man said as Drew neared him.

"Yeah, I remember. What do you want?"

"Need to talk to you, buddy."

"About what?"

"The widow Graham. Saw you walking over from her house. She there alone now?"

Drew bristled. "What's it to you?"

"Don't get nasty with me, boy," the blond said. "I already owe you one from last Saturday."

"Who the hell are you anyway?"

"Name's Calvin. But the man you really want to meet is Zipper."

Drew's stomach knotted. Adrenaline surged within him, urging him to run like hell.

"Okay, where is he?"

"Right here." The voice came from close behind Drew, nearly made him jump out of his socks.

He turned to see a stocky Indian with short hair and a wide face marked down one side by a white scar. Drew hadn't heard the man approach. He looked down at the guy's feet,

expecting moccasins or something, but he was wearing cowboy boots, and Drew couldn't imagine how he'd been so
stealthy.

"You're Zipper?"

"That's right. And who are you?"

"Look, what's this all about?"

Calvin, behind Drew now, reached out and clapped him
on the shoulder.

"Just answer the question, buddy."

Drew shrugged off the hand and stepped sideways, trying
to get out from between the two, but he ended up with his
back against the Jeep. They stood facing him, hemming him
in.

"My name's Drew Gavin. And I don't remember saying I'd
be your 'buddy.'"

The men exchanged a look, and the blond one grinned
again.

"You the sportswriter?" he asked.

"That's right."

"You're just the man we're looking for."

"Is that so?"

"Sure. I think you know our boss, Vicente Sanchez.
Everybody calls him Three Eyes?"

"Yeah, I know who he is. And I know you work for him.
But what are you doing here?"

"We wanted to talk to you," Zipper said. "You owe Three
Eyes some money."

"I do not."

Calvin slapped Drew's shoulder again, harder this time.

"Yeah, see," he said, "that guy Graham, he owed our boss
a lot of money."

"I know that," said Drew, glaring at him.

"Somebody's got to pay. Graham's dead, so we're not
going to get it from him. Either we get it from you, or we

go see the widow."

"You stay away from her."

"Ooh, touchy about her, ain't cha? What's a matter, you doing her? Don't want to share?"

Drew's fist came up so suddenly, Calvin didn't even have time to flinch. It was a big fist, wide and fast, and it smacked Calvin in the mouth and lifted him off his feet. The first thing to hit the ground was his back.

Drew stepped forward, ready to give the fallen man another one, but a *shikk!* sound froze him in place. Zipper had drawn a shiny hunting knife from a scabbard behind his belt and he held it near Drew's face, pointed skyward. Drew could see his reflection in the blade.

"Be still," the Indian said.

Calvin raised up on his elbows, blinking and wincing against the pain. His mouth was covered in scarlet.

"Jesus Christ!" he said, sputtering blood down his shirtfront. "What the hell—"

He spat twice, blood mostly, but something solid came out, too, and landed on the ground beside him.

"Goddamnit!"

Calvin snatched up the bloody item, wiped it clean with his fingers. It was a tooth, bright white.

"He knocked out my tooth!"

He felt his mouth, wiping the blood away, running his fingers over his teeth. Drew could see a bloody hole where Calvin's left front tooth used to be.

"Cut him, Zip!" Calvin shouted, his words muddled by blood and pain. "Cut the sumbitch!"

Zipper seemed to consider it, holding the knife closer to Drew's face.

"Hey!" A woman's voice from up on the road. All three men turned to look.

She was an old woman, wearing a blue housecoat and pink

slippers. She had her gray hair in curlers. In her hand, she waved a cellular phone like it was a gun.

"I see you there!" she shouted. "I've called the police!"

Zipper looked from the woman to Drew and back again, deciding. Then he stepped back and slipped the knife into its scabbard.

"Do him, Zip!" Calvin demanded.

"Shut up, Calvin," Zipper said calmly. "There's a witness. Cops are on the way."

"Goddamnit, he knocked out my tooth!"

"Get up and go back to the car. You can get your tooth fixed. But we don't need cops."

Calvin scrabbled to his feet, his eyes burning. He thrust his bloodied hand at Drew, holding up the tooth.

"See that? You'll pay for that, asshole."

He turned away, brushing the dust off his jeans with one hand, holding the precious tooth to his chest with the other.

The old woman scurried away, clutching her phone, before Calvin reached the road.

Zipper still stood near Drew, just out of reach. He looked him over before he said, "You've made a mistake. You'll be see-ing us again."

Then he followed after his friend, walking with smooth, silent grace.

Drew looked at his fist, which had been cut across the middle knuckle by Calvin's teeth. It hurt like hell. He wiped at the blood, taking deep breaths and watching through the trees as the men climbed into a black Pontiac and roared away.

He felt shaky inside, but he had to move. He didn't want to explain to the police what he was doing near Helen's house. He climbed into the Jeep and got the hell out of there.

THIRTY THREE

Drew watched his mirrors all the way home, but saw no sign of the black Pontiac. Adrenaline gave weight to his gas pedal foot, and he had to force himself to slow down several times. It was the same feeling he once got on the football field, the sense that raw power flowed through his body and needed to find an outlet before he burst. That was easy in football. Just lay into the ball carrier, put him on his ass. In the real world, you could drive fast or go for a run or knock some jerk's tooth out, but none of it was as satisfying as the crunch of your strong body flinging into somebody else.

His hand bled profusely from the ragged inch-long cut. At a red light, he rummaged under the seat of the Jeep and came up with a dirty rag. He wrapped it around his hand, cringing at the thought of germs. The human mouth, he knew, had more bacteria than a sewer. He needed to wash the wound and dress it before he caught something from that asshole Calvin.

He stuffed his injured hand, rag and all, into the pocket of his windbreaker as he entered the lobby of his building. As soon as he was in his apartment, he went to the bathroom to rinse the stinging cut and spritz Bactine into it. That made it hurt more, and he fanned his hand in the air and danced around the bathroom like a lumbering bear while he waited for the anesthetic to take hold. He bandaged the hand with white adhesive tape and a patch of gauze. The bandage wouldn't wear well there, right where his hand bent, but it would have to do.

Then he called Helen and told her about his encounter with Calvin and Zipper.

"They were watching the house?" she asked.

"Apparently. They left after I scuffled with them. But they might come back. They're still trying to get the money Freddie owed them."

Helen was quiet for several seconds.

"Maybe you ought to go somewhere," he suggested. "Stay with friends until this is over."

"No. They won't make me leave my home. Maybe I'll get Daddy to come over tonight."

"I'll call and check on you. If that's all right."

"That would be sweet, Drew. Thank you."

He hung up, thinking about Helen alone in that house, weighing the chances the thugs would come around again. He wondered whether they'd killed Freddie. Didn't seem likely, somehow. He hated to give Lieutenant Buck Moore any credit, but the detective probably was right. Why would a bookie kill the fatted calf? Clearly, the money was the most important thing. They wouldn't have killed Freddie, not unless it was an accident. Maybe they were threatening him and it got out of hand. But he couldn't imagine Freddie doing anything to provoke those two. And, it sure as hell hadn't looked like an accident. You don't whack someone upside the head with a poker unless you mean it.

He felt certain he'd see Calvin and Zipper again. Guys like that couldn't forget such a slight. Violence lives within them. Drew knew that feeling, that inner dynamite, waiting for someone to cross you so you can explode. For a lot of men, every day was a struggle to contain that savagery. Big guys like Drew can't afford to explode, can't take the risk of swinging at some jerk who cut them off in traffic or made a smart remark in a bar. Prisons are full of men who never learned that self-restraint, and cemeteries are full of their victims.

He didn't feel any sense of victory for sucker-punching Calvin and knocking out his tooth. In fact, he felt a little queasy about what he'd done. If Calvin hadn't said those things about Helen, Drew would've tried to talk his way out of it. But the fury had been instant, and it was as if his fist had acted on its own. Now what did he have to show for it? A painful cut on his hand and two goons gunning for him. And he was no closer to learning who killed Freddie Graham.

He leaned back in his La-Z-Boy and closed his eyes, thinking about Freddie's murder. Most homicides, he knew, were solved within a day or two of the crime. If the cops didn't turn up Freddie's killer soon, they might never find him. Or, worse, they might choose the easy way out and blame Drew. He didn't think there was any way Moore could make such a charge stick, but the accusation alone would be enough to ruin him in his hometown. He'd never be trusted by his readers again, and he couldn't imagine living with that.

So who killed Freddie Graham? And why? If it wasn't Three Eyes or Calvin or Zipper, who else had reason to do it?

What was it Curtis had said? Use your reporting skills? Good old-fashioned legwork. Sure, he spent most of his career sitting in press boxes, watching boys play games, but he knew something about doing research, tracking people down, even when they didn't want to be found. What would I do first, he thought, if I were trying to write a big feature on the late Freddie Graham? I'd pull the clips on him—go to the news library and look in the little file drawers for envelopes full of articles. Every time Freddie or Helen or Nick had been in the newspaper in their lives, the librarians would have it stowed away.

Only one problem: The Gazette building was off-limits to him. If he went there, poking around, Benedict would swoop down on him. It would only make Drew's tenuous situation at the newspaper worse.

He could call Curtis or one of the Dwarves, get them to look up the names for him, but he knew how sloppy Curtis could be on such research. And he didn't want the Dwarves to know he was up to something. Then he hit upon somebody else: Teresa Vargas, the police reporter. She'd probably already pulled the clips, had them on her desk for whatever follow-up she was doing on Freddie's death. She was an odd number, with the lipstick and the nails and the earrings, but she was one hell of a reporter. And, he'd bet he could count on her not to tell the brass he'd been sniffing around.

He picked up the phone from the end table, dialed the Gazette's main number and asked for Teresa. He listened to Muzak for a minute, then Teresa came on the phone with a terse, "City desk. Vargas."

"Hi, Teresa, it's Drew Gavin."

"Mr. Gavin," she said, and there was a smile in her voice. "Calling to confess?"

"What?"

"I've always wanted a killer to call me and confess his crimes. The ultimate story for a police reporter."

"Very funny. I don't have anything to confess."

"Too bad. It's a slow day."

"Nothing new on the Graham murder?"

"Not unless you've got something for me. It's all quiet down at the cop shop. I think they're hushing it up."

"Why's that?"

"Something your buddy Buck Moore said. I called him this morning to see if there was anything new. And he grumbled something about the big boys wanting to keep it quiet."

"What big boys?"

"See, that's exactly what I said. He didn't want to talk about it, but I used my feminine charm and wormed it out of him."

He could imagine how that conversation must've gone. Most likely, she pounded Moore with questions until he cried "uncle."

"Seems Nick Casso has been making a few calls," she said, "getting the county commission, the mayor, people like that, to put the hush on the investigation."

"Why would he do that?"

"Again, exactly what I said. You must be psychic."

"Seems the natural question."

"You don't do well with sarcasm, do you? I mean, you don't know it when you hear it."

"Just trying to ignore it," he muttered.

"You ought to loosen up, tiger. Have some fun. If this business isn't fun, how come we all settle for such shitty pay?"

Drew had made the same argument with the Dwarves in the past, but he wasn't in the mood for it now.

"It isn't much fun being a murder suspect."

"Gotcha. Okay, so why would Nick Casso want to keep everything quiet? Seems he has some business deal that might be messed up by the publicity."

"I keep hearing about that, but I don't know what it is."

"You should've done some snooping around. I did. Wasn't even very hard."

She made him wait. Finally, he couldn't stand it anymore.

"Okay, okay, what did you find out?"

"I can give it to you in a word. No, less than a word. Three letters: N-B-A."

"What?"

"Casso's trying to bring an NBA franchise to town."

"Jesus Christ. Where did you hear that?"

"Called up one of the county commissioners. Guy owes me a favor."

"Must be one heck of a favor."

She chuckled.

"Let's just say I kept his name out of print in a most delicate matter."

"Like what?"

"Doesn't matter. No charges were filed. I didn't see any reason to embarrass the man, as long as he knew that I knew and that he'd owe me."

"And this guy—whoever he is—he told you Casso's courting the NBA?"

"'Courting?' Hey, that's good. You made a pun."

"What? Aw, hell, enough kidding around. Have you told Benedict about this?"

"I haven't told anybody yet. Just you."

"Hell of a big story."

"I know. So why would I give it to Benedict? He's an asshole. You said so yourself."

"Yeah, but—"

"I don't have anything on the record anyway. I can't quote this guy."

"Maybe we could run it down some other way."

"What do you mean, 'we,' gringo? You're off-duty, remember?"

"But you're gonna chase it?"

"Sure. In between writing about murders and car wrecks. In all my spare time."

Drew's brain was racing. If Casso's after an NBA franchise, no wonder he didn't want any publicity about Freddie's gambling. Any whiff of impropriety would scare the league away. The big leagues act as if nobody gambles on the outcome of their games. Athletes who are caught gambling face stiff fines or even banishment from the game. Remember what happened to Pete Rose? Christ, they're still keeping the man out of the Hall of Fame. Nick Casso must've shit his pants when he found out Freddie was betting on sports.

"Drew? You still there?"

"Sorry. I was just thinking about Freddie's gambling and what it could mean to Casso."

"I thought the same thing. Looks suspicious, doesn't it? What if Casso found out about the gambling before Freddie was killed? That would be a good motive for getting rid of him."

"His own son-in-law?"

"What's an NBA team worth? Hundreds of millions? I'd kill my own mother for that."

Drew laughed. She sounded so hard-bitten, so old school, yet he could picture her in her purple lipstick and her spiky hair, probably smacking gum, looking like a kid.

"Thanks, Teresa. I appreciate you letting me in on this. It gives me a lot to think about."

"What's the matter? You got time on your hands? You don't know how to keep yourself amused if you're not down here, slaving away?"

"Something like that."

"You figure out who killed Graham, you call me first. Got it?"

"I got it, I got it. Let me know before you print anything about the NBA deal. I don't want to be anywhere near Casso when you break that story. He might burst into flames."

Teresa giggled. "Here's hoping."

Another pause. Drew knew he should hang up and spend some time thinking over what she'd said. But he liked talking to the little smart-ass.

"Why did you call, Drew?"

"I was going to ask you if you'd pulled the clips on Freddie and Nick."

"Nothing in the clips but the usual philanthropy stuff, a few business stories. For such a big wheel, Nick Casso's kept himself out of the paper pretty well in the past."

"But you're going to change all that?"

"I might, if I can get the NBA tip confirmed."

"Thanks for telling me about it. I owe you one."

"I agree. How are you going to pay off?"

"I was being figurative."

"I'm not."

"What do you want?"

"How about dinner sometime?"

"You mean, like, a date?"

"Did I say a date? I said dinner. I'm not a highly paid veteran like you. I can always use a free meal."

"I'll call you."

"That's what they all say."

"I promise."

"I'll hold you to it. So long, tiger."

Drew still held the receiver in his hand, blinking at it, long after it clicked to dial tone.

THIRTY FOUR

Nick Casso smiled as he studied the menu at McGrath's, a posh restaurant on the ground floor of the downtown Hyatt Regency. The back of the menu was given over to a chronicle of Lizzie McGrath, the old-time madam for whom the restaurant was named. Lizzie had run a bordello on this spot back in the days when Albuquerque was a Wild West railroad town. Fitting, Nick thought, that a whore's name decorates the place. In a boomtown like Albuquerque, everything is for sale.

He sat at a quiet corner table, his back to the wall. Friday lunch was a busy time at the restaurant, and Nick waved to a few fellow businessmen, not holding anyone's gaze too long. The NBA guy, Martin Woodward, would be joining him shortly and he didn't want some fawning local in the way.

Nick had deliberately arrived early, making sure he'd get the table he wanted, one away from most of the restaurant traffic. He and Woodward would be lunching with two city councilors and talking over the arena proposal, and he didn't want the whole town's lips flapping about it. He only needed to keep it quiet five more days, until Wednesday night's council meeting. As long as he and Woodward could persuade one of their two luncheon companions that the NBA franchise would be a boon for the city, the vote would be a lock and the public wouldn't have a thing to say about the bond issue.

Nick set down the menu when he saw Woodward gliding

between tables toward him. Woodward was tall and well-dressed and had brown hair slicked back like that coach, what's-his-name, used to be with New York and now was where, Miami? Nick needed to beef up his knowledge of basketball if he was going to be a team owner. He'd never paid much attention to sports until Freddie showed him how much money was to be made.

Fucking Freddie. Too bad the little bastard had to die, especially since he seemed to mean so much to Helen. But it was a good thing in the long run. Freddie's gambling would've nixed this deal. Instead, it would all come together smoothly. Nick would see to it.

He and Woodward shook hands and the lanky man slid into a chair.

"I finished looking over those papers," Woodward said. "A very impressive proposal."

"Sorry it took so long to get them to you. Freddie's death really messed things up. I had to pull some strings to get that laptop away from the cops and get a new copy made up."

Woodward smiled. "Those aren't the only strings that'll need pulling, I'm afraid."

"You mean the City Council? That's no problem. I'm telling you, we've nearly got the votes together already. Wait'll you see these councilors who'll be here in a minute. One of them's Alice Burden. She's this loud-mouthed old lady who always wears hats. She might be tough to swing. The other guy, David Guerrero, fancies himself to be a champion of the little people. But he played basketball in high school. He'll go for it. Wait and see."

Woodward nodded, but said, "Those aren't the strings I meant."

"No?"

"I'm afraid you've got a long road ahead, Mr. Casso. It won't be easy to persuade the other owners that Albuquerque is a big enough market to sustain a team."

"We're big enough. You saw in those papers—"

Woodward smiled again, showing his pointed teeth.

"I believe you. I'm on your side. But you may need some help convincing the owners."

Nick sat back, studying Woodward's lean face.

"Let me guess. You know where I can get such help."

Woodward reached out to the center of the table and fiddled with a saltshaker.

"I might be of service," he said. "You could use somebody on the inside."

Nick felt a grin tugging at his face. He liked this guy, liked the way his mind worked. He was a fucking shark. That had been Freddie's problem—one of many. He hadn't known how to enjoy business, the give and take, the quick offer, the subtle rejoinder. Nick understood it was all a game, one he played to perfection.

"You should be compensated for such help," he said blandly.

Woodward gave him the smile again. "That's what I was thinking. I've been considering leaving the head office, to tell you the truth. I like it here. Nice climate. I think maybe you could use a partner who understands how the league works."

"A partner? I was thinking of something more like a consultant's fee."

"No, that wouldn't do. Might look like a bribe. We wouldn't want that."

Nick grinned. "No, of course not."

"I think I can help the Albuquerque Mustangs become a reality," Woodward said slyly. "But I can't have any connection to the franchise until after it's established."

"And then you'd like to be my partner?"

Woodward raised a shoulder casually.

"Perhaps. You should think it over. It might make a big

difference in persuading the league to go along."

Nick rubbed his palms together, making a dry, rustling sound.

"How big a percentage are we talking about here?"

"There's no hurry to work all that out," Woodward said. "We've got lots of time. First, we have to get your City Council to go along with the plan for the arena."

"I'm telling you, that's not going to be a problem."

"Then you can leave the rest up to me. Once the bond issue goes through, I think I can guarantee the franchise."

"We'll get the vote Wednesday night," Nick said. "I've already got it set up. They'll vote on it as an emergency bond issue, saying they have to act fast to take advantage of this opportunity."

"Good. And you can keep it quiet until then?"

"No leaks," Nick said. "I've got things locked up tight."

"Very good. I think we're in business."

Nick reached over and patted Woodward on the shoulder. "This is going to work out great. Partner."

"I hope so," Woodward said. "I'm really taking a shine to Albuquerque."

Nick looked up and saw the two councilors approaching. Alice Burden wore a wide-brimmed hat that made him think of flying saucers.

"There they are," he said, waving at the councilors.

"Anything else I ought to know about them?" Woodward said, barely moving his lips.

"Just that they both want to stay in office. And I can see to that."

"I like your style, Nick."

THIRTY FIVE

The law firm of the late Freddie Graham was in the 500 Marquette Building, a slick brown monolith across Fifth Street from City Hall. Lawyers in the fourth-floor firm could look out their windows and practically see what was doing in the City Council offices. It took Drew nearly an hour of waiting and badgering receptionists before he finally got a moment with one of Freddie's associates.

He cooled his heels in a conference room until Griffin Bailey entered as if he owned the place, which he did, in a way. The name of the firm was Bailey, Schwartz and Rodriguez, and it had been founded by Griffin's father, whom everyone naturally called the Old Bailey. A portrait of the stern gent glared down at the conference table.

Junior here looked like the kind of guy who'd had everything handed to him his whole life. Maybe thirty years old. Thousand-dollar gray suit, blue shirt with a stiff white collar, muted tie, tassled loafers. Sleek black hair. Movie-star chin. Perfect in every way except, Drew saw as they shook hands, the man had one green eye and one brown eye. The inbreeding of the rich, he figured.

Bailey gestured for Drew to take a seat, then sat across from him and put his feet up on the conference table. He was trying to look casual, but his mismatched eyes darted around the room before they settled on Drew.

"They tell me," he said, "you have some questions about

Freddie's law practice."

Drew tugged at his shirt, an old red polo with "Western Athletic Conference Tournament, '94" printed over the heart, yanking it loose from where it caught under his gut. He was underdressed for a visit to a law office, and he scooted closer to the table, trying to hide as much of himself as possible beneath its mahogany top.

"Sort of. I'm asking around, trying to figure out why somebody would want him dead."

Griffin Bailey narrowed his eyes. "And this is for the newspaper?"

Drew hadn't introduced himself at the reception desk as a reporter. In fact, he'd let the phrase "friend of the family" slip casually from his lips. But Bailey clearly had recognized the name. No surprise there. Anybody reading the accounts of Freddie's death would've noted that a newspaperman found the body.

Drew shook his head. "I'm currently on leave from the newspaper. This is personal."

Bailey steepled his fingers in front of his chest, striking much the same pose as his father in the portrait. He didn't quite pull it off. Maybe in another thirty years he could persuade people he was a respected jurist.

"You were a close friend of Freddie's?"

Drew cleared his throat. "I knew his wife pretty well in college."

"Hm-mm. And you feel some need to look into his death?"

The guy smiled without showing any teeth. He was toying with him, but there wasn't much Drew could do about it. Not like he could grab the guy, shake the truth out of him. All that would get him would be a million trips to court. A lawyer is like a loaded gun. Don't touch unless absolutely necessary.

"The police have been questioning me," Drew said. "I

thought maybe I could help. It's worth a shot."

Bailey leaned forward, brushed at some imaginary lint on his pants leg.

"Frankly, Mr. Gavin, I think your 'shot' is ill-advised. It's a police matter. Perhaps you should leave it to them."

Drew stared at the guy, thinking: You never played ball. You never were part of a team. If you had, you'd know something about supporting your teammates. Freddie worked here, for God's sake. Shouldn't *you* be investigating his murder?

"What's your sport, Mr. Bailey?"

"I beg your pardon?"

"Sports. You like to play anything? I make you for a tennis player."

Bailey's eyes narrowed again, but he said, "I play tennis occasionally. I prefer racquetball."

"You and Freddie ever play together?"

"No, Freddie was a golfer. As I'm sure you know, since you were such close friends."

"What about socializing? Freddie hang out with the guys after work?"

"Not much. To tell you the truth, Freddie was a ghost around here."

"What does that mean?"

"A ghost? Oh, it's a term we toss around. It's a lawyer who doesn't spend much time in the office. Freddie didn't do much for the billable hours around here."

"Why'd you keep him on then?"

Bailey dropped his feet to the floor, adjusted his shirt cuffs. It was as if the guy could see himself in a mirror at all times. Drew glanced around the windowless room. Maybe the guy had a third eye somewhere, a blue one, so he could watch himself looking dapper.

"Don't get me wrong. Freddie could be valuable. He knew

everyone in town. He often heard about business proposals far enough ahead that the firm could, shall we say, take advantage of them."

"Because of Nick Casso."

"If it hadn't been for Nick Casso, Freddie probably never would've gotten on here in the first place. Nick and my father are close."

"Didn't you resent that? Even a little?"

Again the tight smile.

"Of course not, Mr. Gavin. I'm a professional. It's all business."

Bailey looked at his gold Rolex. Drew didn't take the hint.

"I hear Freddie and Nick were working on some deal. You know anything about that?"

Bailey shook his sleek head. "Freddie didn't always keep us informed. We trusted him. We knew he'd let us know when he had something profitable."

"Sounds like Freddie was leaving you out in the cold this time around."

Bailey didn't take the bait.

"Really? Now we'll never know, will we?"

"You didn't know anything about this thing? A sports-related deal?"

"Sports? Doesn't sound like something for us. You clearly know more about it than I do."

"Anybody else in the firm who might know? Somebody else I could talk to?"

"I don't think so. Freddie's secretary, Trish Vandiver, was familiar with his affairs, but Trish isn't here. She took his death hard, I'm afraid. We gave her a few days off."

"What about your father? Maybe I should talk to him."

Bailey's face went slack for a moment. He covered well, smiling at Drew as he rose and moved toward the door.

"Afraid that wouldn't be possible," he said quickly. "Dad's

pretty busy. So am I, frankly. Afraid I've given you all the time I can spare."

Drew walked toward the door. Bailey edged away, didn't offer to shake Drew's hand.

"You said this deal involved Nick Casso?" he asked as Drew reached the doorway.

"That's what I hear."

"Then why don't you ask him?"

"Maybe I'll do that."

THIRTY SIX

Freddie's secretary listed herself as T. Vandiver in the phone book, but Drew was wise to that ploy. He was just glad she didn't call herself Patricia. There were three P. Vandivers and they were spread all over town. Trish, on the other hand, lived nearby, in a cottage off Lead Avenue just west of downtown, not far from the neighborhood where Drew grew up. The neighborhood was gradually gentrifying, and Trish had done a nice job of fixing up her little stucco house. Late-blooming flowers in pots on either side of the front steps, new awnings over the windows, a stained-glass design of a butterfly over the front door. And, beside the door, a nice new mailbox that Drew prowled before announcing his presence. Couple of bills and one letter, all addressed to "Trish Vandiver." He rang the doorbell.

She opened the oak door cautiously and peered around the edge with bloodshot eyes. One hand clutched the collar of her quilted bathrobe. Late afternoon, and Trish wasn't dressed yet. She'd been crying. Bailey was right about her taking Freddie's death hard.

"Miss Vandiver?"

"Yes?"

"My name's Drew Gavin. I was a friend of Freddie Graham's. Could I talk to you for a few minutes?"

She looked him over a long time, glancing past his shoulder to where he'd parked the Jeep at the curb in the shade of an overhanging elm. Finally, she nodded.

The house was tidy on the inside, too, with potted plants tucked onto every shelf and into every corner. Drew followed Trish into a small living room and sat on a cushy blue couch. She took an armchair across the room, tucking her pink bathrobe around her legs nervously. She had a tousled pile of bottle-blond hair, and he guessed she usually wore makeup to hide the sun wrinkles on her sharp-edged face.

"You're the one who found his body, aren't you?"

Drew nodded.

"I saw your name in the newspaper. I cut out those stories about him. I've read them all again and again. It's hard to believe he's gone."

"You and Freddie worked together a long time?"

"Four years." She cut her eyes to the side. "We were very close."

Drew studied her. She seemed edgy. Maybe it was just grief, maybe something more.

"Griffin Bailey gave me your name," he said. Her dark eyes widened at the sound of the lawyer's name. Drew didn't say Bailey had sent him to see her, but he let her draw the conclusion. "He said you were the only one at the firm familiar with Freddie's work."

A glass of what looked to be orange juice sat on the table beside her chair, and Trish Vandiver picked it up and gulped from it, watching him over the rim of the glass.

"I worked closely with Mr. Graham," she said coolly as she put the glass back.

Might as well spring it on her, he decided.

"You know anything about the NBA deal?"

Her eyes widened, but she caught herself quickly.

"Did you say NBA? As in basketball?"

"Right."

She shook her head, but her eyes showed the lie.

"The reason I ask," he continued, "is I think it might have something to do with why Freddie was killed."

"Why would you think that?"

"Lot of money in sports franchises. Maybe somebody got greedy, wanted Freddie out of the picture."

Trish made a show of tucking her robe all around her again. Drew guessed it made her uncomfortable, having a man in her house when she wasn't properly dressed. He wondered if Freddie had seen her in her nightclothes before he died. Wouldn't be a surprise. Even with a terrific woman like Helen at home, Freddie would be the type to mess around.

"I'm not saying I knew anything about such a deal," she said finally. "But if Freddie had been working on such a thing, it wouldn't have gotten him killed. I mean, that doesn't make any sense, does it?"

"Freddie had a gambling problem," Drew said. "You probably knew about that."

She shook her head so slightly it was barely a "no."

"If I know the NBA, they wouldn't give a franchise to somebody caught gambling," he said. "Too worried about their image. Somebody might've seen Freddie as a problem."

She considered it for a moment, but then stood up, shaking her head.

"I'm sorry, Mr. Gavin, but I don't know anything about this. I think you'd better go."

"What about you, Ms. Vandiver? Do you have ideas about who killed Freddie or why?"

She shook her head some more, looking at the door the whole time.

"Had you ever been over to that cabin where he was killed?"

"Sure," she said. "Why do you ask?"

"You said you and Freddie were close. I was wondering just how close."

Trish Vandiver went stiff all over, then turned her glare on Drew.

"What the hell is that supposed to mean?"

Drew tried smiling at her, but it didn't take. This was always the hardest part of an interview, asking the questions the subject didn't want to answer. He always saved those for last. That way, if they booted him out, he already had everything else. A reporter has to be ready to read the reaction when he drops the bombshell, and Drew thought Trish's blush and sputter meant he'd scored.

"You and Freddie had something going, didn't you?"

"You've got a lot of nerve, coming into my house—"

"Answer the question," he said sharply.

"Up yours, mister. I'm not talking about Freddie and me with some stranger. I don't know what you're up to, but you get out of my house right now or I'll call the cops."

"The cops might be interested in talking to you about your relationship with your boss."

She exhaled loudly and her shoulders sagged. Drew nearly grinned. He had her. She knew she was caught and she was ready to admit something.

"You thick bastard," she said, her mouth curving downward. "You think I killed him? You think I know anything about it?"

Drew held out his hands, motioning her back toward the couch.

"Come on," he said. "You can tell me."

"Fuck you, buddy. Get out of my house right now."

He stood and walked to the door, Trish right on his heels. He had to take a final shot. He turned as he reached the porch and said, "You were in love with him, weren't you?"

She slammed the door in his face.

THIRTY SEVEN

When Drew got home, he went straight to the kitchen and cracked open a beer. He'd barely finished a swallow before the phone rang. Probably another TV reporter wanting an interview. He let the answering machine get it.

"Yo, Drew. Curtis here. You recovered yet from that asswhipping I gave you on the basketball court?"

Drew crossed the room and picked up the phone.

"Hi, Curtis."

"Thought an old man like you'd be soaking in a hot tub today."

"How am I an old man when we're the same age?"

"Ain't the age, man, it's the mileage."

"You got that right. Hey, I was just thinking of calling you. You heard anything about somebody trying to get an NBA franchise in Albuquerque?"

"Shit, no. That ain't gonna happen."

"How come?"

"Market's not big enough. And we don't have an arena that would work."

"What about The Pit?"

"Too small. They want twenty-five-thousand seats these days. And that costs more than the town would support."

"What if somebody built a bigger house? Think we'd have a shot then?"

"I don't think so. I talked to an NBA guy about that, back

when the Bulls were here, playing that exhibition game? He made a lot of noise about how the NBA's open to all proposals, but I could see it wasn't going anywhere."

"Didn't you write something about it?"

"Yeah, a little story. I'm surprised you remember. Thought you only read about football."

"Hey, I'm a well-rounded guy."

"Just around the gut. Where'd you hear this? Sounds like something I ought to be going after."

Drew hesitated. Teresa Vargas wouldn't be happy if he tipped another reporter to her potential scoop.

"Just the grapevine. Probably nothing to it."

"Maybe I ought to call that guy—"

"No, don't do that. Give me his name. I'll call him."

"You're on vacation, remember?"

"You said I need something to keep me busy."

Drew waited through a long silence.

"This has something to do with that dead lawyer, don't it?"

"What makes you say that?"

"I told you to go find the killer. Now, you got something about the NBA. What's going on, man?"

"It's probably nothing."

Another silence.

"Come on, Curtis. Trust me."

"Give you a scoop on my beat, that's what."

"How can I scoop you? I'm on vacation."

"What the hell. I'm doing your job, leaving in an hour for sunny Laramie. Might as well let you do mine."

"It's all off the record."

"I've heard that before. Okay, the guy's name is Martin Woodward. He's some kind of development executive for the NBA."

Curtis reeled off a number with a New York area code. Drew fumbled for a pen, then scribbled it down.

"Thanks, Curtis. I'll let you know what I find out."

"Sure you will. I'll read about it in the Gazette."

"It's probably nothing."

"That's what I think, too. Else I wouldn't give you my contact. Nobody gonna sink millions of dollars into a new arena unless the NBA gives them a team first."

Drew thanked him again and said good-bye.

"Wait a minute," Curtis said. "Tell me about this tip you got on Jamal Moore getting arrested. Benedict told me to look into that, too."

Drew told him what little he knew and how his attempt to uncover what had really happened had been fruitless.

"All right, man, I'll check it out. Doing your job is a pain in the ass, you know that?"

"Have fun in Laramie."

"Shit."

Curtis hung up.

Drew figured Curtis was right about the arena, too big of an investment for anybody, even Nick Casso, unless the deal was already done. Albuquerque officials had been trying for years to build a multipurpose arena to host concerts and ball games and such, but the taxpayers had twice voted down the bond issue that would've made it possible. The city had plenty of more pressing needs for tax dollars—sewers and streets and low-income housing. But what if Nick Casso could guarantee an NBA franchise? In a basketball-mad town like Albuquerque, people's priorities could easily get skewed.

Drew dialed the New York number and got a receptionist with a Brooklyn accent.

"Hi there," he said. "I'm trying to reach Martin Woodward."

"I'm sorry," she said. "Mr. Woodward is out of town."

"He'll be checking in, right? Could I leave a message for him?"

The receptionist grudgingly agreed, and Drew identified himself as being a reporter for the Albuquerque Gazette.

"Albuquerque?" she said. "But that's where Mr. Woodward is."

"He is?" Drew felt a bubble of excitement in his chest. "Know how I can reach him here?"

The receptionist went cagey.

"Sorry, I can't give out that information. Would you like to leave a message?"

"No thanks. I'll track him down here."

"Sir? It would be better if you left a message—"

Drew hung up. He hefted the Yellow Pages and turned to the section for "Hotels and Motels."

It took four calls to the biggest hotels in town before he found a desk clerk who confirmed that a Mr. Martin Woodward was a guest at the Hyatt. Drew asked to be connected to Woodward's room, but the NBA official didn't answer.

He downed the last of his beer and headed for the door. Woodward would return eventually. Drew could loiter around the Hyatt's lobby, try to spot him when he returned. Maybe he'd slip the desk clerk ten bucks for a heads up. Somehow, he'd find the guy. Sure as hell beat sitting around his apartment, wondering.

THIRTY EIGHT

It was a rare sensation for Zipper to feel the need to laugh, but it bubbled up within him every time he looked at Calvin's gap-toothed mouth. With his dazzling smile marred, Calvin looked less like a movie star and more like a hillbilly, which was closer to the truth.

Zipper had never seen Calvin so mad. Man was usually mellow, more concerned with getting laid than with getting revenge. But here it was Friday afternoon, the weekend begun, and Calvin was stewing next to him on the seat of the Pontiac; they were headed for the sportswriter's apartment. Calvin was snarling and bitching but trying not to move his lips and show his teeth. Zipper sure felt like laughing, but he didn't want to set Calvin off. Not until it was time.

"I say we just go up there and do the motherfucker," Calvin said, stiff-lipped. It was about the fifth time in the past hour his partner had suggested killing the sportswriter, and Zipper was tiring of it. Normally, he'd say something terse to get Calvin to shut up, but he feared he'd burst out laughing at Calvin trying to talk without moving his lips, like those smart alecks you see on TV, with the talking wooden dummies.

Zipper ignored him. Let Calvin get up a good head of steam, he figured, then turn him loose on Gavin. Be fun to watch.

It had been a snap to find out where the sportswriter lived.

Man was listed in the telephone book, which had surprised Zipper. He'd figured a guy like that, had his name in the paper all the time, would want an unlisted number in case somebody didn't like what he wrote. But not everyone was as careful as Zipper. His address and phone number were closely guarded secrets. Of course, maybe people don't get that angry over what bullshit shows up in a newspaper. Not as mad as the people Zipper dealt with on a daily basis. You break a guy's arm, he might want to track you down, see if you can do it again.

Zipper steered into the parking lot of the Monte Vista and pulled the Pontiac into an empty space.

"Look at this building," Calvin muttered. "Security's for shit. I'm gonna walk right in, go up to that asshole's door. Knock on the door, pop a cap in him when he opens up."

"Don't do anything yet," Zipper said. "Let's think it over for a minute."

"This is horseshit, Zip. We could get rid of the guy, still have some time to party."

"Where you want to go, your mouth looking like that? Think you'll get some pussy tonight?"

Calvin's jaw clenched and he turned away, stared out the car window. Zipper felt the laugh swell within him again, but he swallowed it. He didn't let his face show a thing, but Calvin sure was funny.

Zipper would let Calvin have his fun with the sportswriter, but they'd take their time, find out if he had any money before they killed him. Three Eyes was still hot for that dough. The sportswriter probably didn't have much lying around. No, the money would have to come from the wife or the father-in-law—that rich guy, Nick Casso. The sportswriter would mostly be for fun. Get any money he might have, off him, then maybe go after the widow.

"There he is!" Calvin said. Zipper looked past Calvin's

snaggle-toothed face to see Gavin hurry from the apartment building's lobby.

Zipper waited until Gavin was far enough from the building that he couldn't sprint back inside, then he sped around a line of cars and screeched to a halt between Gavin and his Jeep. The sportswriter's eyes went wide.

Zipper casually rested his revolver on the car door where Gavin could see it and said, "We've been looking for you."

Calvin bounded out of the passenger side and hurried around toward Gavin, who couldn't seem to take his eyes off Zipper's pistol. Calvin ran up behind the bigger man and swung hard at his head with his own gun. The sportswriter went down in a heap, with Calvin standing over him, his marred smile wide.

Zipper almost laughed.

THIRTY NINE

Drew awoke sometime later in the back seat of the Pontiac, lying curled up like a dog. He resisted the urge to sit up. Better that the men in the front seat think he was still unconscious. Pain radiated from a spot behind his left ear. Drew suspected Calvin had taken a few other shots at him, too, once he was down. His ribs ached with every breath.

The car was moving and the two in the front seat appeared to be arguing.

"No, Calvin," Zipper said. "We've got the guy now. The boss'll want to talk to him."

"Why? Result's gonna be the same. Kill this moron and dump him somewhere."

"There's the money. That's what it's all about, remember?"

"This asshole don't have that kind of money."

Calvin's blond head turned to look over into the back seat. Drew quickly shut his eyes.

"Look at this jerk. I say we get rid of him before he starts snoring."

"Sit tight. We'll be at Three Eyes' house in ten minutes."

The Pontiac rolled to a stop, and Drew opened his eyes and saw a red traffic light gleaming through the windshield. Probably the best chance he'd get. Better to make his move when the car was stopped, rather than trying to bail out at forty miles per hour.

He sat up quickly, bringing around his right hand and

swinging hard. The hand was open, cupped slightly and aimed at Zipper's right ear. In the dirt and violence of a football game, a defensive player can pop a blocker over the ear hole of his helmet, set off bells in there that will last for hours. It's called a "shiver," and it constitutes illegal use of hands. In his present situation, it seemed exactly the right move. His hand clapped loudly against the side of Zipper's head, made the driver say, "Unnh!"

Calvin was turning toward him, but Drew swung his arm back the other way, forming a fist in mid-flight. The back of his fist slammed against Calvin's nose and snapped his head back against the passenger side window. Drew felt the nose go squish under his fist, and blood spurted down Calvin's chin.

Drew snatched open the back door of the car and was out of there, running on his bad ankles, the adrenaline coursing through him, making his feet fly. The street was lined with houses and he sprinted across the sidewalk and through the side yard of the nearest home. He vaulted a low fence, surprising a hound dog that was asleep on the other side. He was across the narrow backyard and over another fence before the dog began baying.

A dirt alley split the block behind the houses and Drew ran along it, looking for a hiding place. He spotted a carport holding two battered pickups, ducked inside and crouched behind the grille of one of the trucks. It would be bad if the owner came out to investigate why dogs were barking up and down the block, but better to be caught trespassing than to be spotted by Calvin and Zipper.

He waited there for two hours while darkness fell. Twice, the black Pontiac prowled the alley in search of him. Once the adrenaline wore off, he could feel things again. The concrete was cold on his butt and his head throbbed and his fist was bleeding again, soaking the bandage. But he smiled to himself in the dark while he waited. He'd escaped. Calvin and Zipper could spend all night looking, but they wouldn't find him. And maybe they'd think twice about trying to nab him again.

By the time he decided to move, Drew was stiff from sitting on the concrete. He kept to the shadows as he left the alley, but saw no one hunting him. He found a street sign and figured out that he was south of downtown in the Barelas neighborhood. He needed a taxi and he'd have better luck finding one near the bars and hotels of downtown. He walked north, keeping his arm tight against his bruised ribs. His head snapped back and forth, watching for the Pontiac. But there was little traffic and no sign of Three Eyes' men.

FORTY

Drew awoke late Saturday morning. He started the coffee and fetched the newspaper before going to the bathroom to examine his wounds. He spent several minutes checking the knot behind his ear, using a hand mirror and the one on the medicine chest. It was tough to see behind his own ear, but he felt the knot's dimensions and its tenderness and decided he'd live. He'd had worse bumps from football, had spent many a Sunday morning babying scrapes and bruises and torn tendons. Maybe he'd bounce back slower now that he was older, but he would recover.

After putting a fresh bandage on his hand, he settled in at the dining table with coffee and the Gazette. Teresa had a brief story inside about Freddie Graham, essentially saying the cops were no closer to solving the murder. The story ended by noting that Freddie's funeral was slated for 2 P.M.

When Drew was done with the newspaper, he called Woodward's hotel room again. No answer. He still wanted to talk to the NBA official, but he decided he'd be better off using the next couple of hours to soak in a hot bath and to locate a necktie and a dark suit in his cluttered closet.

He questioned his own motives while he dressed. He certainly didn't feel much grief over Freddie's death. He told himself attending the funeral was part of his investigation. Maybe the mourners would give him some ideas about suspects. But he knew, deep inside, he was going to the funeral because Helen would be there, because he'd get a chance to drink her in with his eyes and to be available if she needed a broad shoulder for her tears. This, he decided, made him one sick puppy, as macabre as the weirdos who attend funerals for people they don't even know. He hitched up his tie and studied his square face in the mirror. No matter how twisted it seemed, he'd be there for Helen.

The graveside service was at Sunset Memorial Park, and Drew thought Freddie had picked a good day for it. The sky was a rich blue scraped with thin, high clouds and the sun was warm enough to make a man in a black suit perspire.

By the time he arrived in his dusty Jeep, a crowd had already gathered around the grave site. A black hearse and a shiny limousine were parked on the gravel drive nearby. A dark-green canvas canopy had been stretched on poles to shield family members from the sun, and a garden's worth of flowers surrounded the fresh hole in the ground.

Drew picked his way between tombstones to join the somber mourners. Big turnout for Freddie, he noted, well over two hundred people here and more arriving by the moment. He skirted the edge of the crowd, spotting the mayor and other dignitaries. He saw the Lobos' football coach, looking uncomfortable in his suit and tie, and exchanged nods with him over the heads of the others. He also spotted the shiny brown head of Lieutenant Buck Moore, who wore his dress uniform and had his hat tucked under one arm.

Moore watched him closely. Times like these, Drew thought, it doesn't pay to be the biggest man in the crowd.

A white-haired priest kept the service short, extolling Freddie's imagined virtues and his civic works and commending him to Heaven. The casket was a shiny pewter lozenge and the priest threw a handful of dirt on it after it was lowered into the ground.

Afterward, Drew angled through the crowd, headed toward the canopy to see Helen, but Moore cut him off halfway there.

"Mr. Gavin. Didn't expect to see you here."

"Friend of the family," Drew muttered, trying to sidestep the investigator. Moore stayed right with him.

"Got a bandage on your hand there. What happened?"

"Three Eyes is what happened. He sent his men after me."

"Is that right?"

"Twice. I punched one of them in the mouth yesterday and cut my hand. Then last night, they tried to kidnap me."

That got Moore's attention. He demanded that Drew tell him the whole story and he took notes. Drew kept it terse and quiet. He could feel nearby mourners leaning his way, trying to hear.

"You report any of this?" Moore asked when he was done.

"Not yet. Thought that's what I was doing now."

"You want to press charges?"

"Sure, if you can find them. I don't even know their full names."

"We'll find them. You can count on it."

"I thought you were going after them once before, too," Drew said. "But you still don't think they killed Freddie, huh?"

"I don't know. Doesn't sound like they're good citizens."

The crowd had begun to disperse, people hurrying away to their cars and their Saturday afternoons full of tennis and golf and TV. The air seemed thinner in the graveyard now, as if the mourners had sucked all the life out of it, doing their civic duty by seeing Freddie off.

"You still asking around about my son?" Moore asked.

"The newspaper put me on leave until this gets straightened out. But I'll get back to it eventually."

Moore scowled at him. The sun made the perspiration on

his bald head glisten.

"I need to go give my condolences," Drew said, turning away toward the remaining crowd encircling the family canopy.

Moore snagged his arm.

"Think that's a good idea?"

Drew yanked his arm loose. "That's why I came."

He strode away, but Moore trailed behind him.

A handful of people were lined up in front of Helen, shaking her hand and murmuring their sympathy. Drew stood behind them, hands clasped, waiting his turn. Nick Casso was at the other end of the canopy, pumping hands and scowling in his grief. Drew noted that Nick drew a bigger crowd than the widow.

He could see Helen over the heads and shoulders of the others, and she looked radiant, even dressed in black from head to toe. Her eyes were red, but her makeup was all in place and her gown was one of those body-hugging numbers that look simple and cost a fortune. She wore black silk gloves, and the fabric glided into his hand when it was his turn in line.

"I'm so sorry, Helen. I hope you're doing all right."

"As well as can be expected," she said, struggling to smile. "I'm glad you came."

"I wasn't sure that I should."

"Nonsense, Drew. Freddie would've wanted you here."

Drew doubted that was true, but it was nice of her to say. He still clutched her hand, staring into her eyes. The moment had gone on a few seconds too long, and he was very aware of Moore and the others watching.

"What are you doing here?" Nick Casso's hiss came from just beside Drew's shoulder.

He quickly dropped Helen's hand and turned to face her father.

"Paying my respects."

"I don't want you here. Get the hell out."

Others who still milled around quickly backpedaled, giving Nick and Drew room under the edge of the canopy.

"Daddy! That's rude."

Nick didn't even look at her. He was too busy jabbing a finger toward Drew's nose.

"I told you to stay the hell away from my daughter."

Drew's face felt hot, but he raised his hands in a gesture of compliance.

"I didn't mean any harm—"

"You got a lot of balls showing up here at all. Now take off."

"Okay, okay. Sorry if I upset you."

Drew practically ran over Moore as he turned to hurry away. The lieutenant followed close behind him.

"Man doesn't like you much," Moore said.

Drew grunted.

"You know, he came by my office to talk about the murder," Moore continued. "He seemed to think you were a good suspect."

"He's always hated me, but I'm surprised he'd go that far."

"Why all the animosity?"

"I wasn't good enough for his daughter."

Moore stopped walking, but Drew moved on, his eyes fixed on the Jeep up ahead.

"Guess you're still not," Moore said.

FORTY ONE

Zipper listened to Calvin read the funeral announcement in the Gazette as he drove to Helen Graham's house.

"See, Zip, this is gonna be a snap," Calvin said. "Nobody's gonna be home. They'll all be at the funeral."

Zipper had to admit it looked as if Calvin was right. No cars were parked in front of the house when they arrived. They slipped out of the Pontiac and circled the house, checking the windows for telltale wires that would indicate a burglar alarm.

They met at the back of the house, where French doors looked out onto a patio and a square of green lawn.

"Looks clean, Zip."

Zipper used his knife to jimmy the lock on the French doors, hardly leaving a mark on them, and they were inside.

"Man's got a lot of nice things," Calvin said as they prowled the empty house. "You'd think he would've sprung for an alarm."

"Probably couldn't afford it," Zipper muttered. "Bastard was too busy giving all his money to Three Eyes."

They wore gloves so they wouldn't leave fingerprints, but Zipper had to keep an eye on Calvin to make sure he didn't slip valuables into his pockets. Three Eyes had instructed them to leave no sign of the break-in, if possible. Just snoop around, see whether there was a safe or some other hidey-hole where Freddie Graham might've kept his money.

"Hey, Zip," Calvin called from the living room, "come look at this stereo system. There's a couple of grand right there."

"Leave it," Zipper shouted down the hall. "We're looking for cash, not goods."

"Still. Push comes to shove, we might have to come back, lift a few things. Repay us for all the trouble."

Zipper wasn't listening. He'd found Graham's study. Man kept money in the house, he figured, this would be the place. Leave Calvin to look through the obvious hiding places like the freezer and behind the artwork on the walls. Zipper wanted to look through Freddie's papers, see where the real money was hidden.

He found it, too, but it took a while. He went through all the drawers in the filing cabinets. Most held legal documents, mumbo-jumbo from Freddie's law practice. Probably a fortune's worth of blackmail there, if a fellow knew how to make people pay to keep their secrets. But the real prize was in a bottom drawer labeled "Household Accounts." Zipper thumbed through the folders until he found one marked "Life Insurance," and he spread it out on the desk to look through it.

It was slow going. Many of the words were too big for him to decipher, but the numbers gave him the gist: five-hundred-thousand dollars to the widow when Freddie died, natural causes or no. Jackpot.

Helen Graham soon would be coming into a lot of money, and that was good news for Three Eyes. Zipper carefully put the folder back where he'd found it.

He looked around the office once more, ready to go round up Calvin, get him out of Helen Graham's underwear drawers. Fucking freak. Calvin had a real jones for the widow. Good thing she was safely at the funeral. Zipper might not be able to keep Calvin off her otherwise. One look at him would scare her into a coma. Tooth missing, nose flattened, both his eyes circled with bruises. The sportswriter had really done a number on old Calvin. Zipper still had a ringing in his ear from where the fool had popped him upside the head. Going to be a big payback for Drew Gavin, and soon.

Zipper looked around, making sure he left everything as he'd found it. He was behind the desk, rolling the chair back into place, but it hung up on something; it wouldn't go all the way under the desk. He bent over and peered into the leg space underneath the desk. A briefcase was tucked under there, keeping the chair from rolling home.

He moved the chair and crouched down to pull out the briefcase. He set it on top of the desk, snapped the latches and opened it. More paper, reams of white paper covered with typing, enough to make a man's eyes blur. Zipper scanned through the pages, picking out a word here or there, the letters "NBA" in a couple of places. What the hell was this? He snapped the briefcase closed and tucked it under his arm.

"Let's go, Calvin!"

FORTY TWO

Saturday night, Drew sat in his La-Z-Boy, morosely slugging beer and listening to the radio as the Lobos lost miserably to Wyoming. When the phone rang next to his chair, he hesitated. The phone had brought nothing but bad news lately. But he picked it up.

"Drew, it's Helen."

"Hi. I didn't expect to hear from you today."

"I needed to talk to someone. I don't know what to do."

There was alarm in her voice. He sat up straight in his chair.

"What's the matter?"

"I think someone broke into my house."

"When?"

"I don't know. Things just feel wrong."

"Have you heard anything? Are you alone there now?"

"There's no one here now. I just, I don't know, I think someone's been in here."

"Is something missing?"

"No, not really. I mean, all the valuables are where they should be. The computer, the TV . . . "

"What makes you think someone broke in?"

"It's just a feeling. Some things seemed to have been moved around, not where I left them."

"Like what?"

"It's hard to describe. My clothes. Freddie's study. I think someone poked around in there. I looked all around, trying to see if anything was taken—"

"But nothing's missing?"

"Well, there's one thing. But I don't know if it was stolen. Maybe Freddie got rid of it—"

"For Pete's sake, Helen, what?"

"Freddie kept a pistol in his bedside table. It was an old one, his father left it to him—"

"And it's gone?"

"Yes, but I don't know for sure that it was stolen. I hadn't seen it there for a long time."

"Call the police."

"No, Drew—"

"If somebody took a gun, they might still be around there somewhere. You can't take a chance—"

"I don't want to talk to the police anymore. I'm sick of the police."

"But Helen—"

"It's probably nothing. But I thought you might know what to do."

"I'll be right over."

FORTY THREE

Drew could feel his heart thumping while he waited for Helen to answer the doorbell. The light filtering through the peephole in the door vanished for a second, then Helen threw open the door, stepped through and hugged him.

"I'm so glad you're here."

"Are you all right?" he asked, one arm automatically going around her.

"I'm fine," she said into his chest. "I'm sorry if I scared you when I called. I didn't know where else to turn."

Helen wore jeans and a green T-shirt and he could feel her ribs. She felt warm through her clothes, and it took Drew a second to remember why he was there.

"I'd better look around," he said.

Only when she broke the embrace and stepped back did she see the Louisville Slugger in his free hand.

"My God, what's that for?"

"Burglars. Have you heard anything?"

"No, nothing. The whole thing may be my imagination."

"Let me look around. Just in case."

He tiptoed around the house, looking into closets and under beds, Helen trailing behind him. He knew he looked foolish gripping the baseball bat, but it felt good to have a weapon. It was a rambling house, and the search took fifteen minutes. By the time he was done, his ankles ached from squatting and peering under furniture. Helen smiled at him.

"You're certainly thorough. You look like a caveman, waving that bat around."

"Hey, you need a burglar flushed out of hiding, I'm your man."

"Satisfied that we're alone?" The smile still played on her face.

He nodded.

"Want some decaf?"

"That would be great."

He followed her to the kitchen and leaned the bat in a corner, saying, "I'll leave that here for you. You might need some protection."

She raised her eyebrows. "You think I could hit somebody with a bat?"

"Somebody breaks into your house, you shouldn't think of it as hurting him. Think of it as swinging for a home run. Knock his fool head out of the park, then sort out how you feel about it."

He sat at the table in the breakfast nook while Helen poured the coffee into mugs.

"Still take it black?"

"Yup."

She brought the steaming cups to the round table. Drew used his foot to push out the chair opposite him, but she ignored the gesture and sat in the closest chair.

"I appreciate you coming to check on me," she said. "After the way Daddy acted today, I thought you might tell me to go to hell."

"Not your fault your old man hates me."

Helen looked down into her coffee cup.

"Maybe it is. I flaunted you in front of him when we were in school together. You weren't the kind of guy he wanted me to date, so I made the most of it."

"Teenage rebellion. At least you didn't bring home a biker

or a bank robber."

"No, but I probably should've. You would've looked good in comparison."

"Guess I didn't hold a candle to old Freddie, though. Nick took to him, right?"

Helen looked away. "I suppose. Though I think, by that time, Daddy would've been happy with anybody who wasn't you."

"I'm that bad, huh?" Drew tried to grin at her, but she still stared into the other room, remembering. When she turned back, it took her a second to focus on him.

"I didn't think so," she said. "I thought we were a perfect match."

"Me, too. It's funny how parents can't see that."

"Daddy can't see anything that doesn't have dollar signs in front of it."

"That leaves me out then. I could barely afford the gas to take you out on dates, much less a place like this."

He waved a hand around the room.

"None of this means a thing, Drew."

"Sure it does. I'd take a place like this in a second over the dump where I live."

She smiled at him primly. Drew noted the dark circles under her eyes, the faint lines on her forehead. Helen had been through a lot in the past few days.

He slurped down a big swallow of the hot coffee, thinking he'd finish the cup quickly and get out of there. It still wouldn't look right for his Jeep to be seen outside her house, no matter how innocent the reason.

Mostly to kill time while he finished his coffee, he told her about Calvin and Zipper snatching him out of his parking lot.

"My God," she said when he was done, "did you tell the police?"

"I told Lieutenant Moore about it today. At the funeral. He wrote some stuff down, but I don't know if he'll do anything about it."

"He could charge them with kidnapping."

"I didn't get the idea that would be a high priority. Moore still seems more interested in pinning Freddie's death on me."

Helen shook her head. "I just don't understand that. How could he let a grudge affect his judgment that way?"

"Cops are human, too, even if they try to act like robots most of the time."

"Are you still trying to figure out who killed Freddie?"

"I've been poking around a little."

"I wish you wouldn't. It's clearly dangerous."

"It's beginning to look that way."

He thought about mentioning the rumor about Nick Casso and the NBA, but he hesitated. What could he tell her? He had no proof. He still hadn't been able to reach Martin Woodward, the NBA rep who was supposedly in town.

"I think it would be best if you left it all to the police," she said.

Helen's eyes were dark and moist, and he noticed she was wearing lipstick. Even as terrified as she'd sounded on the phone, she'd taken time to fix her face before he got there. He felt a smile tugging at his lips.

"What?"

"Just looking at you. Even with all you've been through, you look great."

Their eyes held for a long time, longer than he intended, and he finally broke the spell and downed the rest of his coffee.

"I should go," he said.

"No, don't."

"You're safe here. We've checked the house."

"I might be safe, but I'm lonely."

Their eyes met again, and Drew detected a smolder in hers that hadn't been there before. He still had coffee in his mouth, and it was as if his throat closed up. It took him a second to swallow.

"I'd better go."

She followed him to the door. He paused to say good-bye and she embraced him. She turned her face up to him, wanting to be kissed, and he hesitated only a moment. Then he kissed her, long and deep, and he could feel the years falling away. This was right where he'd wanted to be all these years. Back in Helen's arms. Back where he belonged.

When they broke for air, Drew leaned back from her, looking down into her eyes. He clutched her upper arms in his big hands, ready to pull her to him again.

"Ow!" Helen bent to the side, peeled his hand off her left arm.

"Did I hurt you?"

"I've got a bruise there."

She pulled up the sleeve of the T-shirt and he saw two round bruises on her biceps, each about the size of a quarter.

"What happened?"

She stepped back and looked away.

"Freddie. He grabbed me there the night before he went to the cabin."

"Must've hurt."

"We were arguing. About the gambling debt. I tried to walk away from him, I was so mad. He grabbed my arm and spun me around."

"Did he hit you?"

"No, nothing like that. Freddie was never violent. He was just upset."

Drew felt hot inside at the thought of a man, even a dead man, putting his hands on Helen in anger. Drew wanted to take her in his arms again, but the moment was gone. Freddie had come between them again.

"Thanks for coming and checking the house for me," she said somberly.

"Sure." He opened the door and stepped into the night, feeling trembly inside.

"And Drew?"

He turned back to find her smiling.

"Thanks for the kiss. I needed that."

He felt himself flush.

"My pleasure."

FORTY FOUR

Sunday morning was a busy time at Three Eyes' bookie parlor. Bettors scanned the Gazette sports pages, tapped into ESPN, and they couldn't wait to place their wagers on Sunday's contests. This Sunday was even busier than usual: a full slate of NFL games, baseball play-offs, even a few pre-season NBA games to lure the suckers. The phones had been ringing all morning. Three Eyes sat at his desk, watching his telephone people work, stroking the dachshund who sat whimpering in his lap.

"You don't like all these phones, eh, Oscar? Too much noise for you?"

Three Eyes patted the dog's head absently, his one eye on the telephone men, keeping watch over his business.

It had been a good weekend so far. A couple of the big college teams came up short on the point spread the day before, and Three Eyes would rake in the winnings. Lot of those same bettors would be calling today, trying to make up their losses, getting in deeper. Just like that lawyer had done, that Graham, digging himself in deep. Son of a bitch had to die before he paid off. Three Eyes should've just let it go, forgotten the debt. But sixty thousand was a lot of money, even to a wealthy man like Three Eyes. It irked him that Graham was getting away with something, even if the bastard was dead.

The steel door swung open and Zipper and Calvin entered. Zipper looked the same as always, but Calvin resembled something out of a carnival sideshow, his nose flattened, two black eyes, fat lips around teeth that were missing one incisor.

"Jesus Christ, what happened to you?" Three Eyes exclaimed.

The telephone men swiveled in their seats to look. A few of them grinned at the sight, but they didn't stop working. The murmur of money rolling in continued uninterrupted.

"That sportswriter happened to me, that's what," Calvin said through rubbery lips. "I'm gonna kill that bastard."

The telephone men hunkered down, did their best to look even busier.

"Tell me what happened."

Zipper held up a hand to stop Calvin before he could get started. Three Eyes thought the Indian looked like he was in one of those old Westerns on TV, saying, "How!"

"We saw that guy Gavin leaving the Graham house Friday," Zipper said. "We thought we'd brace him, see if he knew anything about the widow. The guy didn't like it much."

"He blindsided me!" Calvin wailed. "He knocked out my tooth! Look at that."

Calvin spread his lips in a painful grimace. He looked like a jack-o'-lantern.

"I'm gonna have to see a dentist, get it fixed. I can't go around looking like this."

"What happened to your nose?" Three Eyes said.

"Gonna have to get that fixed, too. Son of a bitch."

Zipper took over the story again, explained to Three Eyes about nabbing Gavin in the parking lot and the sportswriter's escape.

"So," Three Eyes said when he was finished, "you just let him walk away?"

"We searched the neighborhood, drove around for hours,

but we couldn't find him."

Three Eyes shook his head. These two dopes couldn't get anything right.

"So you've got no good news for me," he said. "Hah?"

Zipper took a step closer and glanced around at the telephone men before he answered. They all seemed dutifully engrossed in their work.

"We went into the house like you wanted," he said. "Looked around."

"When was this?"

"Yesterday, while everybody was at the funeral."

Three Eyes nodded. Now that was using some brains. Nice change of pace for these two.

"And?"

"Found an insurance policy. Looks like the widow stands to gain half a mil because the lawyer turned up dead."

"Now we're getting somewhere. When's the payoff?"

"Couldn't tell. Lot of paperwork, you know, and we were trying to hurry."

"You take anything from the house?"

The men looked at each other again, but Zipper said, "No. We left everything like we found it. She'll never even know we were there."

"Good."

"Lotta nice stuff there, though, boss," Calvin said. "We could get your money back, just fencing the goods."

Three Eyes dipped his head so the brim of the fedora shielded his eyes.

"No, Calvin. Stay away from there unless I tell you different."

"All right, boss. But keep it in mind. I mean, the stereo alone would bring two grand."

"I said no."

"Right."

"So you didn't leave a trace?" Three Eyes said, looking up at them, studying their faces. Calvin glanced away nervously, but Zipper maintained a level stare.

"Nothing," he said. "I put the insurance papers back where I found 'em."

"Good."

"So, Boss," Calvin said brightly, "you want us to have a little talk with that woman, make sure she gives us part of that insurance money?"

"She won't have it yet. Insurance companies don't pay off this quick."

Calvin blinked his raccoon eyes. Idiot, Three Eyes thought. Probably doesn't follow half of what I say. Maybe I ought to offer Calvin up to the cops. Tell them he bumped off the lawyer. Hell, maybe he really did it. He acted ignorant, but maybe he's just trying to stay out of trouble with me. He could've gone to Graham's cabin alone, trying to make some kind of side deal with the attorney. It would be just the kind of thing Calvin would do. Either way, I could fix it so he looked guilty, and he's too damned dumb to talk his way out of trouble. Calvin goes to the pen, gets out of my hair. The widow gets her insurance payoff. I get my money from her. But Calvin knew a lot about Three Eyes' operation. And he sure as hell couldn't be trusted. The cops start pressing, and he might offer up Three Eyes just to get a lesser charge. And the cops wouldn't have any reason to believe Calvin offed the lawyer on his own. They'd think Three Eyes put him up to it.

Calvin's eyes narrowed.

"What is it, Boss?" he said. "You got a problem with me?"

"No problem. I just want my money."

"We're working on it, Boss."

"Keep after it. This is starting to make me look bad. The word is out the lawyer owed me. Pretty soon, every deadbeat on the list is gonna start thinking he can push us around."

"We'll get it," Zipper said. "I've got some ideas—"

"I don't want to hear about it. Just make it happen."

Zipper nodded once.

"Gonna get that sportswriter, too," Calvin said. "Make him pay."

"That big jock don't have any money," Three Eyes said

"I'm not talking about money. I'm talking about getting even."

The old man shook his head. Calvin made him tired.

"Just go."

He watched the pair walk out the steel door and waited for it to close behind them.

"You ever seen such a couple of dumb shits, Oscar? Hah?"

Several of the telephone men snickered, and a couple turned in their chairs to glance over at Three Eyes.

"Get back to work."

FORTY FIVE

Chuck Gavin had just finished his breakfast when his son arrived at the nursing home. Eating, like everything else these days, was a slow-motion chore, hardly seemed worth the trouble. And the quality of the food didn't help. The nurses swore the yellow mound on his plate every morning was real scrambled eggs, but Chuck knew the powdered stuff when he tasted it. A little jelly on the dry toast would've helped, but he'd learned it's damned near impossible to spread jelly properly with one hand, so he hadn't bothered.

Drew came packing something for Chuck's sweet tooth, though. He was glad to see his son, but he was also eager to see what waited inside the grocery sack under Drew's arm.

"Morning, son. You're here early."

"I was up and around, couldn't sleep. Thought I'd go ahead and stop by."

"Looks like you could use a shave."

"Give me a break, Pop. It's Sunday."

"What's in the bag?"

Drew grinned at him, then dumped the contents on the foot of the bed.

"Oreos and Nutter Butters!" Chuck said. "It's a bonanza. Open one of those for me, will you, son?"

Drew tore open the Oreos and handed a couple to his father.

"Eating cookies in bed," he said as Chuck chomped into

one. "Seems to me I used to get in trouble for doing that."

"Age has its privileges," Chuck said around a mouthful. "And I've got a whole staff of nurses just waiting to change my sheets."

"How you feeling, Pop?"

"Finer than frog hair, now that I've got some sweets. What about you? You said you couldn't sleep?"

Drew's cheeks flushed. He hitched up one hip, sat on the edge of Chuck's hospital bed.

"I've got a lot on my mind. Helen called me last night, had me come over."

Chuck frowned. "Wasn't the funeral yesterday? You know, son, that don't look right."

"I know. It wasn't my idea. She called me all in a panic, thought somebody had broken into her house."

"Anything missing?"

"She couldn't find a pistol her husband had, but I couldn't see any sign that somebody had burgled the place. Maybe he got rid of it."

Chuck grunted. He still held an Oreo in his good hand, but he'd lost his appetite.

"Wish you'd stay away from that woman."

"Come on, Pop. I was just doing her a favor."

Drew scratched at his beard, looked away.

"What happened to your hand?"

Drew glanced down at the bandage on his fist, shook his head slightly.

"Just banged my knuckles on something."

Chuck could tell the boy was lying, always could, but he didn't push it.

"You'd best stay away from that Casso girl," he said. "You'll end up with more than a sore hand."

"What do you mean?"

"Nick Casso doesn't like you. He's made that pretty clear

over the years. He could make it rough for you if you mess with his daughter."

"I'm not 'messing' with her, Pop. I was just helping her out."

Chuck tossed the cookie onto the bedside table. He pushed against the bed with his left hand, struggled to sit up straighter.

"Look, son, I've been thinking about all this, her husband getting killed, and there's something I ought to tell you."

Drew lifted his eyebrows. "You got some idea who killed Freddie?"

"Nothing like that. This is old news. Something that happened a long time ago. I never told you about it before because I thought it might cause problems. And then Helen was married and all, out of your life, so I didn't see any reason to bring it up. But now that she's available again and you're all hot and bothered about it—"

Drew opened his mouth to protest, but Chuck held up his hand to stop him.

"Don't say it. I know. You're just being her friend. But she might have some other ideas. You need to know this."

Chuck took a deep breath. It was a hard thing to tell, made all the harder by the fact that he'd kept it secret all these years.

"Nick Casso loved your mother."

"Say what?"

"Back when we were all in high school. He and Ellie dated for a long time, maybe a year, something like that."

"Get outta here."

"It's the truth. I came along and stole her away from him. I was bigger and stronger and one helluva lot better looking than that sawed-off Greek. And I thought Ellie hung the moon. I worked like crazy to win her over. Sent her flowers I couldn't afford. Asked her to every dance. Nick was nuts about her, but he didn't stand a chance."

Drew's mouth was hanging open.

"Your mother was a beautiful girl. Fair and fragile and bright as a new penny. All the guys were crazy about her. I felt like a million dollars when she chose me."

"How did they know each other?"

"Albuquerque was a small town then, son. Everybody knew everybody else. Hell, wasn't but two high schools in the whole city back then. What've we got now, eight?"

"Something like that. But—"

"Hang on. I'm telling this my way. As you know, Ellie and me got married right after we graduated. Nick never forgave me. Or her, neither. He always had a thing for her, even after we were married. He'd send her birthday presents, things like that. Ellie would just get embarrassed about it, but it made me madder than hell. More than once, I was ready to go pound his ass, but he was becoming a rich man and it would've meant trouble. Besides, Ellie wouldn't let me. She said he didn't mean any harm."

"It would be the first time he ever did something and didn't mean any harm," Drew snapped. Chuck tried smiling at him, but it didn't take. The hard part was still to come.

"We were married four years before Ellie finally got pregnant with you," he said. "Only then did Nick go find his own wife and get her pregnant, too. I don't know if he was trying to prove something to your mother or if he was finally over her. But he went away."

Drew clamped his lips together and cleared his throat. "And then she died."

"That's right. The doctors all said it might be a problem pregnancy. I'm such a big man, and she was so small, you know? We joked about it when she was pregnant, saying it was like breeding a German shepherd and a toy poodle. But then when it was time for you to be born, there really were complications and she didn't make it."

Drew stared at the floor.

"As I've told you before, it's not your fault. Those things happen."

"And then," Drew said, putting it all together, "twenty years later, I start dating Nick's daughter."

"Right. Things work out funny sometimes. I figured it for a fluke, didn't think it would last, so I didn't say anything. But pretty soon, I could see you were head over heels about her. Then I really didn't want to say anything."

"I wish you had," Drew said. "It explains a lot."

"I guess it does. Nick, that crazy bastard, blamed you for Ellie's death, see? If he was going to blame anybody, it should've been me, but he'd been mad at me for years. Too much anger to waste on one man, I guess. So he leveled it at you, too."

"And that's why he did everything he could to break up Helen and me."

"Right. I think he saw it like this: You'd already taken away one woman he loved, even though that woman was married to somebody else and was out of his life. So, he'd be damned if he'd let you take his daughter, too."

All the talking had made Chuck's mouth leak on the right side, where his face pulled down toward his shoulder. He wiped at it with his good hand before he continued.

"He tried to get me fired."

"He what?"

"Guess he figured we'd leave town if I was suddenly out of a job, which was stupid. You were living in the athletes' dorm anyway. Wouldn't have made any difference. But he couldn't get you to go away, so he tried to take it out on me. He worked over the superintendent and some of the school board members, trying to get me replaced at Albuquerque High. But Jim, Coach Hunter, he'd have none of it. Said I was the best damned defensive coordinator in the state and he'd quit before he'd let them run me off."

Chuck smiled.

"We had a winning program back then, remember? Went all the way to the state finals. They weren't going to let Hunter walk out under those conditions. We ended up in a standoff. I was worried to death, but I didn't want to worry you. You were having your senior year in college. You didn't need the distraction."

Chuck could see the muscle twitching in his jaw where Drew was grinding his teeth.

"Helen knew about it, didn't she?"

Chuck took a deep breath, as if he were plunging into cold water.

"I told her. I didn't mean any harm. She came by the house, looking for you. Guess you were late at practice or something. Anyway, I told her she could come in and wait for you. We had some cookies and chatted. I always liked that girl."

"You told her, but you didn't tell me?"

Chuck wiped his forehead.

"I'm sorry. I know I should've said something to you. But I didn't intend to tell her either. She saw I was worried and she asked me what was up and I just blurted it out. A few days later, she dumped you."

Drew looked like he wanted to spit. "That son of a bitch. If I'd known about this then, I would've beaten him to death."

Chuck nodded. He was getting tired, putting together so many words.

"That's the other reason I didn't tell you about it."

Drew stood up and paced around the room. He looked like he was trying to decide what to do. Chuck feared he might race out the door and go confront Nick Casso.

"Take it easy, son. It's all ancient history. And it's as much my fault as it was Casso's. I shouldn't have told her. Maybe things would've worked out if I hadn't said anything."

Drew let out a long breath, and Chuck saw some of the tension drain out of him.

"It's not your fault, Pop. You were doing what you thought was right at the time."

He sat on the foot of the bed again, patted Chuck's leg through the sheets.

"I appreciate you telling me about it. It explains a lot."

Chuck eyed him. "Don't put on an act for me."

"What?"

"You're acting like everything's fine now, but I can see the wheels turning in your head. You're working out some way to get even with him, aren't you?"

"What makes you say that?"

"Don't treat me like a fool. I'm crippled up, but there's nothing wrong with my brain. I know how you think. You're still a football player at heart. Somebody hurts you, you hurt 'em back. That's the way you were trained."

Drew shook his head, but it looked as if he was fighting back a grin.

"You know what you're like, son? An armadillo."

"What?"

"You're just like an armadillo. Trouble comes at you and you jump right in the way."

"What the hell are you talking about, Pop?"

"Don't you know about armadillos? Didn't I teach you anything?"

Drew chuckled and said, "Let's hear it."

"You know how you always see armadillos dead on the side of the highway? They've got that armor, right? And they're low to the ground. Haven't you ever wonder why so many of 'em get run over?"

"Guess not."

"When an armadillo's crossing the road and he suddenly gets caught in the headlights, he panics. Know what he does?"

"Rolls up in a ball?"

"No, that would be the smart thing. Cover his ass, get out of the way, something. But because he panics, he jumps straight up in the air, and boom, he gets creamed by the bumper."

Drew was laughing now.

"You are so full of shit, Pop."

"It's a scientific fact!"

"And that's the way I am?"

"Sometimes. You see trouble coming, you'd best cover your ass and get out of the way."

Drew wiped at his eyes and got to his feet.

"Thanks for the advice, Pop. I'll keep that in mind. I'd better go now. The nurses are probably headed down here, wondering what all the hilarity is about."

"Aw, screw 'em," Chuck said. "They could use a little laughter around this place."

Drew grinned down at him.

"Still, I've got things to do. I'll see you next Sunday, if not before."

"All right, son. Thanks for coming by."

They shook hands and Drew went toward the door.

"And son?" Chuck waited until Drew turned around. "Stay away from those Cassos."

Drew waved, but didn't say anything. And then he was gone.

Chuck let his head drop back against the pillow. Damn, he was exhausted. It had taken a lot out of him, telling his boy the old secrets. He closed his eyes and thought of Ellie, wondering whether he'd done the right thing and how she would've handled it.

Before he came up with an answer, he'd fallen asleep.

FORTY SIX

Drew drove home on autopilot, his mind reeling, hot anger blinding him to the blue autumn skies and the lazy Sunday traffic.

Everything he'd believed all these years about Helen and Freddie and himself was turned on its head by what Chuck had revealed. Helen hadn't simply chosen Freddie over Drew. She'd been forced to do it by her father's conniving. That bastard Nick Casso, manipulating everybody involved. Casso had probably guessed Helen would somehow find out what he'd been doing. He'd probably counted on her acting noble, dropping Drew rather than letting Nick ruin Chuck's coaching career.

He stopped the Jeep outside his apartment building and trudged toward the elevator, so lost in his fretting that he didn't even think to check the parking lot for Zipper and Calvin. Another thought hit him so hard he stopped in the lobby, staring sightlessly at the elevator doors.

When he and Helen split up, friends had told him she'd been seeing Freddie on the sly for weeks, which meant she'd begun that relationship before she knew about Chuck's problem. She was already involved with Freddie. She hadn't been forced into choosing him. If anything, the problem with Chuck's job just helped her make up her mind.

He wanted to call her right away, ask her about the

sequence of those long-ago events, try to determine once and for all what had happened to them. But Helen didn't need that now, while she was grieving for Freddie. Last night's kiss might've been the opening of a door, one that had been closed for a decade. Did Drew want to risk slamming it shut by dragging out all the old wounds and examining them? What could that accomplish now?

He reminded himself of what Chuck had said about armadillos. That glow he'd gotten from kissing Helen might be approaching headlights.

He rode the elevator up to his apartment and let himself inside. He walked over to the phone and stared down at it, willing it to ring, wanting it to be Helen. But for the first time in days, the phone sat mute. Drew cursed and turned away.

He fixed himself a sandwich and ate it without tasting it, the Gazette sports page propped on the table before him. Seeing Curtis's byline over the Lobo story brought him back to his sorry situation — off the job, under suspicion in a murder, pining over a relationship that ended long ago. The fact that Curtis had done a nice job on the article didn't help.

When he was done eating, he picked up the phone, braced once again to call Helen, but he couldn't make himself do it. Instead, he dialed the Hyatt's number from memory. Martin Woodward still didn't answer the phone in his room.

Drew pulled some 1950s records from the collection Chuck had given him and put them on the stereo, thinking he could take his mind off things, but all the songs were about love and devotion and betrayal. He soon shut the stereo off.

He turned on the TV instead and watched two NFL teams slug it out on a muddy playing field, but he couldn't keep his mind on the game.

He drank through the afternoon, one beer after another, trying to silence the voices in his head. It didn't work, and he switched to bourbon at sunset, drinking his supper, finally pushing himself into a stupor that quieted his brain and let him fall asleep in his chair.

He dreamed of Helen.

FORTY SEVEN

Bob Goodman called the next morning, shortly after Drew awoke with a pounding headache and a taste in his mouth like iron filings.

"We need you to come down to the newsroom," the editor said. "There's been a development."

"What's going on?"

"Just get down here. We're meeting in an hour."

Drew tried to cure his hangover with a hot shower and aspirin. He nicked himself three times shaving with shaky hands.

But he felt better arriving at the office, even caught himself whistling a snatch of an old Everly Brothers tune as he went through the door. He figured being summoned to the newsroom could mean one of two things: Either they were ready to break the NBA story, or Drew somehow had been cleared in the murder investigation and could return to work. Work, for all its drudgery, would at least restore some order to his life.

Goodman, Benedict, several other editors and Teresa Vargas were waiting for him in the conference room. It was suspiciously familiar, much like when he'd been shown the door. But he didn't see Manuel Quintana, the attorney, and he took that as a good sign.

As he entered the conference room, Benedict said, "Late again."

Drew smiled at him. He'd even put up with Benedict's crap if they'd let him come back to work.

"Sit down, Drew," Goodman said. "We need your input on something."

Teresa Vargas sat at the end of the table, in Drew's usual chair, so he fell into an empty one midway down, across from Benedict. Goodman, at the head of the table, peered at Drew over his half-glasses. The lights glinted off the old newshound's bald head.

"Teresa has what sounds like one helluva story," Goodman began. "I understand you already know something about it."

Drew glanced at Teresa, not sure what to say, but she smiled and gave him a barely discernible nod. Her lipstick was maroon today, matching her nails, and she wore a dress, which was unusual for her. Drew figured she must be planning to make a splash.

"You mean the NBA deal, right?" he said. "I talked to Teresa about it on the phone."

Benedict's face was bright red as he leaned across the table. "Then I'd like to know how come sports was the last to find out about it."

"I'm off duty," Drew said blandly. "It's Teresa's story."

"You could've called," Benedict barked. "Somebody should've told me something."

"Take it easy, Greg," Goodman said, giving the sports editor a calming wave. "This isn't about turf. It's about getting this story before anybody else finds out about it."

"It's a sports story! Any fool could see that."

Goodman's jaw clenched, and Benedict withered under his glare. He rocked back in his chair and shut up.

"Okay," Goodman said, "if everyone's finished marking his territory, let's hear what you've got, Teresa."

Teresa ran a maroon-tipped hand through her short hair. Then she flipped open a manila folder and made a show of consulting her notes.

"I don't have it all pinned down yet," she said, "but it looks like this: Nick Casso's trying to buy his way into the NBA. He and the late Freddie Graham dreamed up a plan for starting a team here and Graham apparently met with league officials in New York a couple of times. They even have a team name picked out: the Mustangs."

Murmurs rippled among the editors. Drew couldn't tell whether they were excited about the scope of the story or the prospect of attending big-league games.

"You need a couple of things to get a team," Teresa continued. "You need a shitpile of money, which Casso has, and you need a big, fancy arena, which we don't have. Yet."

"What about the Pit?" asked Pete Jurgenson, a bearded assistant city editor who was racing Goodman toward total baldness.

"Not big enough," Teresa said. "And there'd be all kinds of conflicts sharing it with UNM. Casso needs a brand new place to play ball."

"He thinks he can build one?" Goodman nudged.

"Even Casso can't afford to buy a franchise and build an arena," she said. "Probably nobody in the state has that much money."

Goodman held his hands out in a gesture that said, "What then?"

"He wants the lodgers' tax to pay for it," she said.

The editors shifted in their chairs and Jurgenson let a low whistle escape.

"How much?" Goodman asked.

"I don't know exactly," she said. "A lot. Maybe Benedict could tell us."

The sports editor leaned forward and rested his elbows on the table. His high forehead had sprouted a sheen of perspiration.

"They built the one in Charlotte for a hundred million," he said. "It has luxury boxes, the works."

"So figure it's something like that," Teresa said.

Jurgenson looked chagrined. "The voters will never go for it. They voted down an auditorium half that size in the last election."

"Right," Teresa said, smiling. "But nobody's going to ask them."

The editors began talking excitedly, until Goodman banged his hand on the table.

"How's that possible, Teresa?" he asked after it got quiet.

"This is where my sources get cagey. Apparently, there's some way around putting it to a vote. All they'd need is City Council approval."

"Could Casso get that?" Goodman asked.

Teresa shrugged, but Drew spoke up.

"You dangle an NBA team in front of them and they'll snap it up. Casso's got half the City Council in his pocket anyway. He's got a guy from the NBA in town, and I'll bet he's helping Casso persuade the other half to go along."

Teresa looked shocked that he'd somehow gotten ahead of her.

"The guy's in town right now?" Goodman asked.

Drew explained about tracking Martin Woodward to the Hyatt.

"So you don't know this guy Woodward is actually meeting with Casso and the City Council?" Goodman concluded.

"I never got to talk to him. But what else could it be?"

"We need to nail that down, Teresa," Goodman said, and Teresa jotted something in her notes. "Drew, you think all this has something to do with why Graham was killed?"

"I do, but I don't know exactly what. Freddie Graham was in trouble gambling on sports, which would scotch an NBA deal if they found out. But I still haven't figured out who might've killed him. Casso's a possibility, but it seems to me murder would endanger the deal more than Freddie's gambling becoming public."

Benedict spoke up again. "Maybe the two aren't related."

"Maybe not," Drew said, "but it sure seems fishy to me."

"Me, too," Goodman said. "We'll need to pursue that. See if the cops know about Casso's arrangement and if they're investigating it."

"That would fit with something Lieutenant Moore told me," Teresa said. "He said the big boys in city government were leaning on him to keep Casso out of his investigation."

"Is that so?" Goodman said, his eyebrows raised again.

"That's how I got onto all this to begin with," she said. "When I heard that, I figured Casso must have something going on behind the scenes."

"I can see why they'd want to keep it quiet," Benedict said. "If it gets out before Casso nails down a vote, there might be a shitstorm from the public. That could nix the whole deal."

"Maybe that's exactly what's needed," Goodman said.

"I don't know, Bob. I mean, an NBA franchise would be a boon for the city, right? How could it be a bad thing?"

Goodman leaned back in his chair and folded his arms across his chest.

"If it's such a good thing, why are they trying to pull an end run on the voters?"

"Well, you could see it that way—"

"I think you're just excited about the prospect of covering the NBA, Greg," Goodman said, grinning. "I can understand that. I'm sure we'd all like to go see games in a big new arena. But at what cost? Can this city afford something like that?"

"I don't know," Benedict said. "Maybe. I mean, if all this is true, Casso must have some idea about a way to fund it."

"Then why do I have the feeling that Nick Casso's hand is in my pocket?" Goodman's smile had disappeared, and nobody had a ready answer.

"There's one other thing," Teresa said after a moment. "My source says this thing's moving fast. They could bring it to a vote as early as Wednesday night."

"Can they do that?" Jurgenson said. "Don't they need a public comment period?"

"Apparently not when Nick Casso's involved," she said.

Goodman thumped his knuckles on the table, his signal the meeting was ending.

"All right," he said. "We've got to get the story wrapped up by tomorrow if we're going to make Wednesday's paper. Pete, find somebody else to cover Teresa's beat. And get her some help if she needs it. That's all."

The editors pushed back their chairs and filed out into the nearly empty newsroom. Teresa was packing up her notes as Drew said, "What role do I play in all this, Bob?"

Goodman looked at him over his glasses. It was a kindly look, but it brought no good news with it.

"Nothing for now, I'm afraid. You're still on leave."

"I deserve to be part of this."

"I agree. But the lawyers say you're not in the clear in the murder case yet. And you've got a conflict of interest bigger than Texas. You hear anything else we might be able to use, feed it to Teresa. But don't go snooping around unnecessarily."

"I don't have to snoop. I just stand still and this stuff is all over me."

"Go home, Drew. Take it easy. I've got a feeling this will all be over soon."

Goodman left the conference room without looking back.

"Sorry, tiger," Teresa said as she stood to leave. "I'd love to work with you on this one, but doesn't look like it's in the cards."

"This is so stupid."

"You won't get any argument from me. I could use your help. But Goodman has ruled."

She smiled down at him, and he couldn't help running his eyes down her, eventually getting to the legs she usually kept covered in jeans. They were great legs.

"How come you're all dressed up?"

Teresa looked down at her dress and smoothed the front of it with her hands. The bangles on her arms jangled.

"This old thing?" she said, grinning.

"You trying to impress the big guys?"

"Why not? Couldn't hurt. I'm trying to persuade them to run a story that could get us sued by Nick Casso. Thought I'd better look like a grown-up."

"It worked. You look great."

"Thanks for noticing," she said as she headed for the door. She patted his shoulder as she passed. "And thanks for the Woodward tip."

"You're welcome," he said glumly.

She stopped at the door and waited until their eyes met. "We still going to have dinner?"

"Sure. Can't wait."

"Maybe when this is over." She winked. "Call me."

FORTY EIGHT

Lieutenant Buck Moore parked in the shade of an elm and trudged across the sun-splashed parking lot to Drew Gavin's apartment building.

He could've had Gavin brought downtown for questioning, but he wasn't quite ready to place him under arrest. He had something to spring on the sportswriter, and it was better done where there were no witnesses. If he was going to pin the Graham murder on Gavin, he needed to be certain he could pull it off.

Arresting Gavin wouldn't solve all of Moore's problems anyway. Somebody else at the newspaper would be given the job of investigating Jamal's arrest, and he couldn't find a way to lock up all the reporters, could he?

Moore sighed heavily as the elevator doors closed behind him. Keeping Jamal out of trouble had become his life's work. The boy was talented and smart, but he'd always been impulsive. He felt so superior to everyone else, felt entitled to anything he wanted. Buck had tried to beat some sense into him when he was younger, but Jamal was still the cock of the walk, strutting into every situation, expecting to come out a winner.

And the girls remained a problem. They hung all over the boy. They followed him around, called him on the phone. No wonder they'd gotten him in trouble so many times over the years. If a woman throws herself at you, it's difficult to ignore it. Jamal had come to assume that every one of them wanted him. He didn't know how to take "no" for an answer. And his father was expected to clean up what mess resulted.

Moore wondered whether Gavin had experienced the same thing back when he was a football hero. But no, Gavin seemed a sucker for Helen Graham. If anyone was manipulating this situation, it was probably her.

He'd talked the day before with an insurance agent who numbered the Grahams among his clients. Seems Graham had a pretty hefty life insurance policy, which would pay off in the event of his sudden death. Moore figured it wouldn't have taken much of a push for the widow to get Gavin to murder her husband. And a big bundle of money would just make it seem sweeter.

Moore reached Gavin's apartment and knocked on his door. Gavin seemed surprised to find him there.

"Lieutenant Moore. What do you want?"

"Need to talk to you."

"I'm under orders from the paper not to talk to you unless our lawyer is present."

"Didn't stop you at the funeral."

Gavin winced.

"I forgot then. Guess I was too eager to tell you about my run-in with Zipper and Calvin. You have any luck finding them?"

"Not yet. I put out a bulletin on them. Mind if I come in?"

"What for?"

"I got some questions about you and Helen Graham."

Gavin tried to play stoic, but his cheeks colored and Moore saw it.

"Come on in."

Moore looked over the apartment before he took a seat on the sofa. Looked like a bachelor's place. Shoes sitting by the big reclining chair that dominated the room. Empty beer bottles on the table. Magazines and newspapers scattered around. Nice view of the mountains, though.

"Seen Mrs. Graham lately?"

Gavin paused before he said, "I was at her house Saturday

night. She asked me to come over. She thought someone might've broken in."

"She call the police?"

"No offense, but we're a little tired of talking to the police."

Moore nodded his shiny head. "I can see that. It's been a hard time for everybody."

"Especially for Helen."

"Any sign someone had been in her house?"

"No. I checked the doors. No sign of forced entry."

"What made her think someone had been in there?"

"Just a feeling she had. I think she's probably just jumpy."

Gavin looked around the room for a second, and Moore thought he was going to say something else, reveal something, but the sportswriter shut his mouth and waited.

"How long you over there?"

"Less than an hour. I looked around, and we talked for a while."

"Mm-hmm."

Moore tried waiting him out, but Gavin was having none of it. His face flushed again, though, and Moore suspected more than a little talking had occurred at the Graham house.

"Did Mrs. Graham mention anything about her husband's insurance?"

"Insurance?" Gavin looked puzzled. It wasn't the reaction Moore had expected.

"Freddie had a big life insurance policy. Mrs. Graham's about to come into some money."

Moore studied Gavin's face closely, but the sportswriter said only, "I don't know anything about that."

"You sure?"

"You think Helen had her own husband killed?"

"Happens all the time."

"Not this time." Gavin looked angry again. Man sure was easy to read. "I've known Helen for years. She wouldn't do something like that. Besides, she doesn't need money. Her father's loaded."

"Maybe she didn't want to wait on an inheritance."

"You're barking up the wrong tree, Lieutenant. If you're still hunting for a suspect, maybe you ought to look at Nick Casso himself."

That surprised Moore. He waited a couple of beats, but Gavin caught himself and didn't seem ready to say anything more.

"Why Casso?" Moore said. "What would he stand to gain?"

Gavin stood up and paced around the room.

"I can't talk about it," he said. "I just came from a meeting at the newspaper. You can read all about it in the Gazette soon enough."

Moore felt his stomach knot, but he took a deep breath and leaned back on the sofa, trying to look casual.

"Look, this is a murder investigation. I don't give a shit what the Gazette is doing."

"I can't say anything else."

Gavin flopped into the leather chair and said, "You through?"

"Almost." Moore smiled at him. That smile sometimes got suspects sweating, but it seemed to have little effect on the big man.

"So now you think Casso's involved," he said, trying to sound amused. "Two days ago, you were telling me Three Eyes Sanchez had Graham killed."

"It might be him. Hell, I don't know. I don't know anything anymore, except I'm awfully tired of talking about Freddie Graham."

"You got any proof Casso killed him?"

"No. Not yet anyway."

"You planning to get some?"

"I don't know how I'd do that. The newspaper might find something though."

"They do, they'd better tell me before it gets into print."

"Go tell it to Manuel Quintana."

Moore knew Quintana, the newspaper's lawyer. A tough customer.

"Let me make it more personal then. If you find out anything, you'd better call me," he said, getting to his feet.

"Or what?"

"Or I'll find a way to make you pay," Moore said evenly. "You're not off the hook here, Gavin. You want to point the finger at everybody else, but I still don't see any reason not to consider you the prime suspect."

"Think whatever you want."

They stared at each other for a full minute.

"I'll show myself out," Moore said finally. "But I'll be in touch."

He went out the door and closed it behind him, but he didn't go immediately to the elevator. He figured Gavin had a phone call to make. He pressed his ear to the door.

"Teresa?" he heard Gavin say inside after a few seconds. "It's Drew Gavin. Listen, Lieutenant Moore was just here."

Silence for a moment.

"He asked a lot of questions, some about Casso."

More silence.

"I don't know what it means," Gavin said. "Maybe we ought to talk it over some more. You want to stop by here tonight, after work?"

Another pause. Gavin reeled off his address, then listened again.

"I'll see you then."

Moore guessed that "Teresa" was Teresa Vargas, the reporter who'd been calling him daily about the murder investigation. He waited a few minutes more, expecting Gavin to call Helen Graham, too, but he heard nothing else from inside.

He strolled toward the elevator, smiling.

FORTY NINE

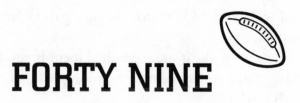

Monday evening, Zipper and Calvin cruised the Northeast Heights in Zipper's gleaming Pontiac. Zipper watched the fast-food joints and neon signs whiz past while he listened to Calvin babble.

"What I'd like to do to that cocksucker, see, is I'd tie him up in a chair. Yeah, then I'd take that big knife of yours and I'd cut him. Just a little at first. Slit his nostrils, so his nose looks like a pig's. Then I'd notch his ears to show he was *my* pig. Then maybe cuts on each cheekbone, give him that warpaint look. Then maybe I'd shave off his eyebrows."

Calvin had been going at it like this for hours, coming up with one elaborate torture after another for Drew Gavin. Apparently, Gavin had made the one mistake Calvin couldn't forgive: He'd marred the golden boy's good looks. Calvin's every plan involved rearranging Gavin's features in such a way that the man would end up in a sideshow if he healed.

"Why don't you just shoot him?" Zipper said.

"What?"

"You're so tough, why mess around? Why not just shoot him?"

Calvin peered over at him. Zipper thought his partner's face looked like a Halloween mask. Black eyes, gapped teeth, flattened nose. Probably could just surprise Gavin—say "boo!"—and give the man a heart attack.

"Shooting's too good for that son of a bitch."

Zipper wheeled the Pontiac through a yellow light, turning off Eubank onto Montgomery.

"All this shit about messing the man up, ruining his face, that's kid stuff," he said. "You want revenge, you don't take any chances. You make him stop breathing."

Calvin thought this over, nodding. "Maybe you're right. Who am I trying to impress, right? Just finish him."

"Now you're talking," Zipper said. "Next time we won't talk to the man. We won't get him in the car, try to take him to Three Eyes. Just pop him."

Calvin looked eager now.

"Take me over to his place. I'll do him right now."

Zipper threaded his way through traffic, not answering. They were near Gavin's apartment building, but Zipper wasn't sure he wanted to go there now and turn Calvin loose. Though it would shut him up for a change. Zipper had a lot on his mind. All of Calvin's chatter wasn't helping him think.

"You don't want to go over there now," he said. "Too much heat hanging around that guy. You pop the guy, gonna be cops all over the place."

"No, there won't. I'll go up to his door, bang-bang, and then I'll run like hell. We'll be out of there before anybody can even dial 911."

Zipper shook his head.

"You've got to plan these things. You gotta be careful."

"I'm sick of being careful. We tried to nab the guy and look what happened."

"He cleaned your fuckin' clock."

"Hey, he whapped you upside the head, too. Aren't you mad?"

"I don't get mad."

"Goddamnit, Zip, come on. Look, there's his place. Pull in there. I'll do it right now."

"You gonna shoot him with your gun? Then what? We

gotta dump it, get you a new one."

Zipper stopped for a red light. They were in the center lane, and cars were close on either side.

"See, that's where you're wrong, Zip. I already got that part figured out."

Calvin leaned forward and reached up under his shirt in the back. He pulled out a revolver and held it up for Zipper to see.

"I got a new gun."

"Put that thing down. You want the people in those cars calling the cops?"

Calvin lowered the gun to his lap, held it in a streetlight beam for Zipper to see.

"Guess where I got this."

Zipper didn't play guessing games, but he had to wonder. He and Calvin had been together practically around the clock for days, and he hadn't seen his partner buy a gun.

"Come on, guess."

"Fuck you."

"All right, I'll tell you. This here gun belongs to the late Freddie Graham."

That surprised Zipper enough that he almost changed the expression on his face.

"Where did you get it?"

"Found it in a bedside table when we were in the widow's house. Nice gun, huh?"

Zipper felt like punching Calvin's bruised face.

"I told you to leave everything where you found it."

"I did, except for this. I figured the widow don't need a gun handy if we go back there. So I took it."

"She's probably called the cops by now, reporting a burglary."

"Nah, I'll bet she don't even know it's gone. It's a man thing. Graham kept the gun there in case of a break-in, probably never even showed her how to use it."

Zipper silently steamed.

"I figured, hey, no sense letting a perfectly good gun go to waste. I can use this thing. I'll pop Gavin and then I'll wipe down the gun, leave it in his place. Let the cops try to figure that one out. It'll look like the lawyer came back from the dead and killed Gavin. Fuckin' cops'll be scratching their heads forever."

"We weren't supposed to take anything from that house."

"What about that briefcase you put in the trunk? You think I didn't notice that? You walked out of there with that thing under your arm, never bothered to tell me what it was. And you didn't mention it to the boss either."

The briefcase. Zipper knew Calvin had seen it, but he figured his partner was too busy checking his swelling in the mirrors to wonder too much about it. Zipper had thought of little else. The papers in that briefcase had to be worth a lot of money to somebody, probably Nick Casso. Zipper had been trying to figure a way to make a bundle off them. Walk-away money, enough that he could give Three Eyes the air and maybe start his own business. The old man wouldn't like it if Zipper quit after all these years, but what could he do? All Zipper needed was a pile of money. Then he could start some new life that didn't include taking Three Eyes' guff. He needed to move on. The pressure of whipping on deadbeats all the time was getting to him. He was feeling murderous these days; only a matter of time before he killed somebody.

He hadn't sorted out how to make those papers pay yet. Hell, he'd hardly had time to think about it with Calvin gabbing all the time.

The light changed and Zipper urged the Pontiac forward. He changed lanes, cutting off an old Plymouth, and turned into the parking lot of a supermarket. He whipped the car into the nearest slot and stopped. Then he looked over at

Calvin, who was still holding the gun.

"You want to go kill Gavin?"

"You heard me."

"Right now?"

"Sure."

"With that gun?"

"Why not? I think it's a helluva plan, don't you?"

Zipper threw the car into gear.

"Okay. I'll take you. You go up there, do your business and come right out. I'll wait in the car. You fuck up in any way, I'll drive off and leave your ass for the cops. Got it?"

Calvin's eyes had gone wide.

"You mean it? Right now?"

"Damned straight."

Calvin bounced excitedly in the seat.

"All right, Zip. Now you're talking."

"No, see. Now *you're* talking. You've been talking about that bastard ever since he knocked out your tooth. I'm gonna take you over there and we're gonna get this finished. And then you're gonna get back in the car and keep your fuckin' mouth shut. I've got to think about some things. I can't think with you talking about Gavin all the time."

Calvin looked a little crestfallen, but he tried grinning at Zipper.

"You got it, Zip. This is gonna be great. I'll show that motherfucker—"

"Just shut up. The shutting-up part starts now. Don't say anything else until I tell you."

"Sure, Zip. I was just—"

Zipper gave him a stony look, and Calvin clamped his swollen lips together. He checked the cylinder on the gun and tucked it into the front of his jeans, under his Hawaiian shirt. He zipped up his black leather jacket.

Zipper roared into Gavin's parking lot and stopped near

an elm.

"All right. Go."

"Okay, Zip, you won't regret this—"

Zipper raised a cautioning finger. "Shut up."

"Okay. I'll be right back."

Then Calvin was out of the car and hurrying across the parking lot toward the lobby.

Zipper sighed. Killing Gavin now was a mistake, he was sure of it. But at least he'd have a few minutes' peace, a few minutes to think.

Maybe Calvin would be more subdued when he got back, once Gavin was dead. Damn well better be. If Calvin came back to the car all juiced from the killing, started shooting his mouth off again, he might be the next one dead.

FIFTY

Teresa Vargas straightened her dress while she rode the elevator up to Drew's apartment. She felt a little wilted after a long day on the phone, haranguing sources and daring politicos to tell the truth for a change. Most days, covering the cop beat felt like combat, and she dressed accordingly. But today, she'd been trying to impress the editors, show them she knew how to dress for a meeting with city councilors. Finishing the story probably would've impressed them more, but she didn't quite have it yet. It was a blockbuster, and she wanted it ironclad before the Gazette printed it.

Maybe Drew had something that would help, though she couldn't imagine what it might be. He'd said on the phone that he'd talked to Moore, but, hell, she talked to Moore three times a day. What could he have gotten that she didn't already have?

Of course, she smiled to herself, maybe Drew hasn't got a thing except the hots for me. This morning, in the conference room, he hadn't been able to control himself, his eyes raking down her body, taking in her legs. Made her glad she'd bothered with the dress and the uncomfortable stockings.

He was a strange one, this Drew Gavin. He had the world-weary air of an old-timer, one of those newsroom coots who've seen it all. But he couldn't be more than five or six years older than her. Maybe working at the Gazette a long time did that to you, knocked all your edges off, left you battered and tired. She'd be more than tired if she had to work for that asshole Greg Benedict. She'd be homicidal.

The elevator doors slid open, and she stepped out into the hall. It was a nice building, quiet and sturdy, not like the rat-trap she occupied near the university. The hall was carpeted and she strolled to Drew's door.

Drew threw open the door after she knocked. He filled up the doorway, his shoulders practically reaching from jamb to jamb. He wore jeans and a blue oxford shirt with the tails out and his big feet were bare. He gave her a crooked grin and stepped out of the way so she could come inside.

The living room was about what she'd expected from a jock like Drew. Newspapers were piled beside a brown reclining chair and a beer bottle sat on the table nearby. The furniture was bulky and worn. The room was dominated by an entertainment center that contained a Sanyo stereo system softly playing some old-fashioned romantic music that sounded like Nat "King" Cole and a large TV that stared blankly at them like a mirror. She smiled at the way Drew's reflection towered over hers, even though she was wearing heels.

"Hey there, tiger. How's it going?"

"Okay. I've been on the phone, trying to find anything that might help on your story."

"Any luck?"

He gestured her over to the sofa, which sank beneath her more than she'd expected. She tugged her skirt toward her knees and kept her feet close together. If she tried to cross her legs, the old sofa might swallow her up.

"A little," he said. "You want something to drink?"

"I could use a glass of wine, if you've got any."

He tromped over to the kitchen that opened off one corner of the living room.

"Bet you could use a drink," he called from in there.

"Imagine you've had a busy day."

"It's been hectic," she shouted back. "But I'm making progress."

"You ready to write it?"

"Almost. I still need to firm up a few things. I don't want any part of it to come from only one source. I'm nailing everything down."

"That's good," he said, returning to the room with a beer for himself and a glass of red wine. He handed it over, and she took a long sip, watching him over the rim of the glass.

He told her about his conversation with Moore, but it sounded lame. He didn't have anything new from the lieutenant, and he seemed to know it. He changed direction.

"I talked to at least one guy who isn't happy about the prospect of an NBA team coming to town."

"Who's that?"

"The athletic director over at UNM. I hinted at what Casso's doing, and he's pissed. Lobo basketball is a money farm for the university. They don't want Casso siphoning off ticket sales."

"Think that would happen?"

"Probably. Lot of people would rather watch the pros."

"Is he willing to talk for the record?"

"I think so," Drew said as he fell into the recliner. "He usually doesn't care much for the press, but he's too worried about this to avoid you. I told him everything was hush-hush for now, so I don't think he'll run to TV with it. You can get to him first."

"Sounds good." Teresa leaned forward, set her glass on one of the Sports Illustrated magazines that littered the coffee-table. "I'll call him tomorrow."

"What about you?" he asked. "What did you get today?"

"I firmed up that Casso's doing what we thought. I got a couple of city councilmen to talk about it, strictly not for attribution. They're all worried Casso will fry them if they're the ones who spill it. I pulled a bunch of paperwork from City Hall, too. Some stuff about the lodgers' tax, looks like the basis for a study to see whether they can fund an arena without taking it to the voters. And I pulled the campaign finance records for everybody on the City Council and the County Commission. Guess who's one of the biggest contributors?"

"Nick Casso?"

"Bingo. He must believe people are stupid to think he can get away with this."

Drew shook his head.

"Rich people just assume everything will go their way. He's been running things in this town so long, he thinks he can get away with this, too."

"What about murder? Think he can get away with that?"

Drew's face went slack. "You got some proof he's behind it?"

"The more I learn about Nick Casso, the more I think he's capable of it."

"But can you prove it?"

She smiled at him. "Not yet."

Drew chuckled under his breath and glanced away toward the balcony doors, which looked out at the city lights.

"You're a piece of work, you know that?" he said, turning back to her.

Teresa took another sip of the wine before she answered. She batted her eyes at him, and said, "Whatever could you mean?"

"You come in the newsroom and you've got the funky hair and the purple lipstick and all that, and you look like a kid, you know? And just about the time they all relax, think they've got you figured out, you come up with this kickass story."

She grinned at his awkwardness. "A kid, huh?"

"A great-looking kid, sure, but still. You'll knock the hell out of 'em with this story and the job offers will pour in, and you'll be out of here quick."

"I don't know," she said. "I like it here."

"I've heard that before. The really great reporters always move on, unless they get trapped here by the sunshine or family or romance or something like that."

"Seen 'em come and seen 'em go, huh?"

"Sometimes I feel like I've been at the Gazette as long as Spiffy O'Neill."

"Just another old man, are you?"

"I'm old on the inside. Know what I mean?"

"You're a terrific sportswriter. How come you're still here?"

Drew ran a hand back over his short hair.

"I don't know. I'm *from* here, you know? My old man's in a nursing home and I've got to look after him. I got some offers over the years, but I never did anything about them."

"Inertia."

"What?"

"You're not stuck. You're just not moving. So you feel stuck."

He grinned at her. "Got me figured out already?"

"Maybe."

Their eyes locked for a long moment before Drew finally looked away. He stared at the blank TV screen, as if it held some answers. Teresa set the wine glass down and folded her hands in her lap.

"Hey, tiger," she said softly, "why did you really invite me over here tonight?"

"What do you mean?"

"You said on the phone you had stuff for the story, but you could've told me what you had on the phone. I thought there might be something else."

"I guess I wanted to see you in that dress again," he admitted.

"Like it that much?"

He looked her over and nodded.

"Too bad. It's back to motorcycle boots tomorrow."

"That's okay, too. I kinda like boots."

"You kinda like me, too, don't you?"

He blushed, and it made her smile.

"Sure, I—"

"The feeling's mutual," she said. "And we should explore that sometime. But right now I'm beat. I'd better get going."

She got to her feet.

"You could stick around a while."

"No, I'm really exhausted. And tomorrow's going to be another long day."

"Okay." He stood and followed her to the door. "Thanks for stopping by. I'm glad we had this little talk."

"Me, too," she said, turning to him. "It was very illuminating."

He looked like an oversized kid himself with that goofy grin. She started to tell him so, but she caught herself. He's nervous enough already.

"You'll call me?"

"You bet. And I'll see you around the office, assuming they ever let me come back."

She nodded and reached for the doorknob. She felt like kissing him, at least a little peck on the cheek. Show him she really was interested. But she restrained herself. Plenty of time for that later.

She opened the door and gasped. A man with wild blond hair and two black eyes smiled crazily at her, showing white teeth with a raw gap in the front. And he pointed a pistol at her chest.

FIFTY ONE

The sight of the pistol snapped Drew out of the shock of finding Calvin in the hall. He grabbed Teresa's arm, tried to spin her out of the way. Calvin gave Teresa a stiff arm to the chest, knocking her backward. Drew tried to catch her, but his eyes were on the gun and she went sprawling to the floor with a yelp.

Calvin stepped across the threshold and slammed the door, keeping the gun pointed at Drew, who felt a tide of alarm surging inside his chest.

Teresa scrabbled backward on the floor, her dress hitched up around her thighs, until her back pushed up against the coffee-table.

Calvin opened his mouth wide to show off the pulpy hole where the missing tooth once lived.

"Remember this?" he said, pointing up at his mouth with the barrel of the pistol. "You knocked out my tooth."

"I remember. Look, put the gun away—"

"I've come to get even."

"What do you want to do? Punch me back? You don't need the gun for that."

Calvin cackled.

"I'm not gonna fight with you, stupid. I'm gonna shoot you."

He aimed the gun at Drew's face. Drew flinched, felt a chill run down his spine.

"Don't do that. The cops'll be here any minute."

He wasn't sure where that came from, but he'd take any quick thinking he could get.

"The cops?"

"We called them a while ago. We've, uh, got some information for them. Isn't that right, Teresa? They're on the way, right?"

Teresa seemed incapable of answering, but she nodded when Calvin glanced over at her.

"I don't care," he said. "You're a dead man."

Drew thought he could see Calvin's finger tightening on the trigger.

"Don't shoot. You've got a witness here."

"Her? Who's she gonna tell? You think I won't kill her, too?"

Calvin looked at Teresa. She still sat on the floor, and tears had sprung into her eyes.

"She's a fine-looking piece," he said. "Maybe I'll see what she's got under that dress before I kill her."

That was it for Drew. He felt the adrenaline flood his body, the heat in his limbs. He charged Calvin, slapping at the gun with his left hand as he ducked his right shoulder into the man's chest.

The gun exploded, and it was as if the loud bang was the sound of their bodies crashing together. Drew kept his feet moving, charging forward, driving Calvin into the door behind him. All the air rushed out of Calvin in a whoosh. Drew pressed hard against him, pushing with his legs, keeping him pinned there, while he tried to wrest the gun away.

Calvin bent his wrist, trying to point the pistol at Drew's head, but Drew grabbed his arm and slammed it against the wall. Calvin's grip didn't loosen. Drew slammed again, and the gun went off, sending a bullet singing away. Slam again, and the revolver fell to the floor.

Now Drew could work without getting shot. He brought his right forearm up sharply, catching Calvin under the chin. Calvin's blond head snapped back, bounced off the door. His eyes rolled, but he wasn't out. He jerked a knee up, trying to catch Drew between the legs, got all thigh. He clawed at Drew's eyes. Drew backed up a step and involuntarily covered his face with his hands.

Blinded, he wasn't ready for the punch. Calvin swung from somewhere around his knees, bringing his fist up hard into Drew's stomach, knocking the wind out of him. Then Calvin flew at him, a ragged scream tearing from his throat.

Drew threw out his hands, caught Calvin's shoulders and turned him the way he once slipped blockers on the football field. As Calvin slid to the right, Drew hit him with a hard left to the side of the face. Calvin's head bounced around on his neck, but he kept coming, crashing into the larger man's midsection.

He wrapped his arms around Calvin, and they did an awkward dance around the room, both men churning with their legs, trying to tip the other over. Calvin pummeled furiously against Drew's body with his fists, but the punches had nothing on them because he kept Calvin's upper arms pinned against his body. Drew tightened his grip, trying to squeeze the man into unconsciousness. Calvin butted with his head, caught Drew in the jaw, hard enough to snap his head back and break his grip.

"Motherfucker!" Calvin screamed as he swung off-balance. Drew dodged the blow, swung two of his own at Calvin's body. He felt something crack when he connected with the left, but Calvin tucked an elbow over the broken rib and kept coming.

Drew grabbed Calvin's jacket and spun him, swinging him toward the glass doors that opened onto the balcony. Calvin's back smashed through the glass, sending shards flying.

Calvin landed on his back on the balcony. Blood streamed from somewhere in his hair, but the leather jacket had kept his body from getting shredded. He stumbled to his feet, still not ready to quit.

Cold air rushed in through the shattered doors. Drew bulled forward, feeling the glass cut his bare feet, and lowered his shoulder as he charged at Calvin. He heard a roar, and realized it came from his own throat. He caught Calvin chest-high with his shoulder, knocked him backward. Calvin's hips caught the balcony rail and he tipped back, up and over. Drew tried to grab the falling man, but he was too late. Calvin disappeared over the edge into the night. He didn't even scream on the way down. Drew heard a dull whump a second later.

He leaned out over the rail and looked down. Calvin had landed in the bed of a pickup truck parked down below. His legs twitched twice and then he was still.

Drew couldn't move for the longest time. He stared down at the broken man. Calvin looked like a scarecrow, his arms bent at strange angles, his straw hair sticking out from his bloodied head.

Glass crunched on the floor behind him and he whirled to find Teresa standing just inside, teetering in her heels among the glinting bits on the floor.

"Are you all right?" she asked.

Drew nodded, but he wasn't sure it was true. His feet were cut up, and his jaw ached from the collision with Calvin's head.

"He's dead?" she asked.

"He's not moving. It's a long way down."

"We'd better call the cops."

"Can you do it? I need to get a towel or something. I'll get blood everywhere."

She hurried to the kitchen and slammed drawers, came

back with a white dish towel.

"Here. I'll call 911."

Drew spread the towel on the floor over the broken glass and stepped gingerly inside. Then he just stood there, looking around his apartment as if it were unfamiliar territory. The pistol lay on the floor near the front door. Glass all over the carpet. Magazines and Teresa's wine glass had spilled off the coffee table. She stood next to his chair, the phone to her ear.

He turned, and looked out into the cool night. The lights of the city sparkled, and the dark mountains loomed beyond. He'd spent many hours staring out at that view. Would he ever be able to look at it again without seeing Calvin Cox tumbling over the balcony rail?

FIFTY TWO

Zipper sat in the Pontiac, waiting for Calvin to finish his business and get out of there.

Finally a quiet moment. Zipper needed time to think about the papers in that briefcase and what they could mean. He'd slaved over them late the night before, reading the legalese a word at a time, parsing out the sentences, until he felt like they were going in one eye and out the other. He thought there might be a way to make all the work pay off.

Nick Casso was the key. Zipper had determined from his reading that Casso was trying to start a pro basketball team, and he'd gathered from the way the lawyer had written it that there were some things Casso wouldn't want public. Like the plan to get a new arena pushed through City Council without a special election. If Casso was trying to keep everything quiet, Zipper might be able to demand a little hush money. Say, a hundred grand. Chicken feed for a rich dude like Casso. But for Zipper, it would be enough for a grub stake.

Zipper felt warm at the notion of that much money. He rolled down the window and let the night breeze drift into the car. He was parked in the shadow of an elm, the darkest and quietest spot available. The peace and the cool air and the anticipated riches gave Zipper an unfamiliar sensation. It took him a few seconds to recognize that he might be happy.

Then he heard two pops and a crash, up high, on one of those balconies. He leaned over the steering wheel to peer up at the building. Couldn't Calvin even kill somebody right?

Zipper looked up at the balconies and saw Calvin's wild blond hair up there in the light that streamed through the broken glass doors. Calvin pitched backward over the balcony rail and plummeted.

You see something like that on TV, Zipper thought, they always run it in slow-motion so you can sympathize with whoever's falling, get that here-we-go feeling of what it must be like to drop several stories. Not in real life, though. Calvin was on the balcony, then whap, an instant later, he was done falling.

Shit. Fucking Calvin would mess up a free meal.

Zipper leaned forward to look up at the balcony again. He saw the square shape of the sportswriter turn to go back inside. He'll call the cops now, good citizen that he is. The cops will come running, too, in a big hurry to see whatever's left of Calvin.

He cranked up the Pontiac and steered toward the street. Time to be someplace else.

FIFTY THREE

Drew sat in his La-Z-Boy, tending the cuts on the soles of his feet, as his apartment filled with cops. Uniforms gave him the hard eye, as if they expected him to confess to something. Technicians took measurements and dug slugs out of the walls and put Calvin's pistol in a plastic bag. The lead homicide detective, a sharp-eyed APD lieutenant named Steve Romero, made Drew tell the story of Calvin's death again and again.

Drew's neighbors came to his door, peering over a beefy cop's shoulders to see inside.

Paramedics showed up, too, and one of them, a woman with callused hands, dug bits of glass out of Drew's feet while he told Romero about his past run-ins with Calvin and Zipper and the events leading up to Calvin's fatal fall. The medic suggested taking Drew to the hospital to have his swelling jaw x-rayed, but Drew wouldn't budge. He didn't want to miss Romero's showdown with Manuel Quintana.

Teresa called Quintana right after she phoned 911, and he showed up half an hour later, looking dapper in a three-piece suit at a time of night when most men have retired to their sweatpants and Monday night football.

Quintana gave up six inches in height and probably fifty pounds to Romero, but he proved a worthy opponent. No, he argued, Drew had no reason to kill the man, except that he was attacked. No, Drew would not go downtown for further questioning. No, he had nothing to hide. And why was Romero trying to blame the victim here?

By the time Quintana was done, Romero looked like he just wanted to go home to bed, maybe pull the covers over his head.

It helped immeasurably that Drew had a witness. Teresa not only could vouch that Calvin had been killed in self-defense, she knew half the cops in the room on a first-name basis. They treated her like a kid sister who'd gotten mixed up with the wrong guy at the prom. Protective and suspicious, but willing to listen. Even Romero showed her some deference.

Once Romero was done with her, Teresa came over to Drew and gently grasped his chin in her hand, turning his head to look at the bruise rising on his jaw.

"You going to be okay?"

"I think so. Doesn't look like I'm going to be arrested."

"They've got no reason to run you in," she said. Then, smiling, "Unless they just need another perp walk for the TV cameras."

Drew grinned at her. She had a way of making him smile, even at the worst times. She gave him a soft pat on the cheek before she straightened up and looked at her watch.

"If you're all right, I should go," she said. "I can get this in the final edition."

"Go. Goodman would never forgive us if we missed this story."

Minutes after she left, Lieutenant Buck Moore showed up. Since Calvin's death occurred in the city limits, it was out of his jurisdiction, but he'd heard about it somehow and he barged into the apartment and made a beeline for Romero. The two detectives whispered for a while, then Moore came over to Drew. Quintana stood nearby, keeping a wary eye on them.

"Guess you were right about those boys being after you," Moore said.

Drew paused in dabbing at his feet to look up at him.

"Still don't believe they killed Freddie Graham?" he asked.

Moore shook his head slowly. "Don't know what to believe anymore. Thought I about had this one figured out."

"By pinning it on me?"

A smile tugged at Moore's lips.

"Maybe. I still don't think Three Eyes would order such a killing, but he probably didn't authorize this thing tonight either. Maybe this boy Calvin, he's gone independent."

"He's not going anywhere anymore."

"Guess you saw to that. How you feel after killing a man?"

Drew tensed. "Not great. But it was him or me."

"Hm-mm. Guess a man could see it that way with Freddie Graham, too."

Quintana stepped between them before Drew could get up, and shoved Drew's shoulder to put him back in his chair.

"You about done here, Lieutenant?" Quintana said quickly. "My client's answered all your questions. I don't see any reason to dredge up the Graham case at this late hour."

Moore looked as if he could take a bite out of the little attorney, but he turned away. He had another whispered conference with Romero, then left without looking back.

Quintana stuck around until all the cops departed. Then Drew was left in the apartment with Sid, a mangy, silent guy who was the building manager. Sid used a roaring Shop-Vac to clean up the shards of glass and pledged to get a glass repairman there the next day to fix the sliding doors. Drew thanked him, but he knew the damage couldn't be undone by glass and putty. His refuge had been invaded, and he wasn't sure he'd ever feel the same about it.

Once Sid left, Drew drank a beer, then turned in. After all the commotion, he felt a little lonely. He thought about calling Helen, but it was nearly midnight.

He wondered how she would've reacted if she, instead of Teresa, had been in the apartment when Calvin showed up. Helen had led a much more sheltered life than the police reporter. She probably would've gone into shock. Or, she would've been more worried about herself than about what happened to Drew. You spend your whole life being told how special you are, you start to believe it. Helen probably would've called Nick Casso before she even phoned the cops.

Teresa, on the other hand, had probably kept his ass out of jail. And she'd been concerned about his injuries and the way the cops treated him.

Lot to that woman, he thought as he turned over in bed. She's deeper than she looks. And softer on the inside than she lets on. He closed his eyes, hoping to dream of Teresa rather than about Calvin flying off the balcony.

FIFTY FOUR

Across town, sleepy Nick Casso was getting into his silk pajamas when the phone rang. He finished hitching up his pants and stumbled over to the phone beside his bed.

"Hullo?"

"Mr. Casso. We need to talk."

"Who is this?"

"You can call me Zipper."

"Zipper? What the hell—"

"Listen, Mr. Casso, I have something to sell you."

"What the fuck you talking about? Call me up in the middle of the night—"

"Shut up, Mr. Casso."

Nick took the receiver away from his ear, ready to slam it down. But there was something about the caller's calm manner that made him listen.

"I have a briefcase here. It's full of papers. I think they belong to you."

A briefcase? Nick snapped fully alert.

"What papers?" he asked warily.

"Legal documents. Think they were drawn up by your late son-in-law."

"Mind telling me where you got 'em?"

"That's not important. You just listen."

"All right, you've got my attention."

"These documents, I think you don't want them to go

public yet. Is that right?"

Nick hesitated. "I don't know exactly which papers you mean."

"These have to do with basketball. Need me to say more?"

"Not on the phone. I understand. You're planning to return these papers to me?"

"Maybe."

The caller let the silence build. Nick fumed, but finally said, "How much?"

"Right to business. That's good. I think we understand each other."

"How much, goddamnit?"

"Take it easy, Mr. Casso. I've got a figure in mind. A nice round figure: A hundred thousand dollars."

"You shitting me? They're not worth anywhere near that."

"I think they are."

"Bullshit," Nick roared. "I've already got a whole new set of those papers. I had one of my people—"

"That's not what we're talking about."

"What?"

"I figured you had another set. But you don't want these to get into the wrong hands."

"What the hell do you mean?"

"If I read these right, it would be a problem for you—a big problem—if these documents showed up at a TV station, say, or at the Gazette. Kinda mess up your plans."

Nick paused, took a deep breath. He felt a pressure deep within his chest.

"Look," he said, "I don't know who you are or what your game is, but I can guarantee nobody's going to believe you. I'll say you're lying. I'll say I never saw those papers before in my life. Who do you think they're going to believe, me or some lowlife?"

"It won't be a matter of believing anybody. They'll have the papers, laying it all out. That's proof."

"Those papers could've been dummied up by anybody. They won't believe you. I know every publisher and news director in this town personally. I'll stall 'em long enough, it won't matter. It'll be a done deal."

Now it was the caller's turn to think it over. Nick waited him out, and he could feel a smile creasing his whiskery cheeks. He'd outmaneuvered this loser.

"I know a guy," Zipper said finally. "Be real interested in this."

"Who?"

"A sportswriter. Name of Drew Gavin. You know him, too, right?"

The smile vanished from Nick's face, chased by a scowl so tight it made his head hurt.

"I know him."

"I thought so. He's got a thing going with your daughter, right?"

"Don't talk about my daughter, you son of—"

"Easy. You get ugly with me, I hang up the phone and take this stuff straight to Gavin."

Nick's grip on the telephone was so tight, he nearly ground it to powder. *That fucking Gavin. Every time I turn around, he's messing around in my life, chasing after Helen, finding Freddie's body. I ought to have that bastard killed. Be worth it, just to make him go away.*

"All right," Nick said once he got himself under control. "I'll buy the papers. But I'm not giving you no hundred grand."

"How much?"

Nick thought the guy was laughing at him, echoing his words back. *Son of a bitch. I'll give you "how much," I get the chance.*

"I'd go fifty."

"Seventy-five."

"Sixty."

"Kinda cheap, rich guy like you. Maybe we forget the whole thing. I'll go see Gavin."

"Okay, goddamnit, seventy-five. When can you deliver the documents?"

"When can you have the money?"

"What's tomorrow, Tuesday? Why don't you come to my house tomorrow? Around noon."

"You trying to set me up?"

"Fuck, no. I just want to get it over with."

"Maybe we'd better meet somewhere public."

"You think I'm carrying around seventy-five thousand dollars, meet you in a park or something, you're outta your fuckin' mind. You want the money, you come here."

"All right. But I smell a cop, and I go straight to Gavin."

"No cops. I don't need the publicity."

"Fine. No tricks. I'll be there at noon."

"Don't you want the address?"

"I know where you live."

The caller hung up, leaving Nick to slam down the receiver and pace around the room, thinking: No way I'm giving some blackmailer seventy-five grand to keep things quiet until Wednesday night's council meeting. He can go fuck himself. I'll be ready for him, though. Put a bullet in his fucking head. Say he was a burglar, broke into my house, found me all alone here. Put that idiot Freddie's papers in the safe before I call the cops, nobody be any the wiser. The bastard. Nobody robs Nick Casso.

FIFTY FIVE

Drew made a mistake on Tuesday morning. He looked in the mirror.

He had a lump on the side of his chin the size and color of a plum, and his eyes were bloodshot and had dark circles under them. Add his sore ribs, the bump on his head, the cuts on his feet and the still-healing cut on his knuckles, and Drew felt like he'd single-handedly taken on the Dallas Cowboys.

He took his flannel bathrobe off its hook on the bathroom door and slipped it on against the chill in the room. His apartment still had more ventilation than usual because of the broken balcony door, and he swore he could see his breath fogging in front of his face. He padded gingerly into the kitchen and started the coffeemaker. A little hot brew would take the cold edge off, then maybe a steamy shower to massage his sore muscles. Then, perhaps, back to bed for a day of rest.

He tried to avoid looking in the living room, where the curtains on either side of the shattered doors snapped in the breeze. Sid would be in and out all day, repairing the glass. Drew's apartment would be like a construction site.

He settled carefully into a chair at the kitchen table with his coffee, trying to think of someplace to go, somewhere to get some peace while he recovered from last night's ordeal. The seat was barely warm when the phone rang, forcing him to get up and tiptoe over to his recliner and the phone beside it.

He flopped into the chair before picking up the receiver. "Hello?"

"Morning, tiger. How you feeling?"

"Hi, Teresa. You're up and around early, aren't you?"

"It's nearly ten. I've been at work three hours already."

"You youngsters don't need sleep, huh? Just bounce up and run into the office to break another big story."

"What is this 'youngster' shit? What are you, thirty?"

"Thirty-two. But today I feel like seventy-two."

"How are your feet?"

"Sore."

"And your chin?"

"Purple."

"How about your attitude? How's that?"

"Shitty. As always."

Teresa chuckled and the sound made Drew smile. He could use some more of that.

"Maybe I can make you feel better," she said. "What would you say if I told you I was ready to nail Nick Casso's ass to the wall?"

"I'd say it's about time somebody did."

"Today's the day. I've already started writing it."

"You've got it all confirmed?"

"Got a city councilor to go on record. Alice Burden, you know her?"

"Seen her name in the paper, that's all."

"Casso's been courting her vote, but she's not sure we need a basketball arena. I think Alice was the kind of girl who skipped physical education in school. And she doesn't like the way Casso tried to railroad her."

"What'd he do?"

"Dinner and arm-twisting. The usual. Guess who was with him?"

"Got me."

"Martin Woodward. The NBA guy."

"So he was involved."

"They apparently worked Alice over pretty good, trying to persuade her a new arena would be the best thing for the city."

"She didn't like that?"

"Not much. When I called her, she spilled the whole thing."

"She'll never win another election in this town."

"Maybe, maybe not. I think she's going to come out looking like a hero."

"And Casso? He'll be the villain?"

"Something like that. He's not a happy man right now, I can tell you that. I called him this morning after I got off the phone with Alice. Ran the whole thing down for him, asked him to comment."

"What did he say?"

"Let's say his comments were unprintable."

"Figures."

"Soon as I hung up, he called Goodman, started yelling at him about invasion of privacy and libel and the works."

"Uh-oh."

"I couldn't hear what Goodman said, but he was kinda red in the face when he came out of his office. I think he gave Casso an earful. He told me to go with the story and he told me to call you. He wants you down here."

"Why?"

"More questions about your involvement in all this, I think. Your fight with Calvin made a big splash. Pardon the pun."

Drew winced, said nothing.

"Have you seen the paper this morning?"

"No. I just got up a few minutes ago—"

"You're all over the front page again. Calvin's become a

public figure. Too bad he's too dead to know about it."

Drew took a slug of his coffee, which had already gone cold. He glared at the missing glass doors, and pulled his robe closer around his bare knees.

"You know the one thing I don't have?" Teresa asked.

"What's that?"

"I still don't know who killed Freddie Graham."

"Nobody does."

"Somebody does. The killer. Unless it was Calvin. If it was him, we may never know for sure. He's not talking."

Drew wished she'd stop joking about Calvin. He knew it was just the black humor endemic to newsrooms, the only places where you'll hear people crow about a "great" homicide. But damn it, he was the one who'd knocked Calvin off that balcony. He wasn't proud of it.

"Sorry," she said when he didn't answer. "Guess that was in bad taste. You all right?"

"I'm okay."

"So what do you think? Any ideas who put Freddie to rest?"

"I don't know for sure. Seems like a lot of suspects. Casso, or one of his people. Calvin or his buddy, Zipper. Maybe Martin Woodward. He was in town early enough to have been there. Somebody with Freddie's law firm. I think he was sleeping with his secretary. Could be her. Hell, it could be anybody."

"That's the only hole left in my story. His death must have something to do with this NBA deal. Sure wish I could prove it."

"Sounds like you've got a pretty great story without it."

"Probably going to take me all day to write it."

"That's okay. You've got all day."

"Not really. They're running everything past the attorneys first."

"That's probably smart."

"I think that's why Goodman wants you in here, to make sure you don't do something else that'll get the newspaper in trouble."

"Me? All I do is throw guys off balconies."

She giggled. "I know. I was there, remember?"

"How could I forget?"

"Okay, tiger. I'll see you soon."

He hung up the phone and let his head drop onto the high back of the reclining chair. The last thing he wanted was to recount last night's tragedy to Goodman. If he knew the editor, he'd have Drew start again at the beginning—with seeing the Grahams at homecoming—and force him to relive everything that had happened in the past ten days. Who needed that?

Talking to Goodman might help Drew keep his job, but it wouldn't do anything to answer the central question: Who killed Freddie Graham? Until the murder was solved, everything else was just so much static.

The phone rang again. Drew sighed. Probably Goodman, telling him to hurry.

"Hello?"

"Gavin? Nick Casso here."

Drew stiffened.

"I'm madder than hell. Your newspaper's trying to ruin me."

"So I hear."

"You behind it?"

"Not me. I'm on vacation."

"They're going to get it all wrong. They're trying to make it look like I'm cheating the public."

"Aren't you?"

"Look here, Gavin, I don't need that shit from you. I called you up because I want to get the story straight."

"Is that right?"

"I know we've got a lot of history. I don't like you, and I'm sure you feel the same way about me. But goddamnit, we've both got a job to do."

Drew felt anger boil up within him at the mention of their "history." He thought about what his dad had told him, how Nick had used his influence to try to ruin Chuck and get Drew out of Helen's life. The man was a devil, and he was tempted to tell him so. But Casso was right about one thing: Drew had a job to do. If Nick was willing to talk, he had to listen. It could help Teresa.

"What do you want from me, Casso?"

"I just want to get the story straight. I figured you might give me a fair hearing. For Helen's sake."

Drew's teeth ground together. The bastard had a lot of nerve.

"You should talk to Teresa Vargas," he said. "It's her story."

"I want to tell it to you."

"So talk."

"Not on the phone," Casso said. "I want to talk in person. There are things, papers, I need to show you that'll make it all clear. You get my meaning?"

Drew wasn't sure what Casso was getting at, but he was willing to see him in person. He wanted to look him in the eye when he told him exactly what he thought of him.

"Where and when?"

"Come to my house. You know where it is. Noon."

"I'll be there."

FIFTY SIX

Nick Casso fondled the pistol that rested on his desk. It was warm in his book-lined study, and his shirt was soaked and his hands trembled. Worst day of his fucking life, no question. The NBA franchise was disintegrating before his eyes. And it was all Drew Gavin's fault. Gavin could play the innocent, say he was on vacation, whatever he wanted to say. But Nick knew the truth. The only way the Gazette could've figured out the deal before tomorrow night's council meeting was if Gavin had seen those documents Zipper was bringing to Nick's house. Gavin and Zipper were in it together, he was certain.

Gavin had acted dumb on the phone, but Nick had it figured out. Gavin or Zipper had killed Freddie and taken those documents from the cabin. The newspaper was using them for the basis of its story. And Zipper was trying to capitalize on it, rip Nick off before the story appeared. Nick didn't know whether Gavin was in on the blackmail scheme or not—maybe Zipper was trying to pull an end run on his own—but wouldn't he be surprised when they both showed up here, only to find Nick Casso pointing a gun at them?

Nick dragged a hairy hand across his forehead. The hand came away wet with sweat. He didn't feel well. He had a pain in his chest; it kept moving around in there. He figured it was heartburn. His left arm hung loose at his side. Had some shooting pains there, too. Must've twisted something. God knows. Fuckers had him so worked up, he was all knots inside.

He looked at the intercom on his walnut desk, then at the clock beside it. Just a few minutes until noon. Zipper and Gavin should be here any minute. Boy, did he have a surprise ready for them.

Nick belched, felt hot pain shoot through his chest again. Goddamn. What was the matter? He hadn't eaten anything all day. He'd been too busy. That fucking reporter, Teresa something, calling him at the crack of dawn, telling him the jig was up on his NBA plans. He'd tried to reason with the editor, but they didn't get it, none of them. They couldn't see what a good deal the team would be for the city. No, they were too busy trying to put the screws to Nick Casso.

He thought about hunting down the Maalox, but the clock ticked onto noon, and he didn't want to move. He had everything right where he wanted it. Just get this business over with, fix Zipper and Gavin, then he could find something to fix his heartburn.

The intercom buzzed. Nick pressed the button, and said, "Who's there?"

"Zipper."

"I'm in the study. Take your first right."

Nick heard the front door click open, then the roar of construction equipment from the street outside. Crews had been putting in new sewer pipes all week, and the noise was abominable. The heavy door blotted most of it out when Zipper closed it behind him.

Nick lifted the chrome-plated revolver from the desktop, but he felt weak and the gun was heavy. He lowered his hand, let it rest on the desk, the gun pointed at the door.

The man stopped in the doorway, his eyes on the pistol. He was a dark man with short black hair, looked like an Indian, with a scar down the side of his face. He had the briefcase in one hand and a pistol of his own in the other.

"Stop right there," Nick commanded, and his voice sounded strong, not betraying any of the weakness he felt. "Drop the gun."

Zipper's expression didn't change. He stared at Nick for a long moment, then let his pistol fall to the carpet.

"That's better," Nick said, and he tried to smile. "Now, come on in."

"What is this, Casso? Thought we had a deal."

"Deal's off. The Gazette's onto my plans. Those papers aren't worth a thing now."

Zipper seemed to take this in stride. "Then why the gun?"

"Don't want you making any mistakes. Looks like it was a good plan, too. You come in here armed. What were you gonna do, rob me?"

Zipper lifted his shoulders. "We had an arrangement."

"Not anymore."

The pain hammered Nick in the chest again, and he winced despite himself.

"What's the matter, Mr. Casso?" The Indian took a step closer. "You don't look so good."

"Just set that briefcase on the desk."

Zipper looked down at the black briefcase dangling in his hand. Nick figured he was disappointed with the way things were turning out, but his face didn't show a thing. He took another step forward, up to the front of the desk, and set the briefcase flat. Nick pulled his gun hand back, keeping the pistol out of reach in case Zipper made a grab for it. The thick briefcase was in the way now, and he lifted the gun to keep it pointed at Zipper's chest. His hand shook.

Where was Gavin? Nick wanted the sportswriter in the room with them when he began demanding some answers. He needed to find out how much the newspaper really knew, and whether Gavin was behind it all. The man gives the wrong answers, and Nick was prepared to shoot him and Zipper. He'd tell the cops they threatened him, and only his quick thinking had saved his life and left them both dead.

He had a lot to settle with Gavin, going back better than thirty years. It was Gavin's fault that Ellie died in childbirth. Big oversized baby, killing the only woman he'd ever really loved. And then the cocksucker had the nerve to take up with Helen when they were in college, try to steal her away from Nick, too. Nick had fixed things back then. Now Gavin was back again, trying to ruin his life, taking the one last thing he'd hope to accomplish.

Damn, the gun felt heavy. He tried to bring up his left hand to steady the pistol, but his arm hung limp. Jesus Christ, something's wrong. I feel dizzy and my chest hurts like a bastard.

Gavin's not going to show, he decided. Gutless wonder. Probably figured out I was onto him and his Indian sidekick here. Better end this thing now, better call a doctor, see what the hell's the matter with me.

"What now?" Zipper asked him.

"Back up," Nick said, and his voice sounded croaky. "Get on out of here. I've got business to take care of."

Zipper watched him for several seconds, not moving.

"I don't like people pointing guns at me."

"Just get out of here. And don't come back. I ever see you again, you're a dead man."

Zipper didn't move.

"Those are big words," he said, "coming from a man who's having a heart attack."

Nick knew it was true. Suddenly, he was scared. Another pain shot through him. He felt like he might vomit.

"I think that's it," Zipper said. "You don't feel so good, right?"

"Just go."

"I don't think so. I think I'll wait a few minutes until you keel over. Then I'll see where you keep your money."

"You fucker. You won't find anything."

A stab of pain took Nick's breath away.

"You want me to call an ambulance?" Zipper was impassive. "Probably not too late. But I'd expect a reward."

"You cocksucker," Nick wheezed. "Get out of my house."

His hand dropped to the desktop, and the pistol's butt went clunk against the wood.

"See? You can't even hold up your gun. I think you're sick real bad."

Nick needed to drop the gun, reach for the phone, get a doctor over here quick. But the Indian wouldn't leave. He just stood there, waiting, like a fucking buzzard. Zipper swam in Nick's vision. Jesus, he thought, if I pass out, this son of a bitch will finish me for sure.

"Get out."

Zipper reached behind his back, slowly, carefully, and Nick figured he was going for another gun. He tried to raise his pistol, but he didn't have the strength.

"Last warning," he gasped.

Zipper's hand reappeared from behind him, holding a shiny hunting knife.

"You're sick," he said again. "I think maybe you need surgery."

FIFTY SEVEN

Drew was a few minutes late when he pulled the Jeep to a stop in front of Nick Casso's mansion. A city crew was tearing up the street, jackhammers pounding and heavy equipment belching smoke. The house itself was just as he remembered it—white stucco, red tiled roof, wrought-iron balconies. The mansion sat close to the street, with a narrow lawn shaded by two giant cottonwoods. The driveway was short and wide, and a Mercedes and an old Pontiac were parked side by side there. It took Drew a second to recognize the Pontiac.

"Oh, shit."

He hurried across the lawn on his sore feet, glancing around in search of the Pontiac's driver. If it was indeed Zipper's car, what did that mean? Was Zipper involved with Casso somehow? My God, was he working for the rich bastard?

He approached the front door and saw it wasn't latched. He gave it a push, peered into the dark entryway. No one.

"Casso?"

He heard scuffling sounds, whispers, then Nick's croaky voice: "In here."

The voice had come from Nick's study, just to the right of the entryway. Drew took a deep breath and stepped into the doorway.

Nick Casso sat behind his desk, pale and sweaty and wide-eyed. Zipper stood behind him, one hand in Casso's black hair, the other holding a knife to the rich man's throat.

"Come on in," Zipper said.

Drew's foot hit something as he edged through the door. He looked down to see a black revolver on the floor.

"Just leave that where it is," Zipper said. "You get any clever ideas, Mr. Casso here might lose his head."

Drew felt a chill rush through him, but he held Zipper's stare.

"What the hell's going on?"

Casso coughed wetly. His arms hung limp at his sides. Drew saw a shiny pistol sitting on the desk, but Casso didn't seem to be in any condition to reach for it.

"Mr. Casso and me had a business arrangement," Zipper said. "I was supposed to sell him the papers in that briefcase. But he decided he didn't want to play. Pointed a gun at me. I don't like that."

Drew reached out toward the men, pleading in his voice: "Look, I don't know what went wrong, but I'm sure we can fix it. Let him go."

Zipper shook his head.

"Come on, what can this accomplish?"

Zipper tightened his grip on Casso's oily hair.

"For God's sake, Gavin," Casso whispered. "Do something."

"Bad idea," Zipper said. "You try anything, I make him dead."

"I'm not gonna try anything. I just want to understand what's happening here. What are these papers?"

"NBA papers," the Indian said.

"Where did you get them?"

"They were at Graham's house, hidden. Me and Calvin found them."

Casso's eyes went even wider at that. He opened his mouth

to speak, but Zipper tugged on his hair and pushed the knife against his throat.

"Mr. Casso promised seventy-five grand for them," he said. "Now I'm going to get my money, or both of you die."

Casso coughed again, looked like he wanted to puke. What was wrong with him?

"I'm," he whispered, then had to stop to breathe. "I'm not giving you a damn thing."

Zipper cocked his head to the side to look down into Casso's face.

"You're a hard-ass now, Mr. Casso? Now that you're dying? Figure you got nothing to lose? I don't know about that. Maybe we could get you to the hospital in time."

"What's the matter with him?"

"Can't you tell? His old, black heart is giving out. I told him we could call an ambulance, get him to the hospital, but he wants to be a hard-ass."

"I'll call."

"Stay right where you are. I'm waiting for Mr. Casso to tell me where the money is."

Zipper watched Drew, daring him to make a move.

Casso wheezed and hacked and swallowed, but he was getting a little color back in his face. Looked like he was getting mad.

"Fuck you," he said, loud and clear.

Zipper looked down at Casso, then back up at Drew. His face split in an unnatural rictus of a smile.

Drew said, "No . . ."

Zipper jerked sideways on the knife, and bright blood gushed from Casso's neck.

His other hand still was in Casso's hair, and he yanked the dying man out of the way and lunged for the gun on the desk.

Drew dove to the floor just as Zipper grabbed up the chrome-plated pistol. He rolled over, flush up against the front of the clawfoot desk, as the gun blew a hole in the wall near where he'd been standing. He wedged his hands under the front edge of the desk and lifted, tipping the heavy desk toward Zipper.

Another shot rang out and the desk crashed backward. Drew scrambled for the pistol on the floor. The wall above him exploded as a bullet hit, spraying white plaster. Drew grabbed up the gun and rolled through the door and into the hall. Another bullet splintered the door jamb, then he was around the corner in the hall.

He weighed the revolver in his fist and pulled back the hammer. Zipper comes through that door, and he'd blast him. Drew backed away, up the hall toward the palatial living room, keeping his eyes on the study door. He needed to find a phone, call the cops, if Zipper would only give him time.

He could hear Zipper crashing around in there, extricating himself from the mess made by the toppled desk. No time for the cops. Hide? Plenty of hiding places in this big house, but Drew had a feeling Zipper would find him.

Before he could make a decision, Zipper came through the doorway, the shiny pistol in his hand.

Drew pointed the pistol and pulled the trigger twice. The bullets blasted holes in the wall, but Zipper ducked back into the study, unhit.

"Come on out of there," Drew yelled. "You can't get away. I've got the door covered."

Zipper let the silence hang in the air for a minute, then he shouted, "Doesn't look like you're much of a shot. I think I'll take my chances."

Drew kept his gun trained on the door, but he crept backward, his feet silent on the thick carpet of the hall.

Zipper ducked his head out the door, but pulled it back quickly and Drew's shot merely chewed up the door jamb some more.

Drew checked the doorknob on the nearest door, found it locked and just had time to press himself into the doorway as Zipper came bounding out, gun blazing.

The bullets whirred down the hall like angry hornets. Drew reached out of his hidey-hole and fired back, but he couldn't see where he was shooting. He needed to get out of this doorway, needed to find a way to escape or at least to put some distance between himself and Zipper.

Zipper fired again and the bullet skipped off the edge of the doorway, throwing splinters into Drew's face. Drew fired back blindly until he hit an empty chamber in the pistol. Uh-oh.

 Nothing to do but attack.

Drew dove out of the doorway, turning to look for Zipper as he bounced off the opposite wall.

Zipper stood in the center of the hall in a perfect shooting stance, both hands steadying the pistol. He took careful aim and pulled the trigger. The gun went "click."

Drew charged him. Zipper hurled the pistol at him, but it flew past his head as Drew went low, driving with his legs. His shoulder struck Zipper in the knees, sent him backward. Drew wrapped his arms around Zipper's legs, pushing forward, lifting, the way Chuck had taught him to make a clean tackle. Zipper crashed to the floor, Drew on top of him.

Drew tried to pin him down, hold him still, but Zipper squirmed and wrestled and managed to get out from under the larger man. Drew rolled away, trying to get to his feet.

Zipper was on his knees, facing Drew, and he reached behind him, going for his knife, but his hand came up empty.

Drew swung hard with a right, catching Zipper cleanly in the jaw. Zipper's head banged loudly against the wall, making a hollow sound, like someone dropping a cantaloupe.

He went limp and slumped to the floor.

Breathing hard, Drew looked around for some way to

immobilize the Indian. A brass torchiere stood in one corner of the foyer, and Drew unplugged it and ripped the lamp's cord loose. Then he flipped Zipper over and used the cord to bind his wrists behind him. He stripped off Zipper's heavy leather belt and strapped it around his ankles, just as Zipper was coming out of it.

"That ought to hold you," Drew said. Then he hurried back into the study to see if anything could be done for Nick Casso.

The place was a wreck. Walls were pockmarked by bullet holes. Drawers had opened when Drew tipped over the desk and papers and pencils had spilled onto the floor. Casso still sat in his swivel chair, but he'd been spun around in the confusion, so it looked as if he was peering out the window into his shady side yard.

Drew stepped around the desk. One look told him it was too late to help Casso. His eyes had rolled back in his head and his shirt was soaked with blood all the way to his lap. The knife was on the floor next to Nick's chair and Drew carefully stepped around it.

The briefcase lay in the mess behind the overturned desk. Drew bent over and picked it up, set it on the desk and popped the latches. It was filled with loose papers, and he could see they all had to do with the NBA franchise, just as Zipper had said. The papers were spattered with brown dots that looked like dried blood.

Drew felt a chill wash through him. He closed the briefcase and left it where it sat.

He went back into the hall. Zipper was awake now, trying to roll over. Drew kicked him in the ribs as he went past to get to the front door. He opened the door a crack and peeked outside. The construction workers still were going at it with the jackhammers. Nobody was even looking his direction. He had some time.

He went back to Zipper, grabbed him roughly by the elbow and rolled him over. Then he straddled the man and sat on his chest.

"Tell me again where you got that briefcase."

The Indian's mouth was clamped tight, but he had to open it to breathe. Drew's weight was pushing all the air out of his lungs.

"Graham's house," Zipper said. "Under his desk."

"When?"

Zipper's eyes ran around the foyer, searching for an escape, some way to get the big man off him, but Drew slapped the scarred face once and the Indian focused.

"On Saturday," he gasped. "While everybody was at the funeral."

"The papers have something all over them."

"Blood. I think they were at the cabin where Graham was killed."

Drew pondered that a moment, then he said, "Go back to sleep," and clipped Zipper a hard one to the chin. Zipper's head snapped to the side and he lay still.

Drew thought about calling the cops, but he knew that would mean hours being grilled about Casso's death. No, the police would have to wait. He thought he knew now who killed Freddie Graham, but he wanted to be the one to pop the question. And it was something he must face alone.

FIFTY EIGHT

Twenty minutes later, Drew rang the bell at Helen Graham's house in the foothills. He trembled while he waited for her to answer.

She opened the door and peered out, smiled when she saw it was him and swung the door open wide. She was wearing clothes like the ones she'd worn when he saw her at homecoming, a black sweater and snug jeans. She looked so good, it made his eyes hurt.

"Hi there," she said. "I was just thinking about you."

"Mind if I come in?"

"Please do." She stepped out of the way to let him enter, then enclosed him in her arms once the door was shut behind him.

Drew stood unmoving, his arms at his sides, feeling her warm body against him and hoping his suspicions weren't true. She leaned back and looked up into his face, her beautiful forehead creased with concern.

"Are you all right?"

"Sure."

"I read the paper this morning, what happened with that man at your apartment. Is that how you got that lump on your chin?"

He nodded.

"That must've been terrible. I wanted to call you, make sure you were okay. But I thought the police might be there again. I worried it would raise a lot of questions."

"Funny you should say that. I've got some questions of my own."

She studied his face, her dark eyes twitching.

"Something's wrong."

"A lot is wrong," he said. "That's why we need to talk."

She stepped away from him and led him into the living room. They sat where they had the first time he'd visited, her on the sofa and him in an armchair with the coffee-table between them. He remembered the last visit, the feel of her in his arms, the warmth of her kiss. Now he knew the kiss meant nothing. She'd been using him, playing him for a fool. He clung to that notion. It was the only way he could make it through what was coming next.

"The day Freddie died," he began, staring at the floor between his sneakers, "you told me nobody knew he was at that cabin."

"I thought no one did."

He looked up at her. Painful as it was, he needed to watch her. He needed to see when her eyes shifted, when the lies came. She sat with her feet together, her hands on her knees. She peered at him, trying to see where he was going.

"Do you have some idea?" she asked. "You think you know who killed him?"

He nodded slowly, still watching her for a reaction. She covered well. She didn't screech or leap to her feet or run to the phone to call her daddy. Her eyebrows raised and she waited.

"You went over there, didn't you?" he said. "To the cabin. You went there before you called me."

Her mouth gaped, and he saw her perfect teeth and her wide eyes, and he felt sour inside. She was acting now, trying to buffalo him again, counting on his old feelings for her. He took a deep breath, steeled himself for her answer.

"You think I had something to do with Freddie's death?"

"Just answer me. You went over there. Maybe the night before. That's right, isn't it?"

She glanced around the room, but then cut her eyes back to Drew.

"Yes. I should've told you about it—"

"What happened when you got there?"

"We talked about his situation. The gambling. That's when he said he'd call me later, after he got everything fixed. But when I didn't hear from him the next day, I called you—"

"It was more than a talk, right? More like an argument?"

Her hands tried to dance, and she clasped them together in her lap.

"The police already asked me these questions—"

"I'm asking now. I know you better than they do."

"We've been friends a long time. I thought we could be together again—"

"Just tell me the truth."

Helen sighed and looked down at her hands. She was picking at her cuticles, and she willed herself to stop.

"Okay," she said quietly. "We argued. Freddie was drunk. He'd sat over there all day, feeling sorry for himself and drinking and doing nothing to solve the problem."

"And that made you mad?"

"I was angry, yes. While he was hiding, I'd gone over our finances, searching through his office for all our debts. We were in bad shape, Drew. Worse than I knew. I was very upset with him for keeping me in the dark. And I found some bills. Hotels here in town, things like that. They confirmed what I'd thought for some time. He was having an affair. His secretary, Trish—"

"You argued about it. And he got physical with you."

Her eyes widened.

"How do you—"

"The bruises on your arm. You got those at the cabin, not here like you told me, right?"

She looked down at her arm. The bruises were hidden by her sleeve, but she rubbed at the sore spot and frowned.

"Yes. He grabbed me. Like I said, he was drunk. He didn't know what he was doing. Freddie never abused me in any way. It was so out of character for him—"

"What did you do?"

"I got away from him and put some distance between us. But he was acting crazy. He didn't like it that I'd gone through his papers. He kept talking about a basketball team and how we'd be 'sitting pretty.' I suppose you've figured that out, too?"

"I had some help," he said. "It's going to be splashed all over the Gazette tomorrow."

She clamped her lips together and looked away.

"Daddy won't like that."

Drew hesitated. He should tell her about Nick. But it had to wait. He had to hear the whole story first.

"I'm more interested in what happened to Freddie. You broke away from him, you crossed the room. I guess you were standing by the fireplace?"

She stared at him with wide eyes for several seconds before nodding.

"Then he came at you again, is that right?"

"I'd never seen him like that, Drew. He was so angry—"

"You thought you needed to protect yourself?"

"Yes," she said, a little too quickly. "I told him to stay away from me. But he kept coming. He said, 'I'll teach you to meddle,' and he was reaching for me."

"So you grabbed up the poker."

Helen closed her eyes and fell back against the sofa. She let her head droop back, and Drew made himself look away from her long, smooth neck. When she spoke, it was toward the ceiling.

"Yes." He could barely hear her. "I did."

She lowered her chin and gave him a steady look.

"I didn't intend to use it. I just wanted him to keep away from me. He was so drunk."

"But he kept coming."

"He was almost upon me when I swung it at him. I didn't mean to do it. It was a reflex."

"And the hook on the poker hit him in the temple."

Tears filled Helen's eyes, but he fought the urge to comfort her.

"That's right," she whispered. "I didn't mean for it to happen. Honest, I didn't."

Drew rubbed his sweating palms against the knees of his trousers.

"So it was an accident?"

She nodded wordlessly. The tears spilled from her eyes.

"Why didn't you tell this to the police?"

"I couldn't do that. They'd never believe me. It would look like I went over there intending to kill him."

"And you didn't? Maybe for the insurance money—"

"God, no. How can you say that? You know me better than that."

"I thought I knew you, Helen."

She met his eyes and held them for a long time.

"I haven't changed, Drew."

"Sure you have. We all have. I wanted to believe it could be like it was before. But time passes and people change and you can't go back."

"We could try, Drew. We could learn all about each other again. Explore each other."

He shook his head. "It's too late for that."

"It's never too late. As long as we keep this secret, we could recapture the past."

Drew stood and stretched and took a deep breath. His

chest hurt inside, and he didn't think it was because of his fight with Zipper.

"People make a mistake with the past," he said. "They think it's real, but it's no more real than a dream. I finally woke up to that. The past is gone. Yesterday's news. All we've got is today and maybe tomorrow."

Helen stood, too, and brushed at the tears with the back of her hand.

"That's not true," she said. "What we had, that was real. You can't deny that."

She took a step toward him and her hands rose beseechingly. Drew sidestepped her and moved toward the kitchen.

"Maybe it was," he said. "But it doesn't change what's happened since. And it doesn't change what happened to your husband."

She dropped her hands to her sides and her face closed up and she hung her head.

"You can stick to your story if you want," he said, "but it's going to be hard to explain how those NBA documents got back here to your house."

"You know about those?"

"People have died because of those papers. Why did you take them?"

"I don't know. I thought Daddy would need them, or I might be able to use them in some way."

Drew thought that sounded pretty calculating for someone who'd accidentally killed her husband, but he said nothing. He reminded himself that she'd taken time to wipe off the poker, too.

"I put the briefcase in the trunk of my car," she said. "It just sat in there for a few days. Daddy was frantic, looking all over for it. But I was so mad at him, I didn't hand it over."

"Why were you mad?"

"I guess I blamed him for what happened. I know that

sounds twisted, when it was all my fault, but Daddy had such an effect on Freddie. You were talking about people changing. Freddie changed. He was becoming more like Daddy every day. Ruthless and mean. He didn't care about anything but money. After Freddie was dead, I wanted Daddy to be there for me, to comfort me, but he threw his weight around and searched through Freddie's study for those papers, and I'd be damned if I'd give them to him. I brought them into the house the day of the funeral. Hid the briefcase under Freddie's desk. That's how I knew someone had been in the house. Later I went to look at the papers to see what they really meant, and the briefcase was gone."

"You told me they'd taken a gun."

"That was true! After I saw the briefcase was gone, I was frantic. I looked all around the house for anything else that might be missing. The pistol was the only other thing that was gone."

Drew remembered what Zipper had said about taking the briefcase during the funeral. He guessed Calvin had taken Freddie's gun, too, and that he'd seen it the night before when the police put it in a plastic bag.

"I'm going to call the police now," he said, moving toward the phone in the kitchen. "It's the only way, Helen. Tell them what happened. Maybe they'll see it was an accident."

"They'll never believe it now. They'll think I was trying to hide it from them."

"Weren't you?"

She came closer.

"Only because I was afraid. I didn't know what to do."

"So you called me," he said edgily. "Sent me over there to find the body. Put me on the spot with the cops."

"I didn't know they'd suspect you. I couldn't bear the thought of Freddie lying over there all alone. I even began to question whether he'd really been dead. My God, what if I'd left him there, bleeding, and somehow he could've been saved?"

Drew shook his head. "You sent me because you knew I'd do anything for you. Maybe even take the blame."

"No, I didn't mean—"

"You counted on me covering for you."

She reached out to him again, but he backed away until his hips came in contact with a countertop.

"Don't, Helen. It's too late."

"Just hold me. Tell me it will be all right."

"I don't believe that, and neither do you. I'm calling the cops. You can take your chances with them. Maybe they'll believe you, maybe they won't, but I'm calling them and I'm telling them what I know."

Her face twisted with rage and fear, and Drew could imagine for a second what it had been like, could see her with the poker in her hand and Freddie falling backward, dead before he hit the ground.

He needed to call the police, get this finished. Lieutenant Moore would be happy to hear that he'd been partly right, that Freddie's death had been a domestic matter. Not as happy as he would've been nailing Drew for the murder, but it would have to do. But first, there was something he had to tell her.

"The guy who took the papers, the one with the scar, tried to sell them to your father today."

Helen went stiff all over.

"So Daddy knows?"

"He doesn't know anything. I sorry to tell you this, but he's dead. Zipper killed him."

Helen's face collapsed into itself, and a sob wrenched from her throat.

Drew dialed 911 and listened to it ring. He didn't look at Helen, not until he sensed movement behind him. He wheeled around to find her swinging his baseball bat at his head. He ducked and the bat missed, glanced off his meaty shoulder. He dropped the phone and backpedaled. She screeched as she swung the bat the other way. It missed him and crashed into the counter. He leaped forward, grabbed the bat with both hands and wrested it away from her.

"What are you doing?" he yelled.

"I can't let you call the police. It's too late for that. You've got to help me, Drew."

"Or what? You'll try to kill me?"

Helen's eyes were wild. She snatched open a drawer in the counter, and Drew saw it was full of knives. He brought the bat down on the drawer sharply, just missing her fingers. The front of the drawer broke away and knives scattered across the floor.

Helen backpedaled, but she was looking down at the knives, searching for a weapon.

"Back up! Get away."

She looked up at him, at the bat cocked by his shoulder, and obeyed.

"I'm sorry." Her shoulders slouched. "I don't know what I'm doing."

"Sit down," he commanded. "Right there on the floor."

She did as she was told, tears streaming down her face.

Drew set the bat on the counter and rubbed his shoulder, keeping his eyes on her.

"Was I going to be an accident, too?"

She said nothing.

The phone receiver was on the floor, dangling on its curly cord. Drew picked it up and put it to his ear.

"Hello? Yeah. I've got a crime to report. A murder."

FIFTY NINE

Curtis White was outside the employees' entrance when Drew arrived at the Gazette on Tuesday evening. Smoke curled from his nostrils as he grinned.

"My man. Been wondering when we'd see you around here again."

Drew raised his chin in greeting, and Curtis zeroed in on the bruise there.

"You look like hell."

"I've been through hell the last few days. Don't you read the paper?"

"Just got back from Laramie, but I saw the headlines. You threw some chump off your balcony?"

Drew slid his card key through the slot to release the lock.

"Not exactly. I'll tell you all about it later. Right now, I've got to talk to Goodman."

"Hold on a second," Curtis said. "I've got something to tell you."

Drew sighed and turned back to his friend.

"I got Jamal Moore nailed," Curtis said.

"You did? Then it was true?"

"Covered up nicely, but yeah, it's true. He was arrested last Saturday. He was whipping up on his girlfriend and she got to a phone and called the sheriff's department."

"His girlfriend?"

"That's right. Sharon Burke. White girl. Lives in the North

Valley, outside the city limits."

"They were at her house?"

"Yeah, her parents weren't home. Guess Jamal wanted to play some games she didn't want to play. So he got rough with her. Slapped her around. She locked herself in a bathroom and called the cops."

"From a bathroom?"

Curtis shrugged his narrow shoulders. "What can I tell you? Rich folks keep phones everywhere."

"So what happened?"

"Couple of deputies showed up, hauled Jamal away in handcuffs. Then his daddy got them to cover it up."

"How did you get all this?"

"Asking around. Turns out Sharon's friendly with another boy on the team. Seth Austin? Defensive back?"

Drew nodded impatiently.

"The cops might've kept it quiet, but Sharon told the whole thing to Seth. He told me about it on the team plane."

"I'm surprised he'd mention it. Loyalty to a teammate and all that."

"Not Seth. He's in love with her. He figured I was just the ticket for getting Jamal out of the picture."

"You're writing it up?"

"Be in tomorrow's paper."

The mention of the next day's newspaper reminded Drew why he was there.

"I've got to go see Goodman," he said, swinging the door open again.

Curtis looked disappointed, but he broke into a smile when Drew said, "Nice work, Curtis. I should've talked to the players. You can't keep any secrets on a football team."

"Ain't that the truth?"

"I'll talk to you later," Drew said as he went through the door.

The newsroom was bustling. This time of evening, most of the desks were occupied and keyboards clacked and phones rang. Drew spotted Goodman's bald head hovering over Teresa's computer. Teresa had a pencil in her teeth. She was nodding, but she looked ready to chew the pencil to splinters. Drew thought: Ah, the editing process.

He'd taken three steps toward them when Greg Benedict popped up in his path.

"Where have you been?"

"I've got to talk to Goodman."

"He's asked me ten times if I've seen you."

"I'm here now."

Benedict wasn't budging, so Drew stepped around him. The smaller man danced backward so he could keep facing him.

"Goodman's mad as hell," he said. "You've really stepped on your dick this time."

Drew leaned toward the sports editor until their faces were only inches apart.

"I'm gonna step on yours if you don't get out of my way."

Benedict's shiny face went red.

"Watch the way you talk to me, Gavin. You're already in enough trouble."

Somebody in sports was chortling. Probably Spiffy, who always enjoyed these little flare-ups.

"I don't have time for this," Drew said.

He reached out and grabbed Benedict by the shoulders. The sports editor tried to dodge away, but Drew's grip was firm. He lifted until Benedict's feet were off the ground, then turned and set him down out of his way. He released him and marched off toward Goodman, ignoring the noise behind him as Benedict sputtered to the others, "You saw that! He put his hands on me! I won't stand for that. That's assault!"

The shouting caused heads to swivel around the newsroom, and the whole staff watched as Drew made his way between desks. He knew he looked terrible. The bruises and the bandages and the limp. He'd had no lunch and not much sleep the night before. He felt hollow inside.

Goodman noticed him before he reached Teresa's desk and peered over his half-glasses as Drew approached. Teresa turned to see, and she looked shocked at his appearance. But she managed to smile.

"Hi, tiger," she said. "We've been looking all over for you. Have you heard the news? Nick Casso's dead!"

"I know. I was there."

Goodman's bushy eyebrows shot up, and he said, "In my office now. Both of you."

They followed Goodman into his office and sat down while he closed the door. Once Goodman was behind his desk, he said, "You were there when Casso was killed?"

"Yeah, but that's not the latest news. Helen Graham's been arrested."

"Casso's daughter? For what?"

"Murder."

"She killed her father?"

"Her husband. They arrested the guy who killed Casso already. I left him trussed up for the cops."

Drew took a deep breath and blew it out loudly. Damn, he was tired.

"Jesus Christ. She killed Freddie Graham?" Goodman apparently was having trouble understanding it all.

"She says it was an accident. They argued. He roughed her up."

"Are the cops buying that?"

"They took her into custody. I think they're going to let the prosecutor sort it out."

Drew waited for Goodman's explosion. But the editor's voice was soft when he spoke.

"How did they determine it was her?"

"I told them. She confessed the whole thing to me."

Goodman cleared his throat. "She volunteered this?"

"No, I figured it out."

Goodman looked at the clock on his wall.

"We've got three hours until deadline," he said. "Don't tell it to me. Tell it to Teresa. We've got to tear up the front page and do it over. This is big."

Drew glanced over at Teresa, found her watching him, concern etched on her face.

"She was your friend, wasn't she?" she said.

"We go way back," Drew said. "College sweethearts."

"Is that why she confessed?"

He shrugged his big shoulders. Every movement, even a shrug, caused him pain.

"She thought I might keep her secret. But I couldn't do that."

Teresa reached out, rested a consoling hand on his forearm.

"Must be rough."

Goodman stood behind his desk.

"I understand this has been tough for you, Drew. But it's one helluva story. I want you to sit down with Teresa, tell her the whole thing. We've got to get this in the paper."

He gave Goodman a level stare.

"I could write it."

Goodman pursed his lips, then shook his head.

"Too much of a conflict. You're a source in this one, a character in the story. Don't worry, champ. We'll make you look like a hero. This thing's a career-maker for sure."

Goodman looked as if he expected Drew and Teresa to leap up from their chairs and hurry to Teresa's desk, but Drew didn't move.

"Does this mean I'm back on duty?"

"Sure, sure. You tired of being on leave?"

"I'm just tired. But I figure it'll do me good to come back to work."

"You've got it. Now go get busy. Time's wasting."

Drew stood. "You'll clear everything with Benedict?"

A smile lit Goodman's face.

"Don't worry about Benedict. He's leaving. He got a job with the Denver paper."

"You're kidding."

"I'm not."

Drew could feel a grin working its way up through his exhaustion.

"We'll talk it over later, Drew. Right now, we've got to get this story. This is the biggest goddamn thing we've had in years."

Drew seemed immobilized, but Teresa gave him a push toward the door.

"You heard the man, tiger. Let's go make a newspaper."

SIXTY

A week later, Drew and Teresa finally had their dinner date. Scalo Northern Italian Grill was jumping when they arrived. The high-ceilinged pastel eatery was full of laughing, happy people wolfing down pasta and pouring down wine. Chefs worked at a frenetic pace in the open kitchen. Drew was glad he'd phoned ahead for a reservation.

A slinky hostess led them up a few steps to a narrow balcony packed full of tables. One wall was glass, overlooking busy Central Avenue, and the hostess directed them to a table that sat squarely in the window.

"I feel like we're on display here," he said once they were seated.

"Might as well be," Teresa said, straightening her dress, the same one she'd worn to the news meeting what seemed like years ago. "Word will get out soon enough in the newsroom that we went out together. That bother you?"

Drew shook his head. His grin faltered. That had been happening a lot lately.

A pale waiter brought menus and reeled off the specials. Drew ordered a bottle of merlot. As soon as the waiter went off to get it, he set his menu aside.

"Tell me about the raid."

She smiled again.

"Is that why you finally brought me to dinner? So you could get all the juicy details?"

"Not at all. But I'm dying to hear about it."

"Don't you want to order first?"

"I always get the pasta special."

"Sounds good to me." She closed her menu. "Okay, so the cops called me first thing this morning, asked if I wanted to be in on the raid on Three Eyes Sanchez's bookie parlor."

"And you said yes."

"Actually, I said, 'You bet your ass.' Anyhow, I rode over there with them. I was a little puzzled when we stopped at this barber shop, but then I remembered what you'd told me—"

"I've been there before."

"Right. So the cops burst into the shop, me right on their heels, and the barber about had a heart attack."

"Guy with a shiny toupee?"

"That's the one. The cops ignored him. They hustled through the shop and kicked open that steel door in the back. And there was nobody there."

"What?"

"Empty. I mean, you could tell it was a bookmaking place. All the phones and the chalkboards and all. But it was empty."

"But I thought they arrested—"

"Wait for it. The cops are disappointed, right? But they start gathering up papers and stuff so they can make their case. Then they hear this yapping sound."

"From where?"

"Couldn't tell at first. It would start, then stop. Then start up again. Finally, the head cop went over to this desk in the corner and got down on all fours and found a trapdoor there."

"I'll be damned."

"The cops all gathered around with their guns drawn, and the boss throws open the door and there's Three Eyes squatting in the crawl space. He's got this little dachshund with him—"

"Oscar."

"What?"

"The dog's name is Oscar."

"Damn, that's a good detail. I'd better phone that in."

"Not until you finish telling me."

"Not much else to tell. They hauled Three Eyes out of his hidey-hole. The cops were all laughing so hard, they could barely cuff him."

"What happened to the dog?"

"Last I saw, that barber was holding him. Three Eyes was shouting as they hauled him away, 'Max! Max! Take care of my baby.'"

Drew laughed loud and long. It felt like a release, something he'd needed for days. He wiped at his eyes, regaining control.

"And Lieutenant Moore? What's happening with him?"

Teresa shrugged.

"It's all with Internal Affairs, so they're not saying much, but it looks like he's in a lot of trouble for covering up for his son."

"Suspension?"

"Worse than that. I've been hearing rumbles about criminal charges. Jamal got arraigned on assault charges yesterday. They may end up sharing a cell."

Drew took little comfort in that. The man had been trying to protect his son, just as most fathers would. But Curtis' story had blown it wide open, and Moore would have to pay.

The waiter brought the wine, and Drew grew subdued while he tasted it and approved it and watched the waiter pour.

"Where'd you go?" she asked after the waiter scurried away.

"Sorry," he said. "That keeps happening lately."

Her smile faded. "Thinking about Helen?"

"About all of it. I'm just glad it's over. I mean, I still have to testify against Helen and Zipper, and that's not going to be easy, but at least they're behind bars."

"She meant a lot to you, didn't she?"

"A long time ago. This latest stuff, it just felt like she was trying to use me."

"Didn't work, though, did it?"

He shook his head and stared out the window, watching taillights rocket by.

"She counted too much on the past," he said, turning back to her. "She thought she could keep riding it. But that never works."

Teresa's smile was mischievous.

"What about you? Don't you live in the past? Still thinking about your glory days on the football field?"

"Let me tell you something, kiddo. Not only have I shaken off the past, but I may have a bright future as well. I had a meeting with Goodman today. He wants me to be the new sports editor."

Her eyes went wide. "You're serious?"

"That's what I said to him. I've never wanted to be somebody's boss. But he thinks I'd be good at it. With Benedict leaving, he thinks it's time to shake things up."

"You're certainly good at that. As you've proven lately."

"Don't remind me."

The ponytailed waiter reappeared, and took their orders. Then Drew waved him away.

"Are you going to take the job?"

"I told him I'd think about it. Maybe it's just what I need. Get me out of my rut, you know? Instead of working for an asshole, I could *be* the asshole."

She laughed, then said, "The sports editor doesn't go to all the games, does he? Wouldn't you miss that?"

"Maybe. But it would also mean some of my Saturday nights are free."

"Is that important?"

"I don't know. I may be needing my weekends open."

She reached across the table and rested her hand on his.

"You making plans for the future, tiger?"

"Let's see how tonight goes."

Drew grinned. This time it didn't falter.